DYING FOR JUSTICE

AN EXTRAJUDICIAL THRILLER

Harry Senthill

QUODLIBET ROCK

Published 2018 by Quodlibet Rock

e-mail: quodrock@gmail.com

ISBN 978-1-9997097-2-3 (hardback)
ISBN 978-1-9997097-3-0 (paperback)
ISBN 978-1-9997097-4-7 (e-book)

CONTENTS

1:	ACCIDENT	1
2:	TRIAL	13
3:	STALKER	29
4:	SKIRMISH	42
5:	PURSUIT	59
6:	KIDNAP	75
7:	ORDEAL	84
8:	MANOEUVRES	96
9:	BATTLE	113
10:	FLIGHT	140
11:	EXECUTION	154
12:	DUEL	169
13:	RESCUE	188
14:	AMBUSH	213
15:	RETRIBUTION	231
16:	LOOSE ENDS	270

1

ACCIDENT

"Undress," said the minder with the shotgun. "Put your clothes on the back seat of the car."

I didn't exactly hasten to obey.

"Please argue," his weight-trained accomplice advised. "Then I can hit you. I owe you for damaging my BMW. Plus you've got sixty seconds or your girlfriend goes over the cliff."

I took off my clothes. What else could I do? As I discarded the final item, Weight Trainer grabbed my left arm, forcing it up behind my back. The shotgun was thrown past me to come to rest on top of my pants, and my other arm was also gripped and pulled up behind me. All very thorough.

The two of them marched me over the grass-covered but stony ground to where Anthony Hartling was waiting with Miranda. I felt the light wind on my skin. It was cold. Not much different in temperature to that February afternoon when this whole affair had started. Except this was well past midnight on a cliff top in Wales. Above us was an almost full moon illuminating the scene, and in the opposite direction was the roaring sea an unknown distance below.

I had it in mind that there was some sort of perversion planned for Miranda and me, but as I drew near it became obvious my suspicion was wrong. Hartling nodded at his two minders, inclining his head towards the edge of the cliff. They picked up speed, almost lifting me off my feet.

At the last possible moment they gave me a final shove and let go, and I went over.

Miranda screamed in horror, a dreadful sound which was cut off almost immediately as I fell out of sight. My life didn't flash before me, but Tanya was there. Waiting for me. I whispered her name. And then I hit the bottom.

*

I don't get thrown off cliffs for a living. It was only by the narrowest of margins I didn't get thrown off for a dying either. This seriously hostile act marked the first time in my life somebody had actually tried to murder me. As an experience it can accurately be considered seminal. People got killed afterwards, some of them at my own hand. It led to the police describing me as extremely dangerous and in urgent need of apprehension. Me! Harmless, law-abiding Ed Somersby. At least that's how I saw myself when the year began. I was just another average citizen, twenty-five years old with a good job, a huge mortgage, and a fiancée whom I loved more than anything else in this world. My life was progressing as most lives do: predictable, rock-solid stable, unremarkable, and — though it seems like a cruel dream now — happy.

But that was before I encountered Anthony Hartling one ghastly winter's day and it all turned to dust.

Put at its simplest it was a case of being in the wrong place at the wrong time. If I'd been going down that road as little as a minute earlier or a minute later there'd have been no accident, no trial, no private war, no finding myself in a desperate situation and forced to do desperate things or go under. But I was neither early nor late for my appointment with disaster. I was there on the dot.

Date: February 14th, a quiet Sunday. Time: 3.22 p.m. The weather was cloudy but dry, with light wind and a temperature about ten degrees above freezing. Ideal conditions if you're on a motorcycle.

Sitting behind me on this occasion, riding pillion on the Thunderbird, was Tanya Matheson, my best friend, lover, and all-round partner in life. We'd been for an alcohol-free meal in the West End of London and were heading home to our suburban end-terrace in Willesden.

Our route had just taken us onto Poole Avenue, a road that begins with a straight section running for about four hundred metres and which then curves to the right, passing out of sight. Parking on the right hand side is forbidden, presumably because of the bend, but the left on the fateful afternoon was solid with residents' cars. There are, incidentally, no trees along this 'avenue', the local council having chopped them all down a few years ago. The only things obviously adorning the pavements since then are the lampposts.

I approached the bend at about thirty miles per hour — the legal maximum — and began to anticipate the change of direction by turning slightly ahead of time, a manoeuvre which took the motorcycle towards the centre of the road. If there's no one overtaking you or coming the other way, it's standard practice because it lessens the shearing force between your tyres and the tarmac. I had of course checked for other traffic and confirmed the road was clear in both directions. There was a pedestrian walking towards me on the pavement, but he was plainly not about to step into the road and so was not something I was paying any attention to.

Nonetheless I had an impression of him stop and look over his shoulder, and at the same moment I saw the car: big and black, travelling much too fast, heading straight for me. On my side of the road! There was no time to reason out what to do. When it comes down to tenths of a second, you experience your decisions rather than think them. I was too far into the turn to back out, and in any case there was insufficient room between the oncoming car and the parked vehicles for me to squeeze between them. All I could do was tip the Thunderbird further over to the right, open the throttle, and attempt to avoid a collision by passing this menace of a driver on the wrong side.

If the guy had done the sensible thing and opted for an emergency stop, I might have managed to get out of his way. But it's pointless to dwell on what might have happened. There's a school of thought amongst some motorists in London (and maybe elsewhere too) which subscribes to the view that when danger looms you sound the horn and apply the brakes. In that specific order. And this was a case of it. He went for his horn. It was still blaring when he struck the motorcycle side-on, some way towards the rear.

I have no recollection of what happened next. There's an interval of time — I don't even know how long it was — missing from my life. I was aware of feeling strangely peaceful, of wanting to lie where I was forever, resting.

And then, like a snowflake in an explosion, the tranquillity shattered. Tanya! My beloved Tanya!

I had come to a halt against a wall — one which marked the boundary of someone's garden where it abutted the pavement — and could see nothing but red bricks. A wave of nausea swept over me as I made an effort to change position. Strong arms were suddenly steadying me.

"Take it easy," the gentleman said. "We've phoned for an ambulance. How are you feeling?"

I tried to reply, but he couldn't make out what I was saying through the crash helmet. That gave him the idea of taking it off, which he did very gently as soon as I was safely sitting with my bottom on the cold ground and my back against the wall.

I could see Tanya at last. She was a few metres away,

lying face up across the pavement, with her right side towards me and her legs from the knees downward in the road. There were several people around her, mostly crouching, and one of them was carrying out mouth-to-mouth resuscitation. I watched. I was in no state to help and simply hoped they knew what they were doing. I felt reassured because I could see no obvious injuries — no blood anyway.

There was a dream-like quality to the way events unfolded at this stage. Certainly the police seemed to arrive very quickly, shortly followed by an ambulance. Somehow I'd managed to get shakily to my feet by then and so was able to join Tanya unaided when the paramedics loaded her on board. They glanced at me and turned all their attention back to her. There was a mask put over her face and wires were attached to her chest. A heart monitor bleeped regularly. I just didn't get what was going on.

And so we sped through the light Sunday afternoon traffic with the siren blaring intermittently, a police car ahead of us clearing a path.

Tanya was unconscious, that was plain, but I didn't know why. Looking at her, I noticed there was a dark stain on her left trouser leg. It wasn't something the ambulance crew were taking any notice of. Because of that, so help me, I thought it must be oil.

When we got to the hospital, they didn't waste any time. She was out of the ambulance on a trolley and into the building in ten seconds flat. And I still didn't get it.

Feeling pretty much ignored, I alighted and set off after her. As I entered what I assume was the accident and emergency department, everything seemed to become very distant. A sensation suddenly gripped me like I was about to die. And Tanya was nowhere to be seen.

At which point I gather I must have fainted. It was probably quite dramatic.

I came to my senses on a hard, narrow bed. Some of my upper clothing had been removed and one of my sleeves rolled up. A female white-coated doctor was in the process of measuring my blood pressure.

"Hi," she said as my eyes opened. "Do you know where you are?"

"Hospital?"

"And what day is it?"

"Sunday."

"Fine. No obvious brain damage. I have to hand it to you. If you've got to go into neurogenic shock, you chose the best place to do it."

Without so much as a pause she went on to examine me generally — stick your tongue out and say aah, that sort of thing — while simultaneously conducting a question and answer session about what had happened and where it hurt. A virtuoso performance.

"You'll live," she announced at length. "There's a police officer over there who wants me to take a blood sample. Are you okay with that?"

I welcomed it. It's normal procedure following bad road traffic accidents, and it would establish beyond doubt that I hadn't been riding my motorcycle under the influence of anything, legal or otherwise.

"We're finished for the moment," the doctor said, having completed the requisite formalities. "I shall need some X-rays to be on the safe side, and we'd better keep you in overnight for observation."

"I'll be okay," I asserted defensively. All I wanted right then was to collect Tanya and go home. Hospitals aren't for people like us.

"You probably will be," the doctor said. "But at the moment you're not okay at all. You've got a headache, you can't remember a lot of what happened, and you're showing signs of confusion. That's classic concussion. I

6

guess it comes from headbutting a brick wall. Your crash helmet saved you from a fractured skull, but I can't rule out a haematoma at this stage, so it's not a good idea to go wandering off. If your vital signs are still normal tomorrow morning, that'll be the time to discharge you. In the meantime, would you like something for the pain?"

"No thank you," I replied. It wasn't a case of playing the tough guy. It was that I didn't want to be drugged while Tanya's situation was undisclosed. She might need me.

This time the doctor didn't argue. She rushed away, leaving me feeling deflated and useless.

A nurse came over and got me to provide details about my pillion passenger: name, address, next of kin. I took the opportunity to ask the obvious question.

"She's in surgery," the nurse said, and hurried off before I could inquire further.

It had me worried. The speed with which Tanya had been rushed to hospital, and now this surgery business, suggested something serious. But she'd come off a motorcycle. That's all. *I* was more or less okay. Surely it couldn't be more than a minor injury she had sustained. Surely.

The uniformed policeman who had been hovering in the background, seeing that the medical profession had retreated temporarily, came over and introduced himself. He wanted a statement from me, which I provided inasmuch as I could recall the details of the accident. The officer maintained throughout an air of questioning open-mindedness. No sympathy. No condemnation. Just the facts.

After that, I was left alone for a while. I watched the door, hoping, believing, that the next person to come through it would be Tanya. Bandaged perhaps, or limping. Ready for me to take her home. Several times I saw her, and as many times I quickly realized I was mistaken. An age passed. I began to think the absence of news was a bad sign.

Eventually they X-rayed me and settled me down in a small ward with three other patients. I kept inquiring about Tanya, and I kept getting evasive answers.

And then, in mid-evening, an elderly male 'white coat' approached my bed, pulled the curtain round it, sat on the one available chair, and asked how I felt. I told him I hurt all over, though not as badly as earlier.

"Was the young lady your wife?" he said.

When somebody dies, I don't think it's possible to break the news gradually to relatives. Whatever you say reveals what's coming. This doctor had done it with his first word. WAS.

"My fiancée," I replied. I didn't say 'was'. Perhaps I'd misheard him.

"I'm very sorry," he said quietly. "We did all we could. In the end her heart just gave out."

"Thank you," I replied, without knowing why.

"Is there anyone you'd like to talk to? A priest or a counsellor?"

"No."

He departed, leaving the curtain in place. It was probably against the rules, because a nurse drew it back after a few minutes and returned implacably to the desk from where she kept her four charges under observation.

I lay there motionless, thoughtless. I didn't dare to think. The enormity of the disaster was too great for my mind to encompass. So what good would thinking do? Instead I watched the clock on the wall, and the slowly turning hands that marked the passage of the seconds and the minutes and the hours. Thus did I pass the longest and loneliest and most desolate night of my life.

*

By the time the hospital got in gear next morning, my memory for the events leading up to the crash had returned, and my various pains had largely gone, except that my head and neck still ached quite badly. At seven, the catering staff brought round a breakfast of uninspiring size which I ate because it was there and not because I was hungry. Shortly after that, another doctor examined me — same routine as yesterday including the blood pressure — and asked me to vacate the bed as it was needed for somebody else.

I got dressed. And then.... What do you do when the point of your life, the focus of it, the centre of your existence, has been taken from you? I needed help. Badly. It says a lot about John Farley that I turned to him. He'd been a good friend of mine since my rebel days before Tanya started working her magic on me. I knew he wouldn't let me down. I rang him, and he didn't.

He must have dropped everything, for he was at the hospital within twenty minutes. By then I was standing in the main entrance, looking out across the car park, trying not to get in anyone's way and watching the first rays of the sun touching some nearby buildings. It was set to be a nice day. Tanya and I love clear, crisp days like this.

I saw John's van arrive and watched as he parked it about a hundred metres away. He got out and came over, spotting me almost at once. Instinctively I knew what he wanted to do, but men don't do that, not in our part of the world. "Come on," he said to me, and we walked in silence back to the van and set off for his home.

When we got there, Judith, his wife, was waiting for us, not inside but on the doorstep. She did what her husband had been unable to do earlier — put her arms round me and hugged me. Long and hard. I fought down a lump in my throat with some difficulty. If I yielded to self-pity I'd be reduced to a pathetic jelly of a man in seconds, and I was determined not to go down that path.

I suppose I had been hoping John would be able to keep me company, distracting my mind or simply commiserating, but it really wasn't a practical proposition. He had a motorcycle repair business to run, and with it came commitments that couldn't be rescheduled at short notice. I wasn't deserted in my hour of need though. He made a point of entrusting me for the rest of the day into Judith's unsentimental care. She was manageress of a local supermarket and awarded herself an emergency day off. "I've got a deputy who can cover for me," she explained. "That's what I pay him to do. It's a matter of priorities. Your need is greater than theirs right now."

I won't deny I initially thought Judith's company was a second-best option. I liked her, certainly, but there was an air about her — quite impossible to define or pin down — which conveyed the message that anyone who messed her about would regret it. It made me wary of her.

But as the morning passed, I gradually told her everything. She listened and commented and queried and never once said anything to make me cry. No one could have done it better. By the time we finished I had a new respect for her, and felt closer to her than I ever had before. She had helped me to believe that yesterday's events were not some awful nightmare, but awful reality. And I had an answer to the question that had tormented me since the previous evening: was it my fault Tanya was dead? Had I made an error of judgement at the fateful moment? I would have sacrificed my life to save Tanya. Could it be that that option had existed and I had failed to take it? Judith went over the details of the accident with me clinically, one by one, and guided me to the conclusion that I had done all I could, and that I was not to blame. Doubts lingered in my mind, of course. Judith said they always would.

After lunch, in which I shared unenthusiastically, Judith continued with her hand-holding ministrations by walking with me the couple of miles to my own house. Going home was something that had to be faced, and she convinced me it was better not put off. There were things needing to be seen to. She spent the afternoon getting me organized.

Among the most urgent matters to deal with were the four messages on the answerphone. The first was Tanya's dad, Bill Matheson, ringing from Nottingham to say he'd heard the news and would be coming to London to deal with various legal formalities. If I wanted to go back with him for a few days, I was welcome to do so. He'd phone again around teatime for a reply. The second was the company, asking why I hadn't turned up for work. The last two were a Detective Inspector Taylor and a coroner's officer. Both wanted to speak to me. Except for the first, I returned the calls straightaway.

Bill duly rang as promised at four. He was the one person I was dreading having to talk to. He had entrusted me with his precious daughter and she had been a passenger on my motorcycle and she was dead and I was alive. What right had I got to be alive? But there was no anger or bitterness in her father's words or in his voice. He was, fortunately, one of the old school like I was: stiff upper lip all the way. It made the conversation easier than I'd expected. I declined the offer of a stay in Nottingham in the kindest way I could. He was probably relieved. We left it we'd get together at the funeral.

And so to Inspector Taylor and the last significant encounter of a bleak day. He paid a visit in the evening after Judith had departed, and made me go through the accident all over again, asking a lot of questions and noting it all down.

I think, on reflection, he was a more sensitive man than police officers generally like to admit to being, for he ended the interview by making a short speech which injected a bit of steel into my fragile spirits. He must have realized what I was desperate for and yet couldn't articulate.

"I might as well tell you," he said, "that we've had the results from your blood sample, and it was negative for everything we tested it for. One hundred per cent pure. We've also given your bike a thorough examination, and there was nothing wrong with that either, apart from the damage caused by the collision. So full marks to you as a responsible road user. We've got two eyewitnesses, a pedestrian and a lady digging her garden, and they both bear out your account closely. And we've identified the make and model of the car from pieces knocked off by the impact. We're going to nail this hit-and-runner, believe me. I trust you'll take good care of yourself, sir. You'll be a star witness in court."

That night, and on other nights too when I was at my lowest emotional ebb, I contemplated suicide. Two things stayed my hand. One was that an impartial observer like Inspector Taylor had told me plainly it hadn't been my fault, and that I was needed to see justice done. The other was that taking my own life would upset Tanya. I had never made her cry before, and I wasn't about to start now.

2

TRIAL

The inquest was opened and adjourned to a later date on the first Friday. A post mortem having been performed, the coroner released the body to the next of kin. Standard procedure.

Six days later in Nottingham, Tanya was cremated and her ashes scattered in a copse of newly-planted trees on her father's farm. Her parents attended with several other relatives and friends, and also four members of staff from the school where she had taught French and Spanish.

Both before and after the forlorn religious service everyone was polite to me but distant, and it only needed the barest insight into human nature to work out the reason. Although my blamelessness had been established privately, it was not yet a matter of public record, and most of those present must have had their suspicions. It mattered a great deal to me. Even though my connection to the Mathesons, and to Tanya's colleagues, was history now, and I would soon be going my separate way and out of their lives, I wanted them to know that Ed Somersby had not killed their loved one. That, so far as I was concerned, was precisely what the inquest was for, and consequently I longed for it to resume.

In the meantime there was life of a kind to be lived. The day after bidding my ceremonial farewell to Tanya I returned to work with the electrical contracting firm which kept me gainfully employed in the North London area. The other electricians and the office staff had done up a nice card. Without exception they were all very supportive. I appreciated it deeply.

To some extent, being able to immerse myself in my job was a blessing. The familiarity of switches and drills and cable runs marked a resumption of normality. There was always, though, the empty house at nights and at weekends to make a mockery of anything normal. And the slow-moving judicial process intruded sporadically to ensure Tanya's absence remained at the forefront of my mind.

The first big intrusion was of course the reconvened inquest, held in May. As I had hoped, it absolved me of blame. It also enabled an explanation to be provided of how Tanya had been killed by an accident that had left me physically almost unscathed.

The old white-coated surgeon who had broken the news of her death to me began the process of enlightenment by detailing the injuries she had sustained. It was a dreadful catalogue: crushed left leg below the knee with compound fractures of both tibia and fibula; ruptured diaphragm; partial upward displacement of the liver through the rupture into the thorax; collapse of the right lung with some intra-lobar bleeding; ruptured spleen; fractures of the right seventh, eighth and ninth ribs frontally. I'm not a medical man, but I understood enough of the anatomical jargon to be unsurprised when the surgeon reported that Tanya's heart had twice stopped beating while he fought to save her life. And after it was all over and she had been sewn up, it had stopped for a third and final time.

Cue the forensic pathologist to reveal how she had come by these dreadful injuries.

"In order to determine the cause of the severe trauma suffered by the deceased," he reported, "I visited the site of the accident. I concluded that only the wounds to the leg were produced by the immediate impact of the car with the motorcycle. The young woman would have been flung off in the collision and almost certainly came rapidly into violent contact with a metal post used for the purpose of indicating the extent of parking restrictions on that side of the road. She appears to have struck the post in a line running from the base of the sternum slightly downward and rightward to the lateral part of the eighth rib."

He went on to give it as his opinion that Tanya's injuries would have proved certainly fatal without medical intervention, and even with it her injuries would have permitted her only a slim chance of recovery. He ended by exculpating the hospital. "Nothing I found," he stated, "led me to believe the treatment undertaken contributed in any way to this woman's death."

So there it was. Sheer bad luck. If the accident had been delayed by a mere seven hundredths of a second — the time it took me to travel a metre — Tanya would have missed the post and suffered nothing worse than a badly broken leg.

Not that that made everything all right. It didn't. There was still a case to answer: Tanya's bad luck had been given a great big helping hand by the driver of the black car. I thought so. Bill Matheson was kind enough to tell me he thought so. The coroner thought so. The police thought so. It was more or less unanimous. All that remained was to convince a jury in a criminal trial.

I began to envision a time when I could lay Tanya to rest in my mind: the day when her killer was punished for the act of careless murder he had committed. Five years imprisonment I reckoned, minimum. Tanya deserved justice, and with my help she was going to get it. In the same way as I had lived for the inquest, I began living for the court case. And after that was over I might possibly, just possibly, start living for myself again.

Naturally you can't have a court case without a defendant, but Detective Inspector Taylor soon solved that problem. He called round to give me the news in person, mainly because it was convenient as he lived only a couple of streets away, but I still think it was a kind touch. He told me an arrest had been made.

"Who?" I asked.

"A young man, name of Anthony Hartling. After the accident was reported on the local news, one of his neighbours contacted us to say he'd noticed Mr Hartling driving his Mercedes with a badly damaged left front wing on the afternoon in question. We already knew it was a Mercedes that hit you, so that fitted. Now the thing is, Anthony Hartling and his father are already known to us. The Hartlings are what you might call a problem family — it's more than my job's worth to be more specific, so don't ask — and that made us particularly keen to check out the neighbour's report. We found the car awaiting repairs at a dodgy garage: the sort whose proprietor can be relied upon to keep his mouth shut. Unless he's leant on by such as myself, that is. After that, it all fell into place."

"It sounds like you should be congratulated."

"We're heading in the right direction, sure enough, but this case isn't over till the judge bangs his gavel. I've seen too many crooks get off."

"This Anthony Hartling character hasn't confessed then?"

"Not a chance. He started by claiming a friend had been driving the car. When asked who, he wouldn't say. Then he announced he'd meant 'friend' euphemistically; he really meant thief. We pointed out we had a witness who'd seen him driving his damaged Mercedes. Witness is lying, he says. Witness will admit to making a terrible mistake. So we ask him if the chap doing the repairs made a terrible mistake too. Scum, he says. Won't testify anyway."

"He sounds very sure of himself."

"He's a cocky brat, right enough. I've got a feeling he's

going to be hard to convict. It doesn't help that his father is very wealthy."

"What's that got to do with it?"

"He'll be able to afford an expensive barrister."

"So? Facts are facts. A barrister can't alter them no matter how much he charges."

Inspector Taylor smiled and looked away. "I'm sure you're right, Mr Somersby. I'll let you know when there are further developments."

I expressed my gratitude. I liked this police officer. He cared.

*

The trial began with Anthony Hartling facing two indictments: firstly, causing death by dangerous driving; and secondly, failing to stop at the scene of an accident. He pleaded not guilty to the former, but had chosen, doubtless on the advice of his 'expensive barrister', to abandon the line of defence that it hadn't been him driving the Mercedes, and so admitted the latter charge.

As Hartling had predicted, the neighbour who had seen the damaged Mercedes had by then retracted his statement, but it didn't matter. By a delightful irony there were two CCTV surveillance cameras videoing the road in question as a crime prevention measure, and Inspector Taylor had in his possession recorded footage in which the car with its buckled left front wing was plainly to be seen entering the road and, an hour or so later, leaving again.

Also as predicted, the owner of the garage where the Mercedes had been taken for repair refused to testify. The evidence he would have provided was peripheral to the case, so the prosecution decided to leave him out of it rather than take a risk with unreliable testimony.

That was the state of play when I found myself

attending the court on Wednesday, June 30th, four and a half months after Tanya's death. I thought of it as the closing act of the drama — a way to say a final practical farewell to the woman I loved and had planned to grow old with, and to enable her at last to rest in peace.

It was in the afternoon I was summoned to take my place in the witness box. Surveying uneasily the strange and somehow foreign scene before my eyes, I saw Anthony Hartling for the first time. Although we were of similar age and height, his physical appearance had little else in common with mine. In contrast to me he had short, neat hair, a clean-shaven face, and wore an expensive suit with a regulation white shirt and a precisely knotted black tie. I couldn't see his shoes but I'll bet they shone. There was a solemn but benign expression on his face. Every mother's ideal son. Inconceivable, to look at him, that this young man had killed someone and tried to evade paying the penalty for it.

Our eyes met briefly as I took the stand. His countenance didn't change in the slightest. Thereafter I was invited to 'tell the jury' and so looked mainly at them.

The prosecution barrister began the questioning, enabling me to give an account of the accident. I had done this several times during the previous months, and relived the events frequently in distressing dreams, so it was almost second nature to me. So far, so good.

Then it was over to the defence barrister. She was, I'd guess, about thirty-five and very attractive, despite having a range of facial expressions which apparently didn't include smiling.

"I'd like to begin, Mr Somersby," she said, "by asking you to provide some background to your life."

What? My fiancée is dead, the man who killed her is in the dock, and she wants to discuss my c.v.? I knew arguing with this woman would be unwise, so I went along with it, but something was way off-target here. I just didn't know what.

It quickly became clear the defence barrister was only interested in particular aspects of my past. For example, she wanted to know if I'd ever been in trouble with the police or other authorities. (No I hadn't.) She wanted to know why I hadn't gone to university. (I'm not academically minded.) She wanted to know how I came to be an electrician. (It's as good a job as any.) She was especially probing about whether I'd ever got into fights (no I hadn't), when the last time was I hit someone (it was at school), how often I get road rage (I don't). And so on.

Then she moved on to my sex life. Once again I found myself having to strongly resist an urge to tell her to mind her own business. How many partners had I had? (Tanya was the one and only.) Why weren't we married? (We hadn't got round to it; neither of us considered it an urgent issue.)

When she didn't get what she wanted from these intrusive, personal and totally irrelevant lines of enquiry, she changed tack, saying: "I'd like to ask you now about your biking activities. How long have you had your licence?"

"I've had a Category A2 licence since I was nineteen, six years ago, and a full motorcycle licence for the last four years."

"So you got on a motorbike pretty much as soon as you could?"

"As soon as I could afford it."

"Did you ever ride a motorbike on a public highway before you got your licence?"

"No, of course not."

"Of course not? Normal teenagers don't generally respect the law, do they? Under-age drinking, getting in to see 18-certificate films, that sort of thing. Having a go on a motorbike would seem a perfectly healthy act of teenage rebellion."

I did consider telling her my father would have been extremely not-amused, and that in any case I didn't actually have access to a motorcycle in those days, but what would have been the point? Instead I simply restated the fact: "I never rode a motorcycle under age."

"How many accidents have you had since you were legally allowed to be in charge of a motorbike?"

"I've been knocked off on a couple of occasions."

"Were you at fault in these instances?"

"No."

"So that's three accidents in six years. Is that usual for bikers? It seems rather a high number."

"I don't know the statistics, but I don't think my experience of accidents is uncommon."

"Have you ever been convicted of a traffic offence?"

I fleetingly considered saying no, but I had a feeling she already knew the answer. If I lied and she could prove it, my credibility as a witness would be destroyed. So I opted for damage-limitation and answered honestly: "Yes, once."

"Would you tell the jury about that, please."

"I was caught speeding on the M4."

"Do you recall how fast you were going?"

I started to feel very uncomfortable. "I'd been trying to do a ton, but I didn't quite make it." (Actually I did, but the police clocked me doing 'only' 94.)

"A ton?"

"A hundred miles an hour. It was stupid, but I was only twenty-one."

"Never mind how old you were. A hundred miles an hour," she repeated in the direction of the jury to make sure they got the message. "Yet despite three accidents and one conviction, you would describe yourself as a good road user?"

"I learnt my lesson from that conviction, so my answer is yes."

"Tell me, have you ever ridden your motorbike while under the influence of any recreational substance?"

"I don't recall."

"Do you mean yes?"

By now I had stopped thinking she was even slightly attractive. "I mean I don't recall. I experimented like a lot of young people do, so I can't completely rule out the possibility."

"We're not interested in 'a lot of young people'. We're interested in you. So let me put it to you directly. Did you use any recreational substance at any time during the week preceding the accident?"

"No."

"You're quite sure about that? Motorbike gangs are — correct me if I'm wrong — notorious for their drug taking."

"I don't belong to a motorbike gang. And I'm not 'quite sure' about it; I'm absolutely certain."

"You must have drunk alcohol, surely."

"No. I only drink occasionally in social situations. There was nothing like that in the week before the accident."

"How about tobacco?"

"I don't smoke."

"You're quite saintly, in fact. But tell me, you'd been out for a meal with your fiancée at the time of the accident. Is that correct?"

"Yes."

"Was it a sumptuous meal?"

"Normal size for a restaurant."

"Most people feel sleepy after a sumptuous meal, don't they?"

"Possibly."

"Is that how you felt as you rode home?"

"No."

"So you're an exception?"

"I was *not* drowsy."

"We'll come back to that shortly. For the moment, let us turn to the machine you were riding. Can you tell us the make and model, please?"

"It was a Triumph Thunderbird."

"And what was its engine size?"

"Nine hundred and eighty cubic centimetres."

"Would you consider that to be a powerful engine?"

"Yes."

"Very powerful?"

"Just powerful."

"Twenty times the size of a moped engine?"

"About that."

"And yet that's only 'just' powerful?"

For the first time, I didn't reply. This woman was earning my contempt. She'd started speaking to me like I was mentally defective.

"Just powerful, Mr Somersby?" she repeated, louder than before.

"I've already made that clear."

"What was the top speed of this 'just powerful' machine?"

"In theory, a hundred and fifteen miles per hour."

"And in fact?"

"In fact, I've never exceeded the speed limit on it."

"Really." She paused to let the jury hear the unspoken words of disbelief in their heads.

Suddenly, in a flash of insight, I realized what was going on. Not one of her questions so far had anything to do with the accident. No. What they were directed towards was an attempt to tarnish my character. Hartling's 'expensive barrister' was endeavouring to create the impression, by means of slur and innuendo, that I was an irresponsible, aggressive, law-breaking tearaway who roamed the highways looking for trouble. The bitch was putting *me* on trial. And no one in this pretentious joke-shop stopped her. They just watched.

"Roughly how many hours a month do you spend riding your motorbike?" she asked.

"None recently."

"I mean before the accident."

"It varied."

"On average then."

"Five to ten, perhaps."

"And how many of those hours were with a pillion passenger?"

"I really don't know."

"You must have some idea."

"I didn't keep a record. Maybe ten per cent of the time."

"So you were much more used to riding the bike alone?"

"Yes."

"I put it to you," she said, pointing at me with her forefinger and feigning suppressed anger like some actress in a soap-opera, "that the presence of the pillion passenger substantially affected the handling of the motorbike and you failed to allow for that at the crucial moment."

"Do you, indeed," I said, responding to her statement literally. I'd had enough of this cow. She couldn't even speak proper English. No one says 'I put it to you' outside of a courtroom.

The judge, who had remained silent throughout this absurd interrogation, now spoke up. "Answer the question, Mr Somersby."

"She didn't ask me a question. *Sir*."

The judge glared at me. "Learned counsel's question was implicit and clear. Answer it."

At this moment I became aware of Tanya's father looking at me from where he was sitting with various other people attending the trial. He appeared to be wincing. It reminded me I was doing this for Tanya. And right now, not doing it well. With an effort I kept my temper.

"On a good motorcycle," I said, "a pillion passenger makes almost no difference."

The defence barrister was obviously going to argue with that answer. "Miss Matheson weighed," — theatrical look at notes — "fifty-eight kilograms. You put that much weight on the back of your machine," — adopt incredulous tone — "and it made no difference?"

"Almost no difference."

"Very well." She gave out a long audible sigh. Oscars don't belong in Hollywood; they belong in English courts. "If we can turn now to your account of events immediately prior to the crash. You state that you veered towards the middle of the road."

"I didn't veer anywhere."

"Shall I read out what you said, Mr Somersby?"

"I know what I said. The word I used was 'steered'."

"Ah yes. There's a subtle difference, isn't there." She switched on the anger again. "I put it to you you veered — I'm sorry, steered — a little too far; that you were in fact over the centre line when the impact occurred."

"Yes I was. I was trying to avoid the car on my side — that's the wrong side — of the road. If I'd been on the left hand side of the road I'd have gone straight into him, head on."

"I put it to you that if you had stayed well over to the left as you approached the bend, you would have seen the Mercedes driven by the defendant considerably sooner, he would likewise have seen you sooner, and consequently the accident would have been avoided."

"I don't think it would have made any difference."

"That is for the jury to decide. Did you apply the brakes, Mr Somersby?"

"The way he was driving, my being further left would not have made any difference."

"That is not an answer to the question I just asked you. Let me repeat it. Did you apply the brakes?"

"No, I did not."

"You saw you were heading for a collision and you didn't brake?"

"If I'd done that on a bend, the Thunderbird would have gone down, and we'd both have ended up being run over."

"How many seconds before the accident did you become aware of the car?"

"I don't know. Everything happened so fast."

"There's a lot you don't know, Mr Somersby. Was it one second, two seconds, three seconds?"

I shrugged. "Maybe one second."

"And how fast do you estimate the car was going?"

"It's very hard to tell. At least fifty, minimum."

"At that speed a car travels, let me see," — quick shuffle of notes — "oh yes, about twenty metres in one second. You didn't see this large Mercedes until it was twenty metres away from you? What were you doing, Mr Somersby? You were in charge of a full Category A motorbike — a machine, by your own admission, of considerable power — but it seems you weren't paying proper attention. Were you falling asleep after your substantial meal? Were you dreaming? Were you being distracted by your girlfriend?"

"That's not how it was."

"Then how do you account for your lapse?"

"There was no lapse. There must be something wrong with your calculation."

"The mathematics is quite simple. Shall I take you through it?"

"I said *maybe* one second and *at least* fifty miles an hour."

"Yes you did, didn't you. Thank you, Mr Somersby. I think we get the picture."

And with that I was abruptly dismissed. No opportunity to reflect. No opportunity to argue. No opportunity to correct a misleading impression. The whole truth and nothing but the truth, but only so long as it suits her hard-faced highness the defence barrister. Otherwise shut your face and clear off. Anthony Hartling was smiling. Everyone else looked impassive. I wanted to crawl away and hide.

Which is roughly what I did, only reappearing in order to attend the summing up by the prosecution and the defence as the trial drew to a close. This turned out not to be an attempt to establish what was truth and what was falsehood; it was theatre, pure and simple.

The prosecution barrister almost apologized for me, asserting that what mattered was that the defendant had been speeding at about seventy miles an hour — so the pedestrian witness said — had not braked but had in fact accelerated as the crash approached — both independent witnesses agreed about that — and had been on the wrong side of the road. The driver was clearly not in control of his vehicle. That was dangerous driving and had caused a death. The accused was guilty.

The defence barrister spoke lyrically about the character of Anthony Hartling: "My client has pleaded guilty to the charge of failing to stop at the scene of an accident. Let me ask you, members of the jury, to consider what this tells us of his moral steadfastness. He fled the scene of the crash for one simple reason: fear for his safety. He believed, rightly or wrongly, that a motorcyclist dressed from head to foot in black leather was someone likely to respond aggressively to being knocked off his machine. Of course, my client should then have reported to the police. He failed to do so and accepts this was wrong and that he should be punished. He stands before this court today ready to pay the penalty. Not, you will agree, an act of cowardice. More than that, it is a display of his fundamental honesty — to own up when at fault.

"Now to the charge of causing death by dangerous driving. He pleads innocent of this crime because he knows he is not guilty of it. His conscience is clear. So let me summarize the alleged facts of the prosecution." She went on to argue that the position of the Mercedes in the road was down to eyewitnesses. There was no hard evidence such as skid marks. The same applied to its speed: people traumatized by shock or injury tend to wildly overestimate such things. Then there was the competence of the motorcyclist. Had he contributed to the accident? She argued at some length that the crash had been more than half caused by my recklessness. Her client's driving may well have fallen short of the ideal standard, but it had not been dangerous, and it had not caused the death of Miss Matheson. Mr Hartling had been greatly distressed by this tragedy and of course extended his deepest sympathy to her family. But the blame did not lie with him. The accused was not guilty.

The eloquence of this lady barrister was, viewed objectively, most impressive. While her opposite number had spoken levelly, with an occasional flourish of an arm to emphasize a point, she, by comparison, had seemed to stride the stage like a prima donna. She commanded attention and agreement. The gestures, the emotion-packed utterances, but above all the intense, passionate sincerity, were to be marvelled at. I could see through it — see it for the dross and irrelevance that it was. I trusted the jury would do the same.

Once she'd finished, the judge had his say, instructing the jury that what they had to decide was a matter of fact: had the defendant been the sole cause of the accident and subsequent death, or was he a contributing factor?

The jury deliberated for three hours before returning to the courtroom to ask about their options in respect of substituting a lesser charge for the one presently under their consideration. Suitably instructed, they went away again. A further hour passed, and they announced their verdict. Anthony Hartling was innocent of causing death by dangerous driving but guilty of the lesser crime of careless driving.

After an adjournment, the judge explained that in the case of a single incident involving two motoring offences, as in this instance, the sentence has to reflect the most serious of the crimes, which was that of failing to stop at the scene of an accident. As punishment for 'this grave breach of the law' he had Anthony Hartling's licence endorsed and fined him what I could earn in eight weeks.

"This is an especially tragic case," he continued, addressing Anthony Hartling directly. "I cannot ignore the fact that someone died as a result of this accident. Had you stopped to help, it would not have affected the outcome for the young woman, but you weren't to know that. And that makes this a particularly serious offence. Consequently I am going to sentence you to six months in prison."

The judge paused and then continued severely: "However, in view of your hitherto good character, I do not believe an immediate period in custody would be in the best interests of society. Accordingly, the sentence is suspended for two years."

Anthony Hartling walked free from the court. He quite legally got into his Mercedes and drove away.

My life fell apart.

3

STALKER

I gave in my notice to the electrical contractors, effective the end of July. The house went up for sale. Tanya and I, with our savings and our combined salaries, had just been able to afford it on a joint mortgage. The loan came with life assurance attached, so it had been paid off following Tanya's death. We had done a fair amount of renovation work on the interior, and several estate agents thought they could sell it quickly. I gave the task to the one with the lowest commission. I didn't have a plan as such. I just wanted to get away. Maybe I'd emigrate to New Zealand.

About a week after the trial Detective Inspector Taylor knocked on my front door one evening, and we sat out on the patio drinking coffee and talking things over.

"I know how disgusted you must be feeling," he said sympathetically. "The best thing is to try and get detached from what happened. Some you win; some you lose. This one we lost."

"Easy for you to say. It's one case to you. It's *the* case to me."

"True enough."

"You know, the worst of it is I feel I let Tanya down."

"You didn't do so badly. You were holding your own until that barrister floored you with her twenty-metre routine."

"Yeh."

"She was muddying the water really. Going by our measurements, you'd have got a clear sight of the car at a distance of eighty metres. Say the car was doing sixty. You were doing thirty. At a closing velocity of ninety miles an hour, eighty metres is covered in two seconds. The dear lady barrister omitted to include your speed in the calculation. I've no doubt it was deliberate."

"And to hell with truth and justice?"

"She was only doing her job. A defence barrister is paid to get the client acquitted. Top line, middle line, bottom line. He or she is not under oath. According to the rules, they're not supposed to deceive the court, but that's the only limitation placed on what they say, and all too often they flout it, especially if it achieves the objective of putting doubt in the jurors' minds. That's all this one was doing."

"It stinks."

"I won't deny the system could be improved."

"Tell me," I asked angrily, "if I was to buy an axe and wave it about violently in a public place so that someone got his head chopped off, what would you charge me with?"

"Assuming you were sane, murder."

"But if I buy a car and drive it about violently in a public place so that someone gets her guts splattered from here to eternity, what am I charged with? Not murder. Never charge a motorist with murder. Only causing death by dangerous driving."

"I don't make the laws, Ed. All I can do is enforce them."

"And would a lawyer try to get a homicidal axe man acquitted by arguing it was the victim's fault for putting his head in the way of the axe?"

Taylor shrugged.

There was a brief silence while I recovered my temper.

"I feel so betrayed, that's all," I said at last. "The jury obviously thought it was my fault."

"Do you think it was?"

"No, I bloody don't."

"Then stuff the jury. Jurors are picked off the street. That means about half are likely to have below average intelligence. In other words, they're thick. Shall I tell you what a canny solicitor will advise a client in trouble? If you're innocent, go for trial by magistrate. If you're guilty, go for a jury trial. It doesn't take a genius to work out the reasoning behind the advice."

"It's irredeemable," I said bitterly. "If there was any justice in this country, the first thing we'd do is hang all the lawyers from the nearest lamppost. How can the system work with people like that running it?"

"Look, Ed, you're going to have to put this behind you."

"I know. Just not tonight."

Taylor took a card out of his wallet. "It's a victim support charity," he explained. "They might be able to help."

"Thanks," I said, taking the card.

He expressed his gratitude for the coffee and, as he was leaving, made a final comment. "Here's one irony that might amuse you. Anthony Hartling is currently in higher education. You'll never guess what he's spent the last two years studying."

"Becoming a driving instructor?"

He smiled. "Law. Some university in Wales. Probably wants to be the Director of Public Prosecutions one day. Funny old world, isn't it."

"Hilarious."

Taylor gave a half-hearted salute and set off into the sunset.

I put the card he'd given me in the rubbish. I didn't want charity.

*

Next afternoon I consulted a solicitor. No, you can't appeal against a jury's verdict. No, a sentence of six months suspended for two years doesn't mean what it says. It actually means the criminal won't go to prison at all as long as he behaves himself until the two years are up. No, an appeal that the sentence was excessively lenient wouldn't succeed. Six months is the maximum for failing to stop at the scene of an accident, and suspending it was reasonable in this case. Yes, a further course of action was open to me: I could sue Anthony Hartling for damages. I said I'd think about that.

When I asked how much I owed him, the solicitor looked benevolently at his watch and said he didn't charge for initial interviews. It wasn't what I expected. My opinion of his profession climbed a little from the loathsome depths to which recent events had consigned it.

*

I spent a couple of evenings a week in the congenial company of John and Judith Farley. They were all the victim support I needed.

Judith particularly was inclined to push me on what I was proposing to do when my electrical employment ended and the house had been sold. I honestly didn't know. I was seething inside, a furious young man with a giant grudge against society, and against one individual especially. I was simply incapable of planning a future while that remained the case.

Curiously, it wasn't Judith but John who, quite inadvertently, crystallized my thinking on what my next move should be. I didn't manoeuvre the conversation or anything. He just came out with it.

"I recall a case a few years ago which is a lot like

yours," he said. "There was this van driver ran over and killed a young lad, then tried to flee the scene. It turned out he had no driving licence and had untreated cataracts in both eyes. They convicted him of reckless driving, but the judge only sentenced him to eighteen months. What sort of value is that to put on a child's life? Anyway, when he came out of prison the boy's father whacked him with an iron bar. Damned near killed him. The father was tried for attempted murder. And guess what? The jury threw the case out. Innocent of the charge. The bigwigs were aghast over that. Open season on taking the law into your own hands, so they claimed. But it wasn't really. In my opinion, the jury were simply saying that, okay you judges and lawyers and suchlike, we pay you to see justice is done. If you fail to deliver the goods, you can't complain if we seek a remedy privately."

"What point are you making exactly?" I asked.

"All I'm trying to get across is that you aren't alone. You're not the first to be kicked in the balls by the English legal system, and you won't be the last. At least you haven't been so badly affected you feel the need to grab the nearest iron bar. That's something to be thankful for."

That remark of John's resonated loudly in my mind. I *was* that badly affected. So much anger and bitterness were festering inside me they left almost no room for anything else. And was it really so surprising I felt that way? I had trusted the law on Tanya's behalf, and it had made fools of us. Those pompous courtroom poseurs had been amusing themselves, playing arcane games with other people's lives. It had been merely an academic exercise to them. They hadn't seen Tanya, pale and motionless in her coffin. They wouldn't carry the scars of her loss with them to the end of their days like those who loved her would. She had been young and beautiful and caring and full of life, and it meant nothing to them. What had they actually known of

Tanya Matheson? Just some woman who got killed on a motorbike. Heaven forbid that a fellow of 'good character' should lose his liberty over *that*. Heaven forbid he should lose his driving licence over *that*. Tanya had cried out to them for redress, and they had collectively shrugged their shoulders and turned their backs. I defy anyone not to be angry and bitter whose companion in life has been treated so shamefully.

Okay then, let me think this through. One. Anthony Hartling had caused a dreadful accident. He had wickedly tried to avoid answering for it by concealing his identity. He had not been 'greatly distressed' as his lying barrister claimed. Two. The courts had washed their hands of the affair. I had no option, far less the right, of appeal. Three. I could seek damages by means of a civil prosecution. Should I do that? It would mean more poseurs, more games. I'd as soon consign my fate to the toss of a coin. And get better odds!

Which left, four: resort to John Farley's symbolic iron bar. There was no other way if I wanted justice for Tanya. So did I truly want it that badly? Badly enough to hazard my future? Yes, a thousand times yes. Unlike everyone else, I wouldn't shrug my shoulders and turn my back. Not me. I didn't yet have any detailed notion of what penalty it would be 'just' to inflict, but one thing I had no doubt about. No doubt at all. I was going to find Anthony Hartling and punish him. Personally.

*

The sale of the house was completed on August 20th. I got a good price. The furniture and most of our possessions went into store, and I moved into a modest bedsit in Kilburn.

The initial steps towards achieving my new goal in life

were taken in one of the main London libraries. From the internet I obtained an address for the Hartlings. It was several years out of date but told me which of the various London councils I should check with first. In the main office of the council in question, I requested to see the electoral register. From that I was able to confirm that the Hartlings were currently at the address I had discovered for them: 47 Hardiman Terrace, St John's Wood. There lived Simeon Hartling, together with his wife and their son Anthony. From the *ancestry.co.uk* online register of births I found Anthony Hartling was twenty-one as of the preceding December and that he had a sister aged twenty-four. I could, however, find no further trace of her and assumed she had left home.

Bearing in mind the two CCTV cameras, I didn't want to walk openly along Hardiman Terrace. Whatever I did to punish Anthony Hartling, it was my intention to get away with it. Being filmed in the vicinity of his home was consequently something to avoid. To that end, I bought the cheapest second-hand car I could find so I could keep under cover whilst checking the street out. It was a little old Mini, pretty much on its last wheels but good enough for driving short distances in London.

Hardiman Terrace, viewed on a map, forms the horizontal bar of an 'H'; that is, it connects two other parallel roads. It is long and straight and runs east-west. On its north side I found well-to-do three-storey town houses. The south side mirrors the north for the most part, but with gaps which have been filled in with large two-storey detached dwellings. No. 47 is one of these. I noted this particular property is fronted by a whitewashed stone wall topped by short steel spikes too close together to get a foot between. Total height of this fortification: two metres. I could discover only one breach in the wall, a gap blocked by an iron grill gate, also two metres high and electrically operated, giving access to a drive leading straight ahead to a double garage. Other points to consider: a burglar alarm bell box and a couple of unusual security extras, namely, active infra-red movement detectors in the grounds, and floodlights. Hardiman Terrace is clearly a crime conscious street, and the residents of no. 47 were particularly zealous in that respect. I plainly wasn't going to get at Anthony Hartling when he was at home.

It was a fair assumption he didn't spend all his time inside his parents' posh residence. Unfortunately, in opting to pursue him when he was away from home, I faced two unrelated difficulties. One was the time it would take. By the beginning of October my quarry would be off to Wales to commence the third year of his law studies. If I hadn't dealt with him by then, he'd be out of reach until the Christmas holidays. The other difficulty was that I couldn't simply sit in the Mini within sight of no. 47 and wait for him to emerge. All parking along Hardiman Terrace was reserved 'for residents only'.

I chose to do the next best thing short of direct observation. By good fortune there are only two ways to leave the terrace, and I decided to watch one of them. I selected the eastern exit because that's the one you'd use if heading into central London. Fifty metres from the junction, along Hilton Road — which forms the right hand vertical bar of the 'H' — is a public seat complete with litter bin and large concrete tub with flowers in it. This I made my observation post.

With my eye very much on the calendar, I took up position for the first time on the morning of Monday, August 23rd. Being out of sight of any CCTV cameras, I sat there openly with nothing more than a broadsheet newspaper to hide behind if the black Mercedes drove past. It sounds terribly amateurish, which is undeniably what it was, but the trouble is no one has written a book on do-it-yourself stalking (not that you can find in a London library anyway). Nor is there anything on the internet appropriate to my situation. It left me having to make it up as I went along.

That first morning I didn't see the Mercedes, but I did notice a metallic-gold-coloured Rolls Royce pull out onto Hilton Road, turning right and away from me at about half past ten. It closely resembled a car of that description I had glimpsed in the drive of no. 47 on several of my Mini-based reconnoitring forays, and one I had assumed belonged to Hartling senior.

The next morning I spotted the gold Rolls at no. 47, parked and probably empty, as I drove along Hardiman Terrace at quarter past ten. Finding somewhere to leave the Mini proved difficult, with the result I didn't get to my Hilton Road seat until quarter to eleven, only to discover a tramp in a sleeping bag flat out on it snoring the morning away. Thinking the Rolls would be long gone, and temporarily nonplussed by not being able to sit where I'd planned, I wandered down to the junction....

And there the damned car was, right in front of me. The sun was bright enough, and high enough up in the sky, to produce impenetrable reflections off the windows, so I had no idea who was inside, but whoever it was could sure as hell see me. Momentarily I froze — about the worst thing to do. Then I carried on as if the Rolls wasn't there, making a mental note of its registration number as it drove away, taking the same route as yesterday.

I still wasn't completely sure it was Simeon Hartling's car I'd seen, so I returned to my Mini, giving the sleeper a good cursing as I went by, and drove once more past no. 47. The drive was now empty. That was conclusive enough for me.

Following the alarming encounter I appeared to have had, I wondered if I should adopt a disguise. I could shave off my beard and have my long hair cut short, for instance. But no, I liked the way I looked. It was 'me' and I wasn't going to change that for Anthony Hartling. I settled for telling myself to be more careful in future.

Wednesday was pretty much a repeat of Monday and very frustrating. Seeing Simeon Hartling in his Rolls Royce might prove useful, I supposed, but it wasn't him I was after. I began to wonder if his son might be away on holiday. I'd been driving along Hardiman Terrace several times a day and had not yet once caught sight of the black Mercedes.

On Thursday and Friday, because Anthony Hartling continued to elude me, I tried tracking the Rolls Royce. On both occasions I was successful. The first of the two days saw me in Maida Vale and, sure enough, the car passed where I was standing. Next morning I watched it turn left off Edgware Road onto Marylebone Road. I didn't know if this activity was getting me anywhere, but it was better than nothing at all.

The three days of the bank holiday weekend I gave a miss as far as stalking was concerned, so it was on Tuesday, August 31st at quarter to nine that I made my first pass of week two down Hardiman Terrace. At last I was rewarded by a glimpse of what I was seeking. The doors of the double garage were open, with the Rolls inside and the Mercedes pulled forward onto the drive.

Much heartened, I parked the Mini in its usual place and took up position on my Hilton Road public seat. At 9.27 precisely the Mercedes appeared at the junction, angling slightly as if to turn right. Suddenly its tyres screamed and it swung round to the left. Hastily I raised my hide-behind newspaper. The car sped past my position, turning off further up the road. On this occasion the sky was cloudy, enabling me to clearly identify Anthony Hartling at the wheel. I wondered if his sudden change of direction was down to him spotting me. I didn't like it, but what could I do?

For the first time, I was conscious of feeling vulnerable out in the open, and decided to go somewhere less exposed. I walked down to Marylebone Road and its intersection with Baker Street, from where I hoped to see the gold Rolls approaching from the west. Assuming it did indeed drive past me, it would take my knowledge of where it was heading one step further. In due course it showed up as expected, drew level with me, and made off down Baker Street. I continued to watch until, some distance away, it disappeared into one of the lesser roads running at right angles.

Studying my *London A to Z*, I felt a rush of excitement. If Simeon Hartling had had much further to go, he would have stayed on either the southbound Edgware Road or the eastbound Marylebone Road. His taking to side streets indicated I was close to his destination.

For the next hour I systematically explored the turnings off Baker Street looking for him. I didn't cover them all. But then, I didn't have to. The Rolls Royce remained elusive, but the black Mercedes was parked for all the world to see in Throckmorten Square.

I couldn't believe my luck. Or then again, perhaps it wasn't luck. Perhaps father and son had left Hardiman Terrace to travel separately to the same destination. Whatever the case, I'd made real progress. If I'd stumbled on a regular parking place — a big if — then I'd found a location where Anthony Hartling was out in the open. Somewhere I could get at him.

Feeling in a superstitious way that I'd be tempting providence taking matters any further that day, I returned to the Mini. The meter had expired, and my little car was adorned with a parking ticket. I was philosophical. The St John's Wood part of London had seen the last of me anyway. It was time to switch my investigations from Hardiman Terrace to Throckmorten Square.

Accordingly, the following morning I made an enthusiastically early start on checking out this new location. The square proved to be accurately named, being exactly that, each side measuring approximately one hundred and fifty metres. Inside the four roads that make up its sides is a large garden with lawns, flowerbeds, bushes and trees. The garden is surrounded by iron railings, and there are several notices on display stating that the open space is private and for the use of residents of the square only. On the outer margins of the four roads are typical central London dwellings: terraced houses with four floors plus basement. On the north side, all the houses have been combined to form a large hotel. The other sides comprise a mixture of genuine homes and properties used as business offices, the latter distinguishable by brass plates and fancy door-entry systems. None of the businesses had a name suggesting a Hartling connection.

Having checked out the environs, I passed a few hours keeping a parking meter happy while I watched for the Mercedes to arrive. I wore dark glasses as my first concession to adopting a disguise. It proved to be a frustrating morning, as neither of the Hartlings showed up. I called off the vigil at midday and drove away.

The next day I turned up after the rush hour to find all the parking spaces had been taken. That wrote Thursday off.

Friday was a little more fruitful. I arrived at sunrise to claim a slot for the Mini and sat there, as on the Wednesday, observing the scene. The Mercedes never materialized, but I saw the Rolls heading south along the east side of the square, and on into Carrington Place. I dashed from my car in the hope of discovering where it was going but was out of luck. By the time I had a clear view along Carrington Place, the Rolls had disappeared.

I wandered about for a while looking for clues as to where it had gone, checking out the various side streets turning off to left and right, but none contained Simeon Hartling's car. I concluded I was wasting my time and gave up. I found myself feeling totally demotivated, to the extent that I returned to Kilburn and spent the rest of the day watching DVDs in my bedsit.

Considering the promising start to my second week of stalking, it was disappointing how little progress had been made since the Tuesday. Given the university imposed deadline of the beginning of October for achieving my goal, I was aware time was relentlessly running out. I was not a happy man.

4

SKIRMISH

Since Tanya's death I had become something of a recluse where social networking was concerned. Our PC had gone into store with most of our other possessions, the landline had stayed with the house when it was sold, and my mobile phone I kept switched off almost all the time. I didn't want to hear from people. If I felt like talking to someone, I'd contact them. My callers gradually got the message and stopped calling. So I was surprised when I switched on the phone on the Friday evening to find a message from Tanya's father.

"Bill Matheson here. Sorry to bother you, Ed, but I found this number in Tanya's effects and I'm hoping it's still current. If you're not doing anything this Saturday, could you get up here for lunch. Say twelve o'clock. I'd like to talk to you. It's important. Let me know if you can't make it. Thanks."

It was like Bill to come across as rather imperious, so it didn't offend me that he was politely giving me an order. Truth to tell, I was intrigued.

Rather than chance it in the rickety old Mini, I caught an Intercity to Nottingham and took a taxi from there to the Mathesons' farm.

It was all small-talk and Tanya-talk before and during lunch. It honestly hadn't occurred to me there were other people on this earth who missed her as terribly as I did. That visit to Nottingham disabused me of the notion that the suffering was all mine.

After the meal, Mr and Mrs and I sat out on the small enclosed lawn which separates the farmhouse from a field in which Bill grows various odd-looking root crops. For early September it was pleasantly warm and sunny.

"There's something I want to show you," said Bill eventually. "Stay there."

He went into the house.

"Don't mind me if I get a bit upset, dear," Mrs Matheson announced, leaving me at a loss for a reply.

Bill returned and handed me a picture frame. The glass had been removed. The picture was a photo of Tanya which had been torn into at least ten pieces and screwed up and not very prettily reassembled.

"We had a visitor," Bill said.

"Someone who did this?" I asked, frowning.

"Yes. And he was at pains to make sure I knew why. It's on account of the action I've been taking. You see, after that smarmy hooligan walked out of the courtroom and drove away, I had a choice. I could either spend the rest of my life howling at the moon, or I could fight. And you know I'm a fighter."

I thought to myself that Bill Matheson and I may not have had much to say to one another in the past, but we had a similar attitude to life's crises. Perhaps that's why Tanya fell in love with me.

Bill continued: "Straight after the court case, we began legal proceedings to sue for damages. You won't mind me saying that as you two weren't married we thought we, as Tanya's parents, had a better chance of success than you would have. Otherwise we'd have involved you from the start."

"Fair enough," I agreed.

"Anyway, things move very slowly in legal circles — about as fast as a heavily loaded tractor with two flat tyres — but we were beginning to get somewhere. Then this....

caller turned up. Knocked on the door Wednesday evening smoking a fat cigar."

"He'd only just lit it," interrupted Mrs Matheson. "It was part of it."

I wasn't sure what she meant by that. "Go on, Bill," I said.

"He started off by asking if he could come in. Naturally I wanted to know who he was first, and he told me he represented Mr Simeon Hartling. Thinking he was a solicitor, I said okay as long as he left his cigar outside. Can't abide tobacco. He completely ignored me, pushed me out of the way, came in puffing on the execrable thing, shut my front door behind him and stood there in the hallway looking about like he was a prospective buyer. That got my hackles rising. I mean, this is my home, damn it. I ordered him to leave or I'd call the police. He advised me not to. I went to the phone, but before I could do anything he grabbed it, pulled the whole assemblage out of the wall, and smashed it under his heel. I squared up to him, of course. He was a dirty hitter, Ed. I went down like a house of cards. After that, it was a lecture on why it isn't a good idea to annoy Mr Hartling. Ruining that photograph was his parting gesture."

"It's the best one we had," said Mrs Matheson, clearly distressed.

"Did you call the police?" I asked.

"Of course I did. After he'd gone, on my mobile."

"And?"

"They haven't the manpower to guard us. If it happens again, they'll give us an alarm which connects to some headquarters or other. Too little, too late. If I was on my own, I'd load up the shotgun and defy these bullies. But I've got to worry about the wife."

"I appreciate that."

"So.... well.... I'm giving in."

"It's probably for the best," I said sympathetically. "There were two witnesses who were set to testify in court who sort of 'gave in'. I didn't understand what they were up to at the time, but I think I can guess. It seems Simeon Hartling knows how to frighten people."

"Awful man," said Mrs Matheson.

"I thought you ought to know about this," her husband went on, "in case you're considering going down the same path. There's no sense in you wasting money on solicitors. If you did decide to take legal action though, despite what you'd be up against, I'd support you financially, one hundred per cent."

And there, spelled out at last, was the reason why I'd been invited to Nottingham. The Mathesons wanted me to pick up the torch they'd been intimidated into dropping, and carry it forward.

I briefly considered taking them into my confidence and telling them my own proposed solution to the Hartling problem, but it would have breached my prime rule. *No one must know.* Whatever punishment I ended up inflicting on our joint enemy, it had to be kept strictly between him and me. His word against mine. If someone else knew what I had done, my continued liberty would rest in their hands. No matter who that someone was, I'd live in fear of the knock on the door for the rest of my life. It was why I couldn't ask Bill for the loan of his shotgun. It was why I had to tell him, when he pressed me as I was taking my leave, that I had come to terms with Tanya's death and was more inclined to get on with my life than to pursue Anthony Hartling. He believed me. I could discern that from the way he deflated. I doubted I would ever see the Mathesons again.

*

The start of the third week of my stalking operation saw me back in Throckmorten Square just after dawn. I went along with a pen and a sheet of paper and wrote down the names of all the companies who had nameplates affixed to buildings overlooking the square. I repeated the process down the adjoining Carrington Place.

Later, after a quick visit to the nearest public library to access the local telephone directory, I began ringing the businesses one at a time using my mobile phone. By then it was the middle of the morning, thus ensuring all the offices were staffed. In each case I asked to speak to Mr Hartling. I got several 'who?' responses, and then the reply I was seeking: "And your name is?"

I hung up. Bull's eye! The company concerned was called High Rise Nightclubs Limited, and it occupied the corner of Throckmorten Square and Carrington Place. I presumed I was dealing with some sort of head office where they process accounts and payrolls and other administrative matters. A nightclub it certainly wasn't.

After going back to the bedsit for lunch, I drove through the square again in the early afternoon and was unexpectedly rewarded by the sight of the black Mercedes, parked and empty. It seemed reasonable to conclude Anthony Hartling either worked for (or with) his father during the university holidays or, failing that, at least visited the premises occasionally. All I had to do was to be patient and catch him between car and office. It meant I was half way to my goal. The question 'where?' had an answer at last.

It was time to face up to what I had hitherto put off: answering the two questions 'how?' and 'what?' In an attempt to be methodical I wrote down a list of possible punishments. They were all intended to inflict injury rather than death, though if Hartling's luck was to prove as bad as Tanya's and he died, I wouldn't burst into tears over it.

I thought of eleven options:

a) Hire someone. Paying a third party to administer a
    sound beating would be a neat solution, but employing
    thugs would violate my no-one-must-know rule. Forget
    it.
b) Poison. Forget that as well. Hartling wasn't about to
    have a meal or a drink with me.
c) Bomb. I could probably find out how to make one if I
    searched the internet hard enough. The trouble with
    this idea was more that it would make me a terrorist —
    bombs are uncontrollably indiscriminate, and I didn't
    want to hurt anyone else.
d) Rifle. Too bulky.
e) Bow and arrow. Too bulky.
f) Shotgun. A certificate has to be issued by the police,
    but they won't give you one until various background
    checks have been carried out and conditions met. I was
    running out of time and couldn't afford the delays
    involved.
g) Handgun. Unobtainable unless you know which
    criminals to ask, and I didn't.
h) Knife. Possible.
i) Car 'accident'. The equitable choice! Another possible.
    However, running Hartling down would be a difficult
    trick to pull off in traffic clogged London.
j) Blunt instrument. Something like a truncheon might
    work. A third possible.
k) Bare fists. I didn't want a fair fight that I might lose.
    Forget it.

Eight options had ruled themselves out for one reason or
another. The remaining three I listed in order of likelihood
of success. Knife was best. Truncheon came second, being
similar to knife but with much less certain effectiveness.

Car accident, the more I thought about it, I was increasingly inclined to rule out. Too many things could go wrong; and if I failed once, he'd be put on his guard and I'd never get a second opportunity.

So I concentrated on investigating knives. I discovered they are freely available in the right shops and over the internet, including types designed purposely for killing people. Finding one I could purchase wouldn't be a problem.

And that brought me face to face with the biggest question of all. Could I really walk up to this guy and stick a knife in him? The more I tried to imagine the actual immediacy of it, the more I doubted. It would be like the first time I chatted up a girl. It was a great idea until I was actually approaching her. Then I wanted to be anywhere but where I was. I'd managed to talk to that girl. Would I manage to stab Anthony Hartling — even assuming he stood still to let me do it? If the answer was no, then the past month had been nothing more than an elaborate fantasy. I could see only one way to settle the issue, and that was to take this thing right down to the finishing line. Metaphorically speaking, I had to get him in my sights with my finger on the trigger. Maybe I'd go ahead. Maybe I'd realize he wasn't worth it. I decided I could accept the verdict of that ultimate moment. And that meant I had to continue with my efforts to bring it about.

To that end, I returned to Throckmorten Square in the evening with the intention of finding out what time Anthony Hartling left the office. Unfortunately, I was too late; the Mercedes had already departed. However, lights were still on inside the building and, having nothing better to do, I elected to hang around for a while and observe the comings and goings. A few people — harmless clerical types — emerged between six and eight, and a little later a not so harmless fat guy came out and apparently locked up.

I'd have gone home at that point except one floor remained illuminated. Was someone still inside, or was it simply that nobody had bothered to turn the lights off?

At ten, one man and five women arrived and went in. From the pattern of lights going on and off and what I glimpsed of these six in the windows, I deduced they were cleaners. It couldn't have been a long job for them, because by quarter to eleven the lights were all out and the cleaners trooped away. With the show clearly over for the night, I followed their example in the Mini.

Next morning I was back in the square early. Now I knew which building to concentrate on, the mystery of the disappearing Rolls was easily solved. A short distance down Carrington Place is a right turn through an archway into a small courtyard behind the High Rise Nightclubs offices. A large grill gate prevents access outside working hours. It was a reasonable conclusion that that was where Simeon Hartling parked his car.

Returning to the front of the building, I noticed something I hadn't spotted before: a small CCTV camera which would film anyone standing at the front door — or someone jotting down details off the adjacent nameplate. I retreated to the Mini and spent a while convincing myself nobody would be watching a monitor at the sort of times I'd been in view, or scanning later any recordings that had been made.

I was still sitting passively in the Mini when, just after ten, Anthony Hartling walked past and entered the High Rise Nightclubs office. I got out of my car and went to find his Mercedes, which was straightforward enough. It was in the square but hidden from where I was parked by a bush in the central garden.

I got back in the Mini and was debating what to do next — go and buy the knife? — when my quarry passed me again, this time presumably returning to his car and intending to drive away. I decided it might be a useful thing to add to my fund of knowledge about him if I could find out where he was going. To that end I decided to try my hand at following his car.

I waited briefly to give him time to get his seatbelt fastened, and then reversed out of my parking slot. As the Mercedes came into view, he obligingly pulled into the traffic.

We set off, heading north. I kept just far enough back that he wouldn't be able to recognize me in his rear-view mirror, and put my sunglasses on as an added anti-identification measure.

I have always thought that tailing someone in heavy traffic would be almost impossible. The way it's shown being done in crime dramas seemed to me to involve an incredible amount of luck. The writers of these stories have obviously never tried to do the real thing. So I was expecting to lose track of the black Mercedes very rapidly. But I was wrong. Anthony Hartling was driving like a senior citizen, following all the rules: no speeding, no gambling at traffic lights, always indicating well in advance of taking turns, showing immense courtesy and consideration to other road users. I was amazed. He was making following him really easy. Maybe the crime film scriptwriters were right after all.

We'd been going for about three quarters of a mile when he took a left turn into a narrow side street. I did the same. About a hundred metres separated us. Totally unexpectedly the Mercedes' brake lights came on. I wanted to keep my distance, so I too braked. There was in any case no room for me to get past his car on either side. The Mercedes came to a halt. So did my Mini. I started to feel the first twinges of alarm. Why had he stopped? Had he spotted me? Was he looking for some kind of confrontation? Considering reversing, I checked in my mirror and saw that a BMW, one which had been behind me since leaving Throckmorten Square, had pulled up across the entrance to the side street, completely blocking it. I honestly thought it was no more than irritating bad luck that the BMW had stopped where it had.

Ahead, Anthony Hartling got out of his car and turned to face in my direction. To my rear, two men were now visible. The driver of the BMW — a weight training fanatic if ever I saw one — was squeezing between the corner of his car and the wall of the building it was up against. His passenger was advancing towards me, a baseball bat swinging from his right hand.

My pulse went supersonic. I knew instantly what was going to happen. And why. I'd been fooling no one but myself. Of course my activities of the past weeks hadn't gone unnoticed. Hartling was well aware of them. This was his response. He wanted a word with me. I could understand that. Break my arms, smash my face in, that kind of word. No wonder he'd been easy to follow through the busy streets. Total sucker that I was, I'd allowed him to lead me like a lamb to the slaughter. I was confronting a blood-spattered catastrophe.

Looking around rapidly, it was plain there was no way out of the trap, either on two feet or four wheels. My immediate thought was to sound the horn, but I knew it wouldn't save me. It couldn't bring assistance quickly enough. Reason told me to stay in the Mini, but beyond that it failed me completely.

Instinct took over. Anything to get away from Hartling. I released my seatbelt, slammed the car into reverse, floored the accelerator, tightened my grip on the steering wheel and let out the clutch.

Logically it was a futile gesture; emotionally there was some compensation in the thought that hurting me was going to come with a price tag. The Mini surged backwards. Weight Trainer had to throw himself against the wall on my right to get out of the way. Baseball Bat took a swing at me in passing, shattering the Mini's rear window.

At the last moment, I pumped the clutch to prevent the engine stalling, and leant my upper half over onto the left-hand seat to avoid whiplashing my neck. There was a screech as I struck the BMW's open front passenger door, followed almost instantly by the impact proper: a severe jolt accompanied by a not particularly loud bang.

I returned to normal driving position. Weight Trainer was running towards me, fury all over his face. I guess what I'd done to his car had just made this personal. I engaged first gear and once again released the clutch. I seemed to feel some resistance, though only momentarily. The Mini jerked forward. There was a clatter as something metallic hit the ground behind me.

Weight Trainer decided to dare me to run him over, positioning himself square in the Mini's path. I was too loaded with fear and adrenalin to show mercy. He jumped out of my way at the last moment, making a grab for the door handle on the driver's side. I'd already engaged the lock. He missed anyway.

Baseball Bat was more sensible. As I approached him, he stood to the left of my car and prepared to take a swing at the windscreen. I tweaked the steering wheel towards him. I was too close to make that much of a difference, but it served to get him to pull the bat up short. He missed his target, striking the window at the side. More shattered glass. Putting the sunglasses on earlier proved to be about the only thing I'd got right so far; it meant none of the fragments went in my eyes.

Hartling must have realized that I was intending next to ram his Mercedes. He was already back inside. Against competition like that, my little old Mini didn't stand a chance. He managed nought to forty in about two seconds, leaving a cloud of burnt rubber smoke in the air.

His hasty retreat surprised me for a moment. But then again, he did have a suspended prison sentence hanging over him, and should his car get damaged it would make it easy for the police to catch him if I accused him of beating me up. In the circumstances it was prudent for him to make off. And he did so with a vengeance. At the far end of the side street was a one-way main road packed with a queue of hitherto stationary traffic which was starting to move forward. He simply drove into the first gap between boot and following bonnet that presented itself. Brakes squealed, horns sounded. Since he was blocking the traffic lane, the motorist he'd cut up had no choice but to let him out. He went.

When I arrived at the same junction, it was just in time to see the Mercedes turning right at some traffic lights a hundred metres away. Behind me, the BMW was entering the side street, both occupants on board. The doors on its left hand side were seriously dented, and it looked like Baseball Bat was trying without success to close the front one.

I was very unhappy about the advancing BMW. Unfortunately I couldn't emulate the Mercedes, because the stream of cars was now speeding past at a good thirty miles an hour. Nor did I reckon I could wait for the next set of traffic lights upstream to create a clear stretch of road for me. The occupants of the BMW only needed a few seconds to drag me from my car. I had to go now. Now. That left only one course of action: to turn into the main road and drive along the pavement, using it as an extra lane. And that's what I did.

It was lucky there were no pedestrians for me to run over. There was, however, an obstacle: a tree about thirty metres ahead. It limited my options. Moving forward I had to gradually angle into the road. As I had hoped, a driver's nerve eventually broke, and he slowed to let me into the flow. He gave me a V-sign out of his window so I wouldn't be under any illusions about what he was thinking of my driving technique. I accelerated and the rear left side window fell out, succumbing by some sort of delayed action to Baseball Bat's second swipe at my car. I pretended not to notice.

When I got to the lights where I'd last glimpsed Hartling's Mercedes, they turned red. Having flouted rather a lot of motoring laws already, I'd have gone through them regardless, but the crossways traffic was beginning to move. In my driving mirror I could see the BMW half a dozen cars back from me. I was relieved neither of its occupants tried to get to me on foot.

When I was cleared to set off again, I decided not to turn right as Hartling had, but to go straight ahead. I was in the wrong lane to do that. The fellow of the V-sign hated me even more if the vigorously waved clenched fist was anything to go by.

It was my intention to give the driver of the BMW a choice: to follow in Hartling's tyre tracks or to come after me. I fervently hoped he'd do the former, because all I wanted at that precise moment was to disengage, get out of the traffic and inspect the damage. Naturally, Weight Trainer chose to disappoint me.

So there I was, doing thirty-five down a wide four-lane London street in a Mini with no rear window, no left-side windows, and heaven knows what missing off its back side, hotly pursued by a couple of thugs in a battered BMW. The inside of the car was now very windy, with the result that my eyes were soon watering copiously. And that was despite the sunglasses. I had to wipe tears off my cheeks every minute or two. I was badly frightened.

I followed all the other drivers; Weight Trainer followed

me. By an irony, I crossed Hilton Road a short distance north of Hardiman Terrace. After that I ended up filtering onto Finchley Road, a fast dual carriageway and one of the main arteries out of London.

On the move, the rear-view mirror had taken to vibrating so badly in the air swirling round the interior that it was practically useless. However, I was frequently stationary at Finchley Road's various sets of traffic lights. (The damned things turned red so reliably as I approached them that it almost seemed deliberate.) I was thus repeatedly able to check on my pursuers. Whenever I halted, I hoped to see they'd gone, but they were always there.

They made no attempt to overtake. They just kept close behind me, their intention obviously being to intimidate. They were succeeding. I couldn't get away from them, and when the petrol ran out — the tank was indicating a quarter full — depending on where it happened, I could be in great danger. I was also heading for parts of London I didn't know. Something else to worry about.

Eventually I came to the North Circular Road. I turned left onto it so as to avoid going any further out into unknown territory where I might come across an empty stretch of highway with no witnesses. The BMW continued clinging like a leech. There were probably a lot of ways I could have got it off my tail, but its very closeness seemed to freeze my thought processes. Fear was paralysing my mind.

It was some distance beyond the Brent reservoir when I passed a police car on the other side of the road. I had completely forgotten that the Mini might attract the attention of law enforcers. They had to find a gap in the crash barrier separating the two streams of traffic, but it didn't take them long, and within a few minutes they were coming up fast behind me, lights flashing. They made it obvious it was me they were after. I took the next left off the North Circular and stopped. The BMW kept straight on and headed away into the distance.

I slumped against the steering wheel, trembling violently. The release of tension, the sheer relief, was overwhelming. I had never been so pleased to be in trouble with the law in my life.

The police car drew up behind me. Both constables alighted, one watching from a distance, the other approaching. I quickly brushed bits of window glass off my legs, got shakily out of the Mini and made my way to the back of it. The damage was quite a sight.

"Are you aware this vehicle isn't roadworthy, sir?" the policeman asked, looking at where the rear lights should have been but weren't.

"Well, I wasn't, no, but on second thoughts...."

The boot lid on an old-style Mini is vertical when closed, and hinged at the bottom. Mine was hanging open. The officer bent down and lifted it slightly, so he could see the number plate affixed to it but I couldn't. He let it drop again. It was the final insult for one of the two hinges, which came adrift; the other one then followed, and the boot lid fell noisily onto the road.

"What would the registration number of this car be?" the officer asked.

I told him.

"And exactly how did you come by this er.... unfortunate re-design?"

"I hit a brick wall. I was reversing, you see, and my feet slipped on the pedals."

"Damage the wall, did you?"

"No actually."

"Just as well."

He moved to the front of the car and inspected that. I saw then that the reason the rear side window had fallen out earlier was that Baseball Bat had hit the car with such force he'd bent the central door strut.

"Licence?" said the policeman.

That was in my wallet. I showed him.

"Insurance?"

I showed him that too.

He noticed my hands were not entirely steady despite my best efforts. His colleague was asked to bring over the breathalyser kit. I did the necessary. It proved, of course, totally negative.

"You know it's a finable offence not to have working rear lights?" the policeman stated in a reasonable tone of voice.

"I'm very sorry if I'm breaking the law," I said, verbally cringing. "I just need to find a garage, and all this can be fixed."

"You should have sent for a breakdown truck."

"Yes, that's a good idea. I'm afraid I'm not much use at emergencies. I've never done anything like this before. I really don't want to get into trouble."

They led me back to their patrol car and made me sit in the rear while they checked over the radio that I wasn't wanted for any crime. That established, the police officer who'd done all the talking looked at his colleague and sighed. "We're supposed to be pretty strict with fines. Bit of an earner really. But we have discretion."

"Hey, steady on," said the colleague unhelpfully.

"Have you got a mobile phone?"

I nodded.

"Give it to me."

I handed it over, puzzled. He keyed in a number and called someone. "Hi. This is your favourite copper. Got a job for you. I need a wreck recovered." He gave the location, returned the phone to me and said: "Let's be clear, Mr Somersby. You wait here for the truck to collect your car. I'm going to be patrolling this area for the next while, and if I catch you driving that car again I'll come down on you like the proverbial. Do we understand each other?"

I thanked him very sincerely. His colleague tutted.

They let me out of the patrol car and drove away. I waited obediently by the Mini until the breakdown truck arrived. Loaded up, we drove to the truck driver's accident-repair garage, where he carried out an inspection. There were several instances of damage underneath that brought forth sharp intakes of breath. (He was an eloquent man.) He said the poor thing wasn't worth repairing and should be pensioned off. I agreed. The car was useless to me now it had become known to the enemy. I settled up with him, leaving him to dispose of the Mini however he thought fit.

Safely back in my bedsit in Kilburn, I found myself mentally re-living over and over again the events of the morning. I had kept my arms unbroken and my face un-smashed in, but my confidence had been shaken to its foundations.

5

PURSUIT

Fact one: Anthony Hartling wasn't an ordinary young man who could be got on his own and dealt with. He had some tough characters supporting him: people like Weight Trainer and Baseball Bat and the cigar smoking hard man who had frightened the Mathesons in Nottingham. I doubted a law student would have the financial resources to pay individuals like them. I strongly suspected therefore that his father was supplying the personnel and the funding. Which led me to....

Fact two: Simeon Hartling was not a typical wealthy businessman. When challenged, he didn't dial 999 or send for a solicitor; he preferred to employ much harsher, and doubtless more efficient, direct methods. His son was made in the same mould. They were both dangerous.

Fact three: I was intending to do something extremely serious but I hadn't been taking it seriously. I'd been conducting the affair like — go on, admit it — like a bungling amateur. It wasn't surprising I'd come close to disaster. For example, every time my presence might have been detected, I had assumed it hadn't been. I should have assumed the opposite and planned accordingly. I'd even been so stupid as to sit in that Mini on three separate mornings and one evening in full view of the High Rise Nightclubs office windows trusting I was unnoticed. Idiot! The price people like the Hartlings pay for bypassing the norms of civilized behaviour is that they have to be constantly on guard against retaliation in kind. Always alert. Always suspicious. To someone with that attitude to their surroundings, I'd have stuck out like a lighthouse on main beam.

The realization that I was up against not simply the unpunished killer of my fiancée, but a violent and ruthless family dampened my enthusiasm for pursuing private justice. I knew now exactly how Bill Matheson felt when they frightened him off. You start to wonder if it's really worth it. Wouldn't it be better all-round if I followed Inspector Taylor's advice and put this affair behind me?

But there was another side to my character: one that reacted to intimidation with outrage and an increased determination to see the matter through. And there was Tanya to consider. What would she think if I succumbed for no other reason than that I was afraid?

For a couple of days I vacillated. But ultimately it came down to this. Anthony Hartling had deprived Tanya of her life. He had inflicted appalling misery on her family and her friends as well as on me. And society, in the shape of twelve incompetent jurors and a lenient judge, had let him get away with it. It was a stark miscarriage of justice, and I wasn't about to passively accept it. I had a score to settle with Anthony Hartling. If he put up a fight, then so be it. I was not going to be bullied into going away.

It was clear I needed a new plan. Now the Hartlings were alerted, an attack in London was out. In all likelihood it always had been; I just hadn't realized it. My thoughts turned to Wales and the university where Anthony Hartling was studying law; and also to the new attitude I was going to have to adopt if I was to take a more 'professional' approach to the task.

My first consideration was an alibi. Obviously I couldn't be in two places at once, but I reckoned I could come close. To that end it was necessary to swap my current bedsit, where my absence would be noticed, for a small furnished flat. There are numerous of those advertised all the time in London, and I was easily able to rent a suitably anonymous one, located in Harrow, on a per-calendar-month basis at short notice. Drawing on my electrical expertise, I rigged the place so that the radio and television came on at appropriate times of day, as did the lights, while curtains were worked by means of electric motors on timer switches. This flat was where I was officially going to be while I was actually in Wales.

My second consideration was that of disguise. The long hair would have to go, as would the beard. T-shirt, leather jacket and jeans would be replaced by white shirt and tie, dark office-worker suit and dignified raincoat. (Autumn in Wales tends to be rather wet.) For the voice I chose a Dublin accent, something I'd been particularly good at since a child and several holidays in that part of the world. I'd keep it at a level which was noticeable enough to provide a mask, but not so noticeable as to attract attention. My false name would be Winston Kelly; Winston from Somersby via Wintersby, and Kelly because it seemed like a common surname for someone from Dublin.

By Monday, September 20th my planning was complete, and I was ready to go. I visited my bank and arranged to transfer my account to a branch closer to my new abode in Harrow. This was so my imminent change of appearance wouldn't be remarked on by the staff — the cashiers at the old bank never seeing the 'new' me, and the cashiers at the new bank never seeing the 'old' one. I also took the opportunity to withdraw a large sum in cash. (Since the sale of our house, I was awash with funds.) With all Ed Somersby's forms of personal identification, and all his possessions that could be traced to him (his mobile phone, for example), hidden in the furniture, I left his electrically powered ghost on auto-pilot and visited a hairdresser. The beard was shaved off later in the toilet of a train as it sped towards Birmingham. That evening a short-haired, clean-shaven, smartly dressed Irish gentleman called Winston Kelly booked into a hotel near Aberystwyth railway station.

Aberystwyth was where one of the Welsh universities offering a law degree was located. I had a look around the campus in the morning and then, on an impulse, went on to South Wales and the town of Caerabont, on the outskirts of which was located the second of the three universities in Wales of potential interest: Deheubarth.

By this time, I had decided Winston Kelly was a freelance journalist. I reckoned this would give me a credible reply if I was spotted snooping about and someone wanted to know what I was doing. I could claim I was gathering information for a series of articles about student life, higher education, and so on. It sounded good to me, anyway.

I checked into a Caerabont hotel of the sort of standard I thought went with my age and choice of occupation; that is to say, small and family run.

Next morning, courtesy of a shop which called itself 'The Print Place', I got myself some business cards. The shop assistant helped me design what I wanted on a PC and then ran off a batch. Considering Winston Kelly had no documentation to prove his identity, I thought a few cards might well come in useful as a substitute.

In the afternoon I explored the Deheubarth campus. The students had mostly yet to arrive for the start of the new academic year, so I felt safe. Hartling would still be in London. In recess or not, though, the place was far from deserted. Fortunately, everybody seemed very engrossed and took not the slightest notice of me. I found the law faculty without difficulty, and also the student halls of residence. What I couldn't find was any proof — a list of students' names, for instance — that I was at the right university. If I wasn't, I'd have to regard what I was doing as a useful trial run.

The rest of the week was taken up with two tasks. One was reading books and performing internet searches in the local library: on student life, law, law-related careers, journalism; anything, basically, a journalist might be expected to know about his job and his latest assignment. The second task was obtaining transport, both for stalking and, if necessary, for escape. I needed a car which was common so as not to be easily distinguishable, cheap so it wouldn't strain my budget and I could ill-treat it in a crisis without pausing for thought, and for sale privately so my lack of Winston Kelly driving licence and insurance could be brushed aside. A twelve-year-old middle-of-the-range Ford estate with a reconditioned engine took my fancy. I paid cash.

On Monday, September 27th I caught a train to London and visited my flat in order to deal with the accumulation of flyers and 'Dear Occupant' junk mail. I also retrieved Ed Somersby's chequebook and called into my new bank in Harrow. That was intended to establish that I, Ed Somersby, was in the capital, and not in Wales. It also enabled me to withdraw some more cash, replenishing thereby Winston Kelly's supply of money, since he had spent most of my previous withdrawal on the Ford. (Winston Kelly of course had no bank account and so had to pay with cash for everything.)

Tuesday morning saw me back in Caerabont. I breezed onto the campus looking my dapper best, and after a few inquiries and internal phone calls found myself interviewing a doctor of law about law degrees and the students who take them. By the time I was well into the conversation with the doctor, he seemed to believe I was genuine, which as far as I was concerned was the object of the exercise. My chosen cover story to explain my presence on the campus had been established. This friendly doctor would be my referee.

In order to facilitate my second stalking operation — either at Caerabont or one of the other two universities — I ended the interview by asking a few questions about day-to-day student routine. It was suggested the best people to consult about that were the students themselves. I went along with the idea because it would have been suspicious had I demurred, and also because it was actually quite a good ploy, notwithstanding that I might end up in conversation with Tanya's killer. The doctor showed me a small room which he said I was free to use after five each evening, and proposed I put up a notice asking for volunteer interviewees. To that end he escorted me to the faculty noticeboard. Studying it hurriedly I noticed one of the sheets of paper already pinned to it was a list of tutors and the students assigned to them for the new year. And there was the name 'Hartling A'. I thanked the doctor warmly for his assistance as we parted. He had been helpful well beyond the call of duty.

I waited a few days to allow the students to arrive and settle in, and then put up my notice at a time when I assumed they'd all be attending lectures. That way I minimized the risk of meeting Hartling accidentally. The notice read:

```
Freelance journalist Winston Kelly
is presently writing a series of
articles on the studying of law,
and wishes to interview a small
number of third-year students about
their life at Deheubarth University
and their aspirations. Interviews
will be one-to-one and will take
place between 5.15 and 5.45
```

I listed Thursday and Friday and all the days of the following week.

Having made a second coffer-refilling trip to London, I returned to the noticeboard to find I had five takers, both Fridays being left blank for some reason. It was a huge relief student Hartling A. wasn't among the five.

I got off to a bad start because the aspiring lawyer who was supposed to show up on the first Thursday didn't. The other four volunteers proved more reliable. By the end of the week I had a good idea of a typical student's routine: what they did and when.

Of the four interviewees, three were males and one, on the Wednesday, was female. I felt I might benefit from having a contact who could provide me with specific bits of information on a continuing basis if I needed them, and so I asked the woman for a date. I was expecting her to say no on existing-boyfriend grounds, but it turned out I was in luck. We agreed to meet the following evening and have a meal in a restaurant near my hotel.

Miranda Kettrick — that was her name — was living in one of the halls of residence, and I collected her from there at the appointed time and drove her to the chosen venue. Not wanting her to get any unwarranted ideas about my intentions, I'd advised her not to dress up, and she hadn't. There was a double advantage to that, in that it poured with rain all evening.

Over the meal we talked mainly about her. She told me some good jokes. I tried, I really tried, to keep the conversation off Winston Kelly, but complete success was never a possibility. What little I said was fabrications, and I loathed myself for doing it. I'm not a natural liar. Nor was my dishonesty limited to what I said. Even the way I said it — using an Irish accent — was a fake. Worst of all, she was so trusting, so obviously taken with me, and so damned likable. If only I could have been honest with her. But for all I knew, she and Anthony Hartling were close friends. I had to lie.

In a way, I marvelled at the effect she was having on me, because she was utterly unlike Tanya in almost every respect. Tanya had been physically beautiful, five feet seven inches tall, slim, with long naturally blonde hair, blue eyes, a down-to-earth self-confident personality and an 'ordinary' voice. To my adoring eyes she had been female perfection. Miranda, in contrast, was someone who would never stand out in a crowd. She had gorgeous innocent pale green eyes and a very sexy mouth (hard to describe, but you know it when you see it), yet somehow overall her face wasn't especially attractive — a case of something being less than the sum of its parts. She was three inches shorter than Tanya but must have weighed as much; not that she was overweight — she wasn't — rather she possessed a curvier sort of figure. She had a flighty and much less assured personality and spoke like she had been taking elocution lessons. To cap it all, Tanya would be twenty-seven next month; Miranda was still only twenty.

After the meal, I drove her back to the hall of residence. Before getting out of my car she said she'd like to return the hospitality. There was a local restaurant the students used. How about meeting there Saturday evening? We agreed a time and parted. We didn't kiss, and the only touch was her hand briefly on my forearm.

The next day, Friday, October 15th, was when I commenced stalking Anthony Hartling in earnest for the second time. I caught sight of him in the distance entering the law faculty in the morning but totally failed to locate his Mercedes. It certainly wasn't in any of the university car parks. His whereabouts for the rest of the day remained a mystery.

Saturday I wasted, fretting over the slow progress I was making. I'd been in Wales for three and a half weeks, and all I had to show for it was that I had found the right university. I didn't know where Hartling lived, where his car was stabled, what he did at weekends, or any details of his weekday movements. I also found myself thinking rather too much about Miranda. It was loneliness of course now that John and Judith were out of touch, but the distraction was one I would have been better off without.

Come the evening I drove to Miranda's restaurant, which was only a short walk from the campus and obviously survived on the student trade. I parked the Ford and went inside to find her waiting for me. She'd dressed specially for the occasion and had her hair done. It was made very clear she was pleased to see me.

I praised her appearance because it would have been rude not to, but I was feeling uneasy. I'd have to put her straight or I'd end up hurting her, and I didn't want to do that.

We found ourselves a table. After a short wait, a waitress came over, handed us the menu and asked if we'd like a drink. A three-way conference ensued. I never mix alcohol and driving — on a motorcycle, that'd be close to committing suicide — and Miranda, who initially fancied wine, chose to have what I was having. The waitress duly brought us a bottle of alcohol-free, sparkling 'white grape and elderflower' water and two glasses. Duty elsewhere called her away, and we were left alone to decide what we were going to eat.

We had just begun discussing our options when somebody called: "Hey, Miranda."

We both looked in the direction of the voice, over towards the entrance. A thump of adrenalin hit me like a blow in the stomach. It was Anthony Hartling. He was with a couple of presumed friends, and all three sauntered across to our table. "You're Winston Kelly," I said to myself. "Believe it!"

"Haven't seen you in here for ages, Miranda. You on a date?"

"Hello, Tony," she replied resignedly.

"Whatever have you done to your hair?"

One of the friends chipped in with: "Hairdresser must have made a mistake."

That set them laughing. Miranda put a smile on her face that wasn't a smile.

"Yeh, that must be it," said Tony, warming to the joke. "Mistake like that, you should sue. You know, inconvenience, pain and distress caused. Might make you a lot of money."

"You could act for her, Tony," said the friend.

Miranda's smile was locked in place. Even in the subdued lighting I could see she was blushing.

Unhurriedly I reached forward and gripped the bottle the waitress had brought us — which fortunately was made of glass not plastic. I used my left hand, thumb upward.

The three of them continued to laugh, apparently not noticing me.

"Tell you what," Tony continued, "I've got a better idea. Why not come back to my place? Let me sort you out with a pair of scissors."

More guffawing.

"How about it, darling?" He pulled a few strands of her hair aside with his fingers. "These bits ought to go for a start."

With a flick of my wrist I could grasp the neck of the bottle with my right hand, thumb down. Ready by now to do exactly that, I stated calmly in my assumed Irish brogue: "You've said enough."

I was aware all their taunts had been directed at Miranda. Her guest hadn't been mentioned even indirectly. Their knowledge of me was nil, so it followed their omission was based on wariness rather than contempt. Bearing that conclusion in mind I looked squarely at Hartling. Yes I was scared, but if you show it you're lost. I thought of Tanya and let the rage hide the fear.

"We didn't mean any harm," said Hartling. "Me and Miranda, we get on fine, don't we, Miranda?"

"If you say so, Tony," she agreed.

"Tony," I said, staring straight at him with an expression on my face that was definitely not warm, "I'm not putting this any stronger in front of the lady, but I'd like you to go away now."

The two friends fell silent. They stopped smiling. And more to the point, they moved to stand a little behind Hartling. The body language was clear. He couldn't rely on them.

He looked at me intently, his own grin fading, and asked: "Don't I know you from somewhere?"

"I doubt it. You don't sound like you grew up in Dublin."

"Come on, Tony," said the quieter of his friends. "We came in here for a drink, remember?"

"Yeh, right," said Hartling, pretending not to be glad of an excuse to back off. He gave me a final stare I didn't like at all. "Enjoy yourself," he said to Miranda, and followed his two companions through to the bar, where fortunately they were out of sight.

My heart went out to Miranda, but I didn't know what to say. There was a silence between us.

"I'm sorry, Winston," she said at last. She looked how you'd expect a woman to look who'd been anticipating a nice evening which had seemingly just been ruined.

"Let's get out of here," I suggested firmly.

Tactically it was imperative. That was because I didn't know if Hartling had recognized me. Probably not. But once he got tanked up on alcohol there was no telling what he might do. Beating him half to death in a drunken brawl had its attractions, but not in front of so many witnesses. I paid for the bottle, keeping it with me in case of further trouble, and escorted Miranda to my car. I had visions of Hartling pursuing me outside, so I was jittery.

Miranda wanted to go home.

"Miranda," I said earnestly, "will you please get in the car. I've been looking forward to this evening ever since Thursday. Don't let that ape spoil it. Please."

She did as I asked, and with great relief I drove off. I took the main road heading out of Caerabont, stopping briefly on the way to buy us some takeaway fish and chips. After that, I kept going until we came to a kink in the road which had been straightened out, leaving the kink to form a fairly secluded layby. By then the Ford smelt of frying.

We ate mostly silently in the dim illumination provided by the car's interior light, swigging the sparkling water directly from the bottle and listening to the whoosh of occasional cars driving past.

I still didn't know what to say to her, and she didn't seem to know what to say either. The few words which passed between us as we consumed the fish and chips seemed tense and strained.

We finished eating and I deposited the various remains on the rear seats. In the course of doing that, I found I was facing sideways towards her and saw her in profile. The words came to me. And they had the merit of being something I could say to her that was actually true. I reached up and touched her hair lightly with the back of my fingers (so as not to get it greasy) and said: "I don't think your hair is a mistake. It suits you. It makes you look really nice."

"Thank you, Winston," she said, sounding almost relieved.

I couldn't bear to be called that by her any longer. "My friends call me Ed."

"Ed? Is that your middle name?"

"No, it's my real first name. I use Winston solely for journalistic purposes. The idea is to make me more memorable."

"Oh right. You have a nom de plume."

"No I don't. It's not that. It's a pen name."

She looked at me like I'd just said something really stupid. I smiled at her. Her face lightened and she smiled back. "Watch it, mister, or I'll tell you what it is in dog-Latin legalese."

"Promise me though, Miranda. Only call me Ed in private. In public, stick to Winston. I don't want to confuse people."

"I promise," she said and giggled. "Ed Kelly; wasn't he an Australian?"

"That was Ned. No relation." I continued gently stroking her hair. "You know, I think that Tony fellow must either be blind or totally lacking in taste."

"I believe," she remarked gravely, "that his eyesight is quite good."

It took me a moment to realize this was a Miranda-joke, and then we both burst out laughing. The pleasant evening was back on course.

"Tell me about him," I said. "As a prospective lawyer he seems to lack suitability."

"I can see how you might arrive at that conclusion. But the thing is, law students are selected on their ability to soak up facts, not their good character. A crook with brains can enter the profession if he wants to."

"Are you saying Tony is a crook?"

"Is this Ed the friend or Winston the journalist who's asking?"

"I don't even have my tape recorder with me. Let's say this is a.... what do you legal bods call it...? a privileged communication."

"Ah, but which of us is the privileged one?"

"I am, to have your company."

"You don't have to say things like that, Ed. It takes more than that obnoxious oaf to make me feel bad about myself."

"Don't be daft. I said it because it's true."

Suddenly she had her hand behind my head — never mind the greasy fingers — and her face was very close to mine. We kissed. I was surprised to find she approached oro-lingual stimulation in a vigorous and enthusiastic way. I was temporarily at a loss for words again. Eventually I settled on: "Wow!"

For a while we sat looking at reflections in the windscreen.

"Do you know something?" she said after an interval. "Your accent has gone."

That's what comes of relaxing your guard! "Why sure and begorra it has," I said in the thickest Irish accent I could manage. "It's another trick of mine. Memorability again."

"That's funny. I don't think you need tricks to make you memorable."

That sounded like a compliment. It wasn't a route I wanted to go down any further with her. I dropped the accent, deliberately this time, and asked: "You were telling me about Tony. Is he a crook?"

"Oh yes. He's already been in court once. I don't doubt he'd break the law if it suited him."

"Given his choice of career, I think that's despicable."

"Well, don't think I'm going to sit here and defend him."

"I'm glad to hear it. Assuming he gets his degree, do you know what he's going to do with it?"

"His father owns some sort of entertainment business, and I guess he'll join it. Work his way up to company solicitor. Something like that."

Her answer wasn't unexpected. It made sense.

"You haven't asked what he was in court for?" she remarked.

"No. What was it?"

"He killed a girl on a motorbike. She was being driven by her boyfriend, and they were doing about ninety. You should have heard him after the event. Like they were the dragon and he was St George."

"No remorse?"

"Remorse? Tony? You've got to be kidding."

"What's his car?"

"Some big black thing."

"Do you know where he keeps it?"

"Not off hand. Near his flat, I suppose."

"He lives in a flat does he?"

"Yes. His daddy got it for him on a short lease."

"Any idea where it is?"

She hesitated. "You're not thinking of starting something, are you?"

"No. I promise I won't be starting anything. Blame it on the journalist in me. You sometimes find yourself following a trail like a bloodhound."

"Well, if that's all it is, it must be near the campus because he walks in in the mornings. Probably Hillside somewhere."

I decided if I asked any more questions I'd make her properly suspicious. Time to seal her lips. "You won't mention this conversation to him, will you?"

"Of course not. Privileged, remember. Anyway, I don't talk to Tony unless I have to."

The moon, half full and well up in the sky, came clear of the clouds to the south, and we were treated to a display of beautiful greyness illuminating the fields alongside our layby. The scene turned our thoughts in a more romantic direction. We got out of the car and stood, holding hands and chatting about things we liked: films, plays, music, and so on. In the distance by a stand of trees, we could just make out an owl flying low as it hunted.

It was only a brief gap in what was mostly a cloudy sky. All too quickly the moon disappeared again. It started to rain as I drove Miranda back to her hall of residence. We kissed on parting, more of a peck this time, and agreed a third date.

After she had gone, I permitted myself a smile. My going out with Miranda had certainly paid off brilliantly in terms of information about Hartling: a veritable break-through. Yet in a different respect I was disturbed. She and I were developing an affection for one another. In the circumstances, it was an invitation to tragedy. Every time I thought of her I had a premonition to that effect. With the utmost unwillingness, I was going to break the poor girl's heart.

6

KIDNAP

At first light next day (Sunday) I motored around the suburb of Hillside. Now I knew where to look, finding the black Mercedes was easy. It was parked in an entirely unremarkable residential through-road. Learning from my mistakes in London, having identified the street, I was careful not to hang about and risk being seen.

At nightfall I returned and went on watch from inside the Ford. I hoped to catch sight of my quarry either out in the open or else in a lighted window. After four hours I decided I wasn't going to be successful, and that if I ever did this again I'd need a blanket to wrap around my legs.

It proved to be an example of a needless waste of time, for the following morning I was able to locate Anthony Hartling's probable residence without his coming into view. Trusting that he'd be at the university, I walked along the street where the Mercedes was parked, looking to see if any of the houses had been converted into flats. Only one had. What gave this away was the presence of a door-entry system. There were six buttons, so six flats. No residents' names were on display.

Noting the address of the property, I checked on who lived there by examining the electoral register in the local council offices. All six of the flats were occupied. It proved to be flat 4 which had against it the name I was seeking: Hartling, Anthony.

Having memorized the names of the other people living in the building, I bought a bunch of flowers and called round, pressing the button for flat 6. No one responded. I tried flat 5. A lady answered via the intercom and I told her I had a delivery of a bouquet. She released the lock to let me enter. I noted on my way up that there were two flats on the ground floor and two, including no. 4, on the first. The top floor was occupied by flats 5 and 6. I handed the flowers to the lady, who turned out to be quite elderly. She was obviously puzzled, particularly when she discovered there was no accompanying message to give her a clue.

On the way out I took a quick look at Hartling's residence. The door had a Yale lock and an eye-level spyhole, and if it matched the one I had seen into upstairs it also had a security chain and opened directly into a living room with other rooms off. Further points to bear in mind were the fire-alarm button on each landing and the absence of a fire-escape. I could see no CCTV cameras and no hiding places. The entrance giving overall access to the flats needed a key, or else an in-situ resident who could operate the door-entry system. This latter was utterly standard. Nothing unusual or sophisticated. It would be easy for electrician Ed Somersby to bypass it from the inside, but to do the same thing — swiftly — from the outside wasn't an option.

My nerves were badly strained by my being right outside the lion's den, and I was glad to get out into the fresh air.

From a local street map I worked out the simplest route from university to flat, and parked where I could see Hartling enter the building without having him walk past my car. He obliged just before dark. That concluded Monday's investigations.

Tuesday I spent in a state of paralysing indecision. I had discovered a location where Hartling was vulnerable. All I had to do was get on with it: run him down with the car or go and buy the hunting knife. I did neither. I did nothing at all except berate myself for being so irresolute. The truth is, I was on the verge of calling the whole thing off.

On Wednesday, partly to put off making the decision, I bought a day-return train ticket to London and called into my flat in Harrow just as I had the previous week. I also took the opportunity to cash a cheque at my bank, making sure the video camera inside got a clear shot of me.

I had a pre-arranged third date with Miranda in the evening, so I was back in Caerabont by nightfall. We had decided to go to the theatre in Swansea, and I drove us to a multi-storey car park near our destination.

Miranda greatly enjoyed the play. I would have too if it wasn't for my being severely distracted. One thing bothering me was my forthcoming on/off appointment with Anthony Hartling. I could feel the stress and tension growing inside me. Whether or not to attack him was proving a nearly impossible decision to make. My other more immediate concern was what to do about Miranda. If I went ahead and my punitive endeavours succeeded, my subsequent disappearance was essential. Winston Kelly would simply cease to exist. And if I abandoned my quest for justice and went home, my future lay in London, not South Wales. Whichever way you looked at it, my law student friend and I were going nowhere. I had to tell her that, and it had to be tonight.

After the play we went for a late meal. All through it my mind was elsewhere. It was something Miranda was aware of, and it obviously worried her. I decided to put off informing her that our short relationship was over until we were back at the hall of residence.

It was close on midnight when we returned to the multi-storey car park. There were no people about and very few cars left, though by chance one of the few was parked immediately to the right of mine. My car was face in to a wall; its neighbour was face out. There was about a metre gap between the two cars so access wasn't a problem. I strolled up to the driver's door and inserted my key in the lock.

The driver of the other car opened his door wide so it clunked into the side of my own car, and I was trapped. I'd been so busy thinking about other things, I hadn't even noticed in the dim lighting that he was there. Or his companions. I was completely off guard.

As I turned in surprise I was punched in the solar plexus, which doubled me up and briefly robbed me of my senses. I heard Miranda cry: "Eddie!"

The driver manhandled me into the rear of his car. His two accomplices must have seized Miranda, for she was quickly bundled in beside me. When my wits returned, we were already on the move.

I looked up, still gasping for breath, my mind momentarily unable to believe this was happening. And then, in the glow of the street lighting, I recognized the front seat passenger and knew it was all too real. Anthony Hartling turned sideways and stared back at me.

He ordered me to put my seatbelt on. I made no move to obey.

"Let me explain the position you're in," he said. "The rear doors are locked, so if you try to open them we'll have plenty of time to stop you. Unpleasantly. My colleague here," — he nodded to someone sitting directly behind him on the other side of Miranda to me — "has a sawn-off shotgun which is currently pointing at Ms Kettrick's pretty midriff. If you make a grab for any of us, or do anything else of a seriously stupid nature — well, it'll make a hell of a mess inside this car."

"Tony," Miranda began, "I...."

He held up his hand. "Just a minute, darling. Let me finish explaining things to your vigilante boyfriend." He resumed addressing himself to me. "For lesser infringements, like not doing exactly what you're told when you're told...." He paused. "Hurt her, Gerry."

"All right," I shouted, panicking. Miranda screamed anyway.

"You bastard," I said as I fastened my seatbelt.

"Don't worry. You just saved Miranda from a lot of discomfort. That was terror, not pain."

"You were saying?" he remarked to Miranda.

"Look," she said, her voice unnaturally high pitched and tremulous with fear, "I don't know anything about him being a vigilante. I don't want to know. It's nothing to do with me. Just let me go, Tony. I won't say anything. You know I won't say anything."

"I thought you were fond of this fellow. You'd go for help."

"I wouldn't. I swear I wouldn't. He doesn't mean anything to me. I was just passing the time."

"You hear that?" he said to me.

Miranda began to cry quietly.

Hartling seemed to soften. "I really am sorry, darling," he said. "I hoped to keep you out of this, but there's no way. Look. I promise you, as long as Mr Death-Wish here does what he's told, we won't be nasty to you. Take the gun out of her side, Gerry. We'll have no trouble from them now."

"You could still let her go," I said. "Drop her out in the countryside somewhere miles from anywhere. She wouldn't be able to do anything."

"Afraid not," he said. "I'll give you nine out of ten for the disguise, Ed. I wasn't at all sure it was you last Saturday. But nought out of ten for the brains. We let you off too lightly in London. I didn't think you'd get the message. In any case, I always keep an eye open for strangers, so it seemed particularly sensible to watch for you around these parts. That Winston Kelly notice asking for interviewees set me wondering. Probably perfectly innocent, I thought, but worth checking on. When word got about Miranda was meeting up with you Saturday evening, it provided a good opportunity to have a look at an unexpected face on the campus. I admit you almost had me fooled. Still, I sent for one of my minders here just in case. He was watching my flat when you turned up on Monday morning. He saw your second visit with the flowers too and took quite a pretty picture. So what, I wondered, was Winston Kelly doing delivering flowers to the building where I lived? It had to be you, Ed. All the same, I was concerned how we were going to make absolutely certain we'd got the right man. Sweet Miranda solved that problem for us when we jumped you. Didn't she, *Eddie*."

I had to admit it to myself again. In London I'd made about every possible mistake; in Caerabont I'd done a lot better, but I was still totally outclassed. And now it looked like I was going to pay for it. The thought in my mind that I could get out of this situation by denying I was Ed Somersby I reluctantly abandoned. It didn't stand a chance of working. Hartling was certain who I was. He had no doubt at all. Surely though, it wasn't necessary for Miranda to be punished as well. I tried once more to get her off the hook.

"Yes, okay," I said. "You've got the right guy. You don't need Miranda. We can settle this without her. She's just an innocent bystander."

"Oh please," she sobbed.

"Sorry darling," Hartling repeated. "It's unfortunate, but I need you for a prop."

Then his voice took on a harsher tone. "But you," he said, staring at me, "I don't need at all. You stake out my street in London. You stake out my father's office. Now you turn up here staking out my flat. What would you do that for? You know what I think? I think you have a lot of trouble with the concept of forgiveness, Eddie. I think you're out for revenge. Isn't that right?"

I didn't answer.

Hartling nodded at Gerry. There was a rustle of movement next to me. Miranda cried out.

"That was for real," Hartling said. "Answer the question."

"Maybe I'd have had a go at you and maybe I wouldn't. I wanted the option, that's all."

"A loser. Right down the line you're a loser. We followed you this evening all the way from the campus to the multi-storey car park, and you didn't have a clue. You pick a fight with me and then carry on as if my dad and I are nobodies. You're a loser, Eddie, and I've had more than enough of you."

Miranda suddenly announced she was going to be sick. Gerry grabbed her by her hair and forced her head between her legs. She vomited.

"Shit!" said Hartling. He sighed. "We'll clean it up later."

He'd apparently finished what he wanted to say to me, for he turned his back.

Gerry opened a window.

We travelled on, the quiet marred only by the sound of the engine, the noise of the wind, and Miranda weeping.

I felt utterly wretched. I had failed Tanya a second time. She would never get justice now. I didn't know whether Hartling intended to kill me or merely beat me senseless. The former, as long as he was quick about it, didn't bother me that much. Tanya would be with me. But I felt unbearable pity for Miranda. If I could give her a chance to escape, that would be my first priority.

After a while, she recovered her composure and whispered in my ear: "Sorry, Ed." I took her hand and held it after that.

For a time we headed north on the M4 and then west on a fast dual-carriageway. It must have been an hour before we turned off onto minor roads — roads which became progressively narrower and more isolated.

"Not much further," Hartling announced as he began giving directions to the driver. This latter individual I had identified by then from his large build. He was the fellow who'd driven the BMW in London: the one I called Weight Trainer.

The moon, three-quarters full, appeared ahead of us, shining brightly in a cloud-free sky. I deduced we were now heading south. We eventually came to a sharp left turn in what had become a narrow lane with a hedge bordering both sides. The car halted. Weight Trainer turned off the headlights and got out. I made to undo my seatbelt.

"Not yet," said Hartling. "This won't take much time if you cooperate. Then you'll be free to go."

"Just Miranda, or both of us?"

"Both of you."

I felt a glimmer of hope. But there was something false in his words. He hadn't gone to all this trouble and driven all this way to let us loose with no greater inconvenience than a long walk home.

The moonlight revealed a five-barred gate being opened. Weight Trainer returned to the car and drove us into a field. We proceeded to lurch and bounce our way across it on a gentle down-gradient before coming to a halt again. Hartling and his two minders got out.

Gerry, holding the sawn-off shotgun, beckoned to Miranda. "You sit still," he said to me.

Hartling took Miranda's hand and led her to stand in front of the car. Beyond her I could make out a faint shimmering and a few points of light in the far distance. I realized we were on a cliff overlooking the sea.

Gerry crouched in the open doorway to my left, the

double barrels pointing intimidatingly at my chest.

"Didn't you have a baseball bat last time I saw you?" I asked.

"That's right," he replied. "You should have taken what was coming to you then. Probably wouldn't be here now if you had."

There was an altercation between Hartling and Miranda. I couldn't make out the words. She spat at him. He turned to look at Gerry. She said something else and began to take off her clothes.

My hand moved to my seatbelt release button. "Just keep calm," Gerry advised. "It's not what it looks like."

When she was down to bra and panties she stopped. Hartling spoke again. She undid the bra and flung it at him. Then the panties. Hartling grabbed her by her wrist and walked her the short distance to the cliff edge.

"Your turn," Gerry said. "Slide across and get out this side."

Weight Trainer meanwhile had gathered up Miranda's clothes and now put them in the car where I had been sitting. He joined Gerry so they were standing either side of me.

"Undress," said Gerry.

Very aware of the shotgun pointing at me, and with Miranda obviously under threat, I reluctantly obeyed.

Once that was sorted out, they didn't mess about with last wishes or speeches or anything else that might have prolonged matters. In a way they were mercifully quick. The two minders marched me past Hartling with his naked captive and unceremoniously threw me off the cliff. I was falling for about three seconds. Not long enough to make my peace but enough time to die with Tanya's name on my lips.

I settled for that.

7

ORDEAL

The shock of impact forced some of the air from my lungs. Everything was cold and black. And I was still alive.

Surprise gave way almost instantly to confusion — I'd been sure I'd hit rocks either on the way down or at the bottom — and then comprehension. The cliffs were vertical and there was water at their base. I was in no worse predicament than being submerged.

I struck out for the surface. As my head broke through into the air, two things happened simultaneously: a wave slapped into my face and set me choking; and something big impacted with the sea very close to me. A large rock?

Breathing was proving impossible. Incoming waves and waves reflecting off the cliff were combining to make the sea turbulent and unpredictable. I was almost blinded by water repeatedly splashing into my eyes, preventing me judging when it was safe to inhale. I began swimming out, aware that the air in my lungs was almost used up.

After ten metres or so the surface became less troubled. Treading water, I found timing when to breathe was much easier.

My first thought was that Hartling had made a mistake and by sheer incompetence had picked a place where someone thrown off the cliff wouldn't be seriously injured or killed. But then I thought of his words: "You'll be free to go." It was his idea of a joke. Free to go and drown, ha ha. He'd also said: "*Both* of you."

I knew then that it hadn't been a rock hitting the water

near me; it must have been Miranda. I looked about and quickly located her, bobbing on the surface. Fortunately she didn't appear to be in urgent need of my assistance. I shouted to her and she swam over.

"Oh god, oh god," she said. "We're going to die. We're going to die."

I could tell she was very close to panicking. I was afraid she'd grab hold of me, which would probably make her prophecy rapidly true, but instead she just trod water, voicing her fears.

I reached out and touched her lightly under her chin, raising her head a little. It got her attention, but at that moment a wave slapped me in the face and I needed both arms to right myself again.

"We're going to die," she repeated.

I touched her shoulder, and had better luck with the waves this time. "Listen," I said. "Forget about dying. Forget about being afraid. Concentrate on staying afloat and alive. I'll get you out of this, I promise. Just do what I tell you."

She looked at me and waited for me to make good on what I'd said. The truth is, I was almost as close to panicking as she was, but I knew I had to appear confident and in control. If I cracked up, she'd crack up, and that would be the end. But get us out of this? If only appearing confident and in control were enough.

"How good are you at swimming?" I asked her.

"Above average," she replied. That was an answer she couldn't have bettered. It was one less thing to have to worry about.

Okay, I thought, take stock. In the moonlight the cliff face was uniformly black. Level with us it was quite unclimbable. To the west the geography seemed to be unchanging into the distance — a solid, vertical wall of rock, at a guess fifty metres high. No way out. To the east the picture was nearly as bleak, but when I was on the peak of passing waves I thought I could glimpse white water in the distance. No telling how far away or what it signified.

"Watch the cliff," I said to Miranda. "Can you make out if we're in a current?"

We trod water for a couple of minutes. I couldn't detect any movement on our part, east or west. It was simply too dark and the waves were moving me around too much. The problem we faced was that if there was a current, we didn't want to end up swimming against it. If that happened we could well exhaust ourselves staying more or less in the same place.

"What do you think?" I asked.

"I don't know," she replied, sounding panicky again. "I'm getting cold."

This being October 21st, the sea temperature wasn't in fact that low. Even so, my calves were aching with the chill sufficiently to make me worry about cramp. It was time to decide.

"We'll head east," I shouted, pointing. "Okay?"

Her reply was to set off. I followed. She was correct about being an above average swimmer. I was left in her wake. I knew I couldn't keep up with her for long, and I had to be concerned about our losing contact with each other. She agreed to go at my speed.

We swam together side by side. Interminably. With no landmarks to judge by, we couldn't be sure what headway we were making. It was all down to whether the current, if there was one, was with us or against us.

Slowly, with each stroke of my arms, my optimism — the little I'd managed to summon up initially — drained away. I began to think exhaustion was going to overcome us. Or me at any rate. And then, just as despair was giving way to resignation, we practically bumped into a sizable low-lying rocky ledge sticking out jaggedly seawards.

86

Waves were breaking against it — probably the white water I had seen earlier — and I knew immediately it was this or nothing. We had to get out of the sea.

Calling a halt, I told Miranda what we needed to do. Cautiously we approached. The ledge was mercifully only about thirty centimetres above the surface of the sea, and the wave crests were washing over it. In theory, getting onto the ledge should have been no harder than getting out from the deep end of a swimming pool. In theory. In practice the waves were a severe complication, dashing us against the ledge rather than up onto it. Several times I was in position, feeling for an underwater foothold, only to be thumped into the rock face and washed back from it as another wave struck and reflected.

But desperate determination wouldn't let me give in, and I was rewarded at last. With one foot suitably anchored, I got my stiff, sluggish body half out of the sea. Another surge swirled around me, lifting me onto the ledge. I lay flat on the surface, relying on friction between my upper body and the rock to keep me in place as the water retreated. And it worked. I was on the ledge. Home if not dry! I almost cried with the triumph of getting onto firm ground.

Miranda came in to my yelled instructions. She tried. A wave caught her, and she submerged. She tried again with the same result. And a third time.

I got as low as possible on the ledge and shouted to her not to worry about footholds but just to reach up to me.

She obeyed and I was able to grasp one of her wrists as the next wave lifted her up. But then, as the wave retreated and she began to drop lower, my strength failed. So did my muscular coordination. Instead of releasing my grip I kept hold. The next thing I knew I was falling on top of her, and we both went under.

A feeling of utter despair overwhelmed me. I was back

in the sea. We were going to drown or get battered to death against the rock face, and I didn't care any longer. Resisting the inevitable was no more than going through the motions.

As I floated beside her, numbed into hopelessness, I heard Miranda wailing in distress. Her cries tore at my heart like nothing before in my life. Oh to hell with this, I thought bitterly.

I found the foothold again, positioned myself and called for her to come in closer. She hit up against me at precisely the moment another wave washed past. As it lifted us, I got my arm under her buttocks, shouted: "Go!" and pushed her upwards. Somehow I found the strength. The action drove me beneath the surface. My open mouth filled with salt water. Submerged rocks contributed a few bruises to add to my misery.

Resurfacing yet again, I saw Miranda's pale form in the moonlight. She was out of the sea and safely on the ledge.

In what was now a familiar routine, I relocated the foothold and braced myself for the next incoming wall of water. It seems I learn more quickly in dire situations. My timing was perfect and I joined Miranda without further difficulty.

With that accomplished, I got stiffly to my feet and began to explore. The ledge we were on was a sort of platform, about a hundred metres from side to side and maybe ten metres wide from where it emerged from the sea to where it joined the cliff proper. I walked the full hundred metres, looking, begging for the cliff to give us a break. A way up. A cave. Anything. But it was hopeless. The damned thing was a featureless slab of rock. No shelter. No passage to anywhere.

It was all too much. I turned so Miranda couldn't see my face, sank to my knees and wept. Partly it was frustration and partly just sadness that our lives were going to end like this. By getting out of the sea, all we'd done was exchange hypothermia for drowning. We were still shortly going to be every bit as dead.

After a few minutes of this appalling self-pity, I got to my feet and walked to the eastern end of the ledge. To a degree I was beyond emotion now, but some part of my being wouldn't give up. I was still alive, right? I could still think, right? Well then, think, damn you.

The cliff seemed to disappear a short distance away. Trying to make sense of what I could discern in the dim moonlight, I began to wonder if the cliff turned a corner, and, if so, what was round that corner. We'd probably only find more of the same: an unclimbable rock face. If that proved to be the case, we'd had it. But then if we stayed in our present location, we'd had it anyway. When you're down to your bottom dollar, that's the one you have to bet with.

I walked over to Miranda. She was on her knees, moaning and rocking back and forth. I cupped her cold face in my cold hands to get her attention. She carried on moaning but looked at me nonetheless.

"This is no good," I said. "You see," — I pointed — "we have to swim over there. It may be a way out."

"I can't. You go. I'll be all right here."

Like hell she would. "You'll die if you stay here. We've got to swim further."

"I can't," she repeated, her voice rising in pitch. "Not in the sea. Not again."

I wasn't so much cupping her face in my hands now as gripping it. "I hate the thought of getting back in the sea too. But we don't have a choice. We have to."

She tried to shake her head, but I was holding it too tightly. I realized I was hurting her and let go.

"I'm not going to make it," she said. "I'm too cold. And so tired."

"Look, Miranda, I promised I'd get you out of this. I've got you this far, haven't I? I'm not leaving you now."

When she didn't react, I took her hand and tried to pull her to her feet. She struck out at me, crying: "No. No. Go away. Leave me alone."

I was doing my best to help her, to save her life, and getting no thanks and no cooperation. I discovered I wasn't as beyond emotion as I thought; for a few seconds anger got the better of me.

"That's right, give up," I cursed. "Typical useless woman. Nothing better than a millstone around a man's neck. I can do without it."

I turned my back on her and took the few steps to the edge of the ledge. I had to look round. She was motionless, watching me. "Miranda," I shouted through gritted teeth, "come *on*!"

"I hate you," she yelled, but to my immense relief got to her feet and started to follow.

Physically, re-entering the sea was much easier than leaving it. Mentally, the opposite was true; I experienced an involuntary repulsion that very nearly stopped me. I don't doubt Miranda felt the same.

We soon discovered the cliff did indeed turn a corner. Following it round, we could see in the distance ahead of us something white. A building? On a beach? We swam towards it.

As we slowly drew nearer, the waves began breaking as they surged past us. I put my feet down and felt sand. We staggered ashore, finding ourselves in a bay backed by dunes. In amongst the dunes, unmistakably, was a house.

When we were clear of the water, I pulled Miranda to me, put my arms round her and held her tightly against my body. I did it as an expression of my utter relief, and for warmth and for comfort — mine as well as hers. She responded, nestling her head, face inward, on my shoulder and with her hands holding my back tightly. I could hear her crying.

We clung to each other like that for a while, both shivering vigorously. Presently she became quiet. Those areas of our skin that were pressed against each other began to feel a little warmer. I couldn't help registering how different the shape of her body felt compared to Tanya's.

"Just a little way to go now," I said. I looked in her eyes in the moonlight and speaking very gently added: "You've done brilliantly. I'm so proud of you. We've made it. We've really made it."

With my arm around her and keeping her close for support and to mutually reduce heat loss, we stumbled up the beach. The house, I could soon see, was in fact two white-rendered semi-detached bungalows, probably built on piles driven into the sand. The front of the building, which faced the bay, had a veranda reached by climbing a set of wooden steps, six in number.

Leaving Miranda sitting at the foot of the steps out of concern for her modesty, I went up to the nearest of the two front doors and rang the bell. It occurred to me these might be holiday homes and empty at this time of year. If that was so, I'd have to break in.

Fortunately such drastic action proved not to be necessary. A dog started barking somewhere inside. I rang the bell again. A light came on in what I assumed was the hallway, followed by a porch light over my head.

The door opened slightly, as far as the security chain would permit.

"Who's there?" a gruff male voice called out, peering out at his extremely self-conscious nocturnal caller.

"I'm sorry to disturb you," I said, slurring my words slightly because my jaw muscles were too cold to work properly, "but I've lost my clothes, and I don't know where I am."

"Stone me!" the man exclaimed.

The door shut. I heard the sound of the chain being unfastened, and then the door re-opened wide to reveal a gentleman in a dressing gown. Full head of grey hair and a moustache. Sixty maybe. He invited me in.

"There's a young lady as well," I explained.

He unhooked two coats off the wall by the door and handed them to me. A raincoat and an anorak. I awkwardly put the former on and took the latter to Miranda.

Her arms were so cold they were almost paralysed, but somehow I managed to get them into the sleeves. The zip, though, defeated me. It was too dark to see what I was doing and my fingers were dead.

The gentleman came down the steps from the house, doubtless wondering what was taking me so long. "Never mind about that," he said. "Let's get her inside."

Between us we picked Miranda up and helped her walk indoors. (I say 'between us'. A lot more him than me!) He led us through into what proved to be the kitchen.

The warm air in the room felt like the greatest sensual pleasure imaginable.

"I can heat some milk. Would that do you?" he asked, having sat Miranda down on a chair.

"That would be fine."

"I'll put a shot of whisky in it."

"No alcohol," I said. "Not for hypothermia."

"Right enough."

He set the milk to heat on the hob.

"So how'd you lose your clothes?"

"We er.... Well, we couldn't get back to where we left them in the dark. A student acquaintance of ours set it up as his idea of a joke. Except it wasn't very funny."

"Which seat of learning would that be?"

"Deheubarth University."

He tipped the milk into two mugs. One he passed

cautiously to me, fearing I might drop it. I was indeed surprised by how weak and unresponsive my arms were. I had to use both hands. As the heat soaked into my fingers they became intensely painful. In contrast, the feeling of warmth produced in my stomach as I drank was indescribably good.

Miranda, shivering uncontrollably, was using her hands to keep the anorak wrapped tightly round her, so the gentleman held her mug to her lips. She sipped.

"Been raining, has it?" he asked, referring to our wet hair.

"No. We've been in the sea."

He smiled. "You went swimming off this beach? Are you sure it wasn't the incoming tide that got your clothes?"

"It wasn't off this beach. We swam here from.... wherever we were."

"In that case you must have covered quite a distance. No wonder you're cold."

Miranda continued sipping from her mug. She seemed to be reviving slowly.

The gentleman asked: "What do you want to do? I don't think it would be a good idea for you to leave here tonight, but it's up to you. I've got a phone you can use if there's someone you'd like to call."

I shook my head. Frankly, I had no idea what I wanted to do next. At this moment, I didn't have a Plan A, let alone a Plan B.

"I tell you what," the gentleman said. "The wife and I have a spare room at the back for family when they stay with us during the summer. I can let you have it for the rest of the night, and we can sort everything out in the morning."

"We'd be very grateful. Thank you."

He turned back to Miranda and asked her concernedly how she was feeling.

"Freezing," she whispered through chattering teeth.

He got out a large bowl and ran some hot water into it, setting it on the floor by Miranda's chair. He explained: "You're not getting between my clean sheets with those feet."

I watched as he washed off the sand, taking care to be gentle. I could see her legs were scratched and bruised from when we'd got onto that totally useless ledge. My legs were in a similar state.

"I'm not sure the young lady oughtn't to see a doctor," he remarked.

"I'll be okay," Miranda said softly.

He refilled the bowl so I could wash my own feet while he administered first aid to Miranda's grazed knees. He also put a plaster on a laceration in my left hand, an injury I had no recollection of acquiring.

With the first aid sorted out, he showed us to our room, which contained two single beds. I said to him before he left us: "You've been very kind. And very trusting too."

"Trusting?" he responded. "Young man, if you meant to rob me or harm me or the wife, the last thing you'd do is come up to my front door stark naked at two o'clock in the morning and ring the ruddy bell."

After he'd gone I spent a few minutes drying our hair on towels he'd provided. Miranda, still shivering, got into one of the beds, keeping the anorak on. I got into the other, in my case putting my coat aside. I turned out the bedside light.

I was still very cold and in a lot of pain, particularly from my arms and feet as they thawed out. And my mind was restless as the events of the night ran round and round. Sleep would be a while coming.

After about ten minutes, Miranda called to me.

"Ed?"

"Are you okay, Miranda?"

94

"It's really hurting."

"I know."

"Come and cuddle me."

"I'm not sure."

"I just want you to hold me. I'm so lonely and frightened."

I slipped out of my bed and into hers. We snuggled up together, clutching each other tightly, the anorak between our two bodies.

She whispered: "What are we going to do? I thought I was going to die."

"Tomorrow," I answered. "We'll sort it out tomorrow. It won't look so bad then."

"I didn't mean what I said about you in the car."

"I never thought you did. Not even for a second."

"Thank you for saving my life, Ed," she said, her voice catching.

"Hey, come on. Don't cry. Shall I tell you the truth? You saved me too. I made you a promise that I'd get you to safety. If you hadn't been there, I'd have given up. It was you that kept me going."

"Is it all right if I kiss you?" she asked.

In acceding to her request I found the anorak wasn't covering her bottom. The discovery triggered off a partial erection. I did nothing about it and neither did she, though she must have felt it. Presently it subsided, the pain became more bearable and exhaustion overwhelmed me. I fell asleep.

8

MANOEUVRES

I was awake again by half past seven according to the clock-radio on the bedside table. While Miranda slept on, I sat wrapped in the duvet off my bed, looking through the window at the start of a glorious day. Not a cloud in the sky.

If you hunt a lion with your bare hands, you can expect to get mauled. Occupational hazard. That was the first thought to strike me. It was a way of saying I'd brought last night down on my own head. I'd asked for it. Yet surely to blame myself was to defy logic and morality. Suppose, instead of trying to beat me up in London, Hartling had come to me and said, in a convincing and genuine way, that he was sorry. Would I have pursued him to Wales? No, of course not. What would have been the point? I'm not a vindictive man. The only reason I felt unable to put this affair behind me was because Hartling was neither sorry nor punished. The faults lay with Hartling and the legal system respectively for that, not me.

Assigning responsibility had in any case been rendered a purely academic exercise by what had happened. What mattered now was that the option I had been seriously considering only the day before, of walking away and forgetting the whole thing, was closed to me. I had no doubt Hartling would never settle for an *attempted* murder. He'd want to finish the job. The conclusion was unpleasantly clear: a private war had broken out, and I either had to fight or make arrangements for my funeral. As for the rights and wrongs, I'd have to leave that for my conscience to sort out later. If I survived.

I needed a plan. But there were so many difficulties to face, trying to decide which one to tackle first had me running round in mental circles. The only decision I'd made by the time Miranda woke up shortly after eight was 'no police'. I had no faith whatever in the judicial process their involvement would set in motion.

After she'd opened her eyes and worked out why she was in a strange room with a man she'd only known for a few days, I asked her how she was.

"Much better than when I went to sleep," she said. She momentarily peered beneath the bedclothes and added: "I'm not presentable."

I grinned and said: "I don't think you've got anything I didn't see last night."

"I don't mean *you*."

"No. A bit of a problem, isn't it."

Before we could discuss our lack of clothing further, there was a knock on the bedroom door. I opened it cautiously, half fearing it was Anthony Hartling and his two thugs paying a call. But no. It was the grey-haired gentleman.

"Both all right?" he asked.

I said yes.

"Just been on the local news. They found two piles of clothing on the beach at Warren Bay. Would they be yours?"

The question took me completely by surprise. "Er...."

"Tenby lifeboat's been launched, you see, and a helicopter."

"Where's Warren Bay?"

"A couple of miles west of here."

"Yes," I told him, "it sounds like us." It was a gamble, but only a small one. The chance that two other people would pick last night to go swimming and get swept away was very slight.

He went to telephone the coastguard.

"I don't get it," said Miranda.

Unfortunately I now did. The two piles of clothes were the key. I grudgingly had to give Hartling nine out of ten for the brains. But nought out of ten for the humanity. The unwelcome thought struck me hard that my dispute with Hartling had nearly cost Miranda, an innocent bystander, her life. *He* wouldn't be feeling guilty about that. But I did. Suddenly I couldn't look at her.

"I think I understand some of the things that happened to us last night," I began, keeping my eyes fixed firmly on the view through the window. "You see, Tony has obviously got it into his head he wants me dead. Throwing me off that cliff and hoping I'd drown was quite a clever way of going about it. That explains why we had to take our clothes off. The idea was obviously to make it look like we'd been at Warren Bay, gone skinny-dipping and got into trouble. Inquest verdict: misadventure. No murder inquiry. Neat solution to a problem."

"But that doesn't make any sense. Why does he want you dead? It couldn't be because you told him to clear off when he was poking fun at me. He may be nasty, but he's not that nasty. And it's not just you he tried to kill; he tried to kill me too. Why would he do that? I've never done anything to him."

"You remember in the car he said he needed you for a prop? I didn't know what he meant by that at the time, but it's clear now. He meant a prop like in a theatre. Think about it. He could have waited till you were out of the way before seizing me if he'd wanted to. He needed to bring you along because it's very implausible I'd go swimming alone in the dark at the end of October. If, however, I was amorously aroused by the prospect of a frolic in the waves

98

with a girl.... Well, you get the idea. You were just a convenient means to an end.”

“That’s downright sick. I can’t believe anyone.... Ed, would you please stop staring out of the window when I’m talking to you.”

I turned to face her.

She looked me straight in the eyes and said: “You’re avoiding the big question, aren’t you? You and Tony have a quarrel of some sort, that much is obvious, but I don’t know what it’s about. I’m guessing it started before I met you. This is a movie I’ve come into half way through, isn’t it? He said in the car you’d been stalking him. He said you were out for revenge. Is that true?”

I knew then there was no way I was going to get away with keeping Hartling’s motive to myself. I could either lie to Miranda, making some story up, or I could tell her the truth. And I’d had it with lying to her. So let her hear the truth, I thought. The worst she can do is hate me.

But there are ways of revealing the truth, and they’re not all equally productive of a good outcome. (Or in this case, more probably, the least bad outcome.) I wanted time to think out the best way to explain. And, to be honest, time to summon up the courage. “Let’s get away from here first,” I said. “We have to find somewhere safe and private where we can decide what to do next. I promise I’ll tell you the whole ugly story then.”

“Will you?”

“You know I keep my promises.”

We had breakfast dressed in raincoat (me) and anorak (her). I decided she ought to wear an anorak with nothing underneath more often. Her body filled it out in a highly erotic way and it showed off her legs, which were world-class. I explained this to her after we’d returned to our room. She wasn’t in the mood for that kind of talk — not surprising — but I knew she wouldn’t forget.

I heard a car turn up. A quick check revealed it was one of the constabulary variety.

"Go along with the official story," I hastened to advise her.

"But he tried to kill us."

"I know. But this isn't something the police are going to be able to help with. We haven't got a shred of proof. They won't believe us in the first place, and even if we do somehow manage to convince them, it'll be our word against Hartling's. He's bound to have an alibi. You can bet on that."

"So you want to let him get away with it?"

"Absolutely not. Just give me a chance to explain. Then if you want us to take this to the police, that's what we'll do."

She looked away.

The policeman knocked on our door and entered. He was carrying two large plastic bags inside which were our clothes.

"Please examine the contents," he instructed us. "I'd appreciate it if you'd confirm everything is present and correct."

We did as we were told. Everything was, including money, cards, Miranda's mobile phone and my car keys.

He proceeded to enlighten us about how much of everyone's time we'd wasted, not to mention taxpayers' money and RNLI donations. We were informed we should grow up and start behaving like responsible adults.

The pièce de résistance was kept till last. He took out of his pocket an opened packet of condoms. "These were found near your clothes. I take it they're yours."

"Yes," I agreed, never doubting they were another of Hartling's so-called props.

"Stick to the bath in future, sir," I was instructed. "You're less likely to get carried away."

100

I won't deny my face was burning.

"I suppose you'd like a lift into Pembroke," he remarked.

"Yes. That would be very helpful. Thanks."

"Get dressed then and better be quick about it. I'm a busy man."

As soon as we were alone again, Miranda said: "We should have told him."

Our clothes were cold and damp, but compared to last night the discomfort of wearing them was trivial.

Now properly dressed, I went along to the kitchen to settle up with our host of the night, and found him chatting over coffee to the policeman, who didn't look all that busy to me. The coffee and the chat were plainly not to be hurried.

A while later, Miranda and I found ourselves being driven along the pretty lanes of Pembrokeshire.

"One thing I don't understand," our temporary chauffeur asked, "is how you two got to Warren Bay to start with?"

"We were dropped off," I answered, which was literally true, if misleading. The remark actually brought forth a short sharp chuckle from Miranda.

"And no one waited around to take you back?"

"Apparently not."

"Dear oh dear," he said, shaking his head gravely.

Despite his air of disapproval over what Miranda and I had supposedly been up to, I detected a degree of ill-concealed amusement in his manner. There was a tale here that would have his fellow officers in the locker room laughing their heads off for years to come if it was told right. He was doubtless rehearsing it in his mind while he was driving.

He left us at Pembroke station from where we caught a train, not to Caerabont, but, at my insistence, to Cardiff.

Once there I found a reasonably expensive hotel and booked Miranda in under a false name.

It was with a degree of trepidation I accompanied her to her room. Since the start of the morning she had gone along with my various instructions without argument but with increasing ill-temper. She was holding back, waiting for 'the explanation', and it had better be a good one.

And of course there was the little matter of last night. Both of us having recovered psychologically from our maltreatment, we were in a frame of mind to apportion blame. In my case I knew exactly where the blame lay. She, though, judging by the set expression on her face, was keeping her options open. I could tell I was under consideration for at least a share.

I sat her down and told her my story, beginning with Tanya: how the dragon that Tony 'St George' Hartling had slain was my beloved fiancée; how we'd been doing thirty miles an hour, not ninety; how the court had let him off with nothing more, in effect, than a fine; how I'd stalked him in London and narrowly escaped a beating for my efforts; how I'd adopted a new persona and followed him to Wales; and worst of all, how I'd lied to her about who I was and misled her about my initial motive for meeting her in the evenings.

She heard me out in silence, something, in its way, which was more unnerving than if she'd responded by thumping me. When I finished she said: "You realize I ought to be furious with you?"

I looked at the floor and nodded.

She waited a few seconds and then said: "Oh, don't look so glum. From the sound of things, there's been more than enough sadness in your life this year without me adding to it. But you lied to me, Ed. I'm not sure I can cope with being lied to. Not by you."

"You've no idea how ashamed I am about that. But at

the time, what choice did I have? You and Hartling might have been buddies."

"Hmm. Well now you know we're not."

"Now I know. And it's a relief to be able to tell you the truth, believe me."

"I'll have to think about whether I believe you. One question. A few days ago you said it was a privilege to have my company. Was that one of the lies?"

I looked her in the eyes and answered honestly: "No. I meant that."

"All right. So. Can I make a suggestion?"

"Yes of course."

"We've got to decide what we're going to do about Tony. We can plan our moves separately or together. I'd like it to be together."

"That's fine up to a point, Miranda. But ultimately it's not your fight. I have to sort this out on my own."

"Not my fight!" she exclaimed, suddenly releasing the anger she'd been suppressing. "Not my fight! I can't believe I heard that. Are you seriously proposing getting thrown off a cliff is a part of everyday life, the sort of thing a girl has to expect once in a while? Am I supposed not to be offended when someone compels me to strip off by threatening to shoot my boyfriend? And I wasn't going to tell you this, but after they'd disposed of you I got so terrified I was crying and pleading, 'Please don't do this. No, no,' all that sort of stuff, whimpering like a dog, and he handed me over to those two hatchet men regardless. Are you suggesting I deserved that?

"And another thing. I've put a lot of effort into my law studies. I've got a good career in prospect. How can I go on with Tony Hartling in the same class? He's regularly made my skin crawl over the last twenty months. Now it'll be even worse. And that assumes he doesn't need me for a prop again. So don't you tell me it's not my fight. We both have a score to settle with that so-and-so. Right?"

"Okay. Keep cool. I take your point. What do you think we should do?"

"I don't know," she said, somewhat undermining the effect of her admonition. "All I can say is your current approach is counter-productive. The most you've achieved by stalking Tony is to get him annoyed. Thanks to which, I might add, I've just had by far the most traumatic night of my life. I don't call that a policy success. Do you, Ed?"

"No," I agreed. I didn't like to admit it to myself, but the criticism was irrefutable. She was spot on.

She continued: "What we've got to do is come up with an effective means of striking at him; something that'll get him off our backs."

I listened to her talking her way around the problem, thinking out loud. She had been trained in law, and it was naturally to law that she turned for a remedy. The notion that we should use illegality never occurred to her. Mostly her ideas ran along the lines of getting Hartling's prison sentence unsuspended. Nothing she put forward struck me as viable. In any case, having him locked up for six months would only defer the day of reckoning. The sad thing was I couldn't tell her my own plans. I had my prime rule. *No one must know*. And that still applied to her, all the more so since I had concluded after last night that merely punishing Hartling wouldn't work. Besides, one doesn't invite a casual acquaintance, albeit an affectionate and highly likable one, to become an accomplice in a murder. It's simply not what one does.

Miranda finally realized I wasn't going along with any of her proposals. They just weren't practical. I watched her deflate like Bill Matheson had when I'd told him I was going to let him down too.

"Well, if you don't like my ideas, what do you suggest?" she asked irritably.

"I'll talk to him. And when I've finished he'll leave you alone and I shall disappear." One lie and two truths.

She frowned. "You really think that'll work? *Talking*?"

"Take it from me, I can be very persuasive when I want to be."

"Yes, I've noticed."

"The thing is it's not in his interests any more than it is in ours for this business to be prolonged or to escalate. We need to bring it to a conclusion. And swiftly at that. How else can we hope to achieve that than by talking?"

"Okay. Have it your way. For now. But what's this about you disappearing?"

"I won't want to be found afterwards."

It was the biggest hint I dared give her, but she inevitably took it as meaning 'found by Hartling'.

"I can appreciate you'll need to keep out of his way, but you won't disappear completely, will you? I mean, how can I see you again?"

"I don't think you will." I couldn't imagine how it could work out any other way. It was better to be cruel to be kind.

She straightened up, an air of wounded dignity about her. "I ought to be going. I don't want to waste any more of your time."

"You haven't been wasting my time. And I need you to do me one last favour."

"Do you a favour? When you're dumping me?"

"It's not like that. One day you'll understand."

"Don't patronize."

"Look. It may take a day or two before I have my word with Tony. I'd like you out of circulation until then. That's all I'm asking. Stay in this hotel for a few nights. That way I can be confident he won't find you."

"I don't think that's necessary," she said, though a look of fear flitted across her face.

"He's a killer, Miranda. Talking to him is going to be

hazardous. I don't want him getting to you before I get to him. It really is best you stay in hiding."

"All right," she agreed sullenly.

"Don't forget to use the false name I've registered you under. That's in case Hartling takes to ringing round the hotels asking for you. He doesn't know where you are right now. Let's keep it that way."

I checked she had enough money to pay her likely hotel bill and told her I'd call her with the all-clear when it was safe for her to return to Caerabont. She gave me her mobile phone number to that end.

We parted without any show of affection.

*

The hesitation and dithering that had afflicted me earlier in the week were at an end. It was undeniable my brush with an imposed death had changed my mindset, freeing me from the restraining effects of self-doubt. As of now, I was keenly determined to settle the matter as quickly as possible.

Unfortunately, immediate action was out of the question because everything was in the wrong place. I was in Cardiff, my car was in central Swansea (since the keys had been left with my clothes at Warren Bay, it was reasonable to assume the Ford hadn't been moved), and Anthony Hartling was in Caerabont.

It was clearly necessary to deal with the car urgently. At first it puzzled me that it hadn't been parked near our clothes at Warren Bay. I suspect the explanation was simply laziness on the part of the minders. They'd have had to drive back to Swansea to get my car, then drive both the Ford and their own car to Warren Bay, then drive to Caerabont *again*. Tedious in the extreme. Given the distances involved, they'd have been going back and forth all night. Since it wasn't crucial that a car be found at Warren Bay, they'd decided not to bother. If my conjecture was correct, it meant retrieving the Ford would be trivially easy.

However, that would only be the case while I was believed drowned. Once the enemy knew I had survived, they'd put the Ford under observation in order to make another attempt on my life when I showed up to reclaim it. In other words, I either had to fetch it immediately or write it off.

Getting to Swansea from Cardiff was easy enough by train. Entering the multi-storey car park was harder. Psychologically, that is. The place was busy, which helped because it meant there were plenty of witnesses to act as a deterrent, but it also hindered in that it was impossible to spot if there was a wolf amongst all the sheep. I didn't know how soon Hartling would learn I had escaped a watery grave, and consequently had to be alert to the possibility of a second kidnap. Being out in the open in a place where it could be predicted I'd show up was a nerve-racking experience.

The Ford was where I'd left it. When I drove away, no one obviously followed. After a spell of dodging about in the town centre I was convinced no one was following unobviously either. I set course for the hills.

Pausing only to buy a blanket and some food in Port Talbot, I spent the afternoon cruising sedately along the roads which pass through the forests lying broadly to the east of Neath. I found several sites suitable for the purpose I had in mind. The final choice, however, I decided to leave till tomorrow. When it got dark, I made for the coast.

Hartling would know by now I was still alive. His two minders would have been recalled to duty. They couldn't find Miranda and they couldn't find my car. So what would they do? My guess was they'd ring each hotel in Caerabont in turn until they contacted one who'd take an innocuous message for Winston Kelly. That accomplished, they'd go on watch and wait for me to put in an appearance. In consequence, I could only return to my hotel when I was ready to do battle. That would be within twenty-four hours, but not yet. For one night only I'd need to bed down in the car. Hence the purchase of a blanket.

I parked in Porthcawl and had a meal.

Later, I sat on the seafront, looking out to sea and feeling increasingly miserable. My conscience was bothering me, and I knew I was going to get little sleep unless I took remedial action. What was troubling me was my treatment of Miranda. I'd made a mistake, and a vile one at that. If I succeeded in my endeavours, she already knew enough to single Ed Somersby out for the police whether I saw her again or not. As long as she couldn't testify that I had stated I was going to murder someone, and as long as she was not aware of anything incriminating that the murderer alone could have told her, she would only be able to arouse suspicion. Not enough to get me convicted. So why shouldn't we meet in future?

At ten o'clock I rang her mobile phone from a phone box. She answered almost at once.

"I'm sorry, Miranda," I began. "I said a horrible thing this morning. I wasn't thinking straight and I didn't mean it at all. Please will you forgive me? I do want to see you again. Lots of times."

"What makes you think I want to see you?" she said coldly.

She had a well justified right to respond that way, and I'd already anticipated it. "Can you note down a number?" I asked.

There was a pause and she said: "Go ahead."

Since I was dependent on payphones in Wales — Ed Somersby's mobile phone being in my flat in Harrow — I gave her John Farley's business number. "If there's an emergency or you need to get in touch, phone that number. If there's no one there, you'll be able to leave a message on the answering machine. It's a phone belonging to a friend of mine. I'll call him every day to check."

"Emergency?" she said. "I thought you said I'm safe here."

"Well, you are. I just meant...."

"Look, Ed. You want me to talk to you, *you* call *me*. Okay?"

"You're right. I will."

"I assume I've still got to hide," she remarked.

"Yes. For a day or two."

"It won't work, you know."

"What won't?"

"Talking to Tony."

"It's worth a try."

"Oh God, this is such a mess."

"I've got to go now. Take care, Miranda. I'm missing you already."

"Speak to you soon," she said and broke the connection.

I felt better after that. If things went badly for me over the coming days, I didn't want the last words I ever said to her to be a rejection. Cruel to be kind it might have been, but sometimes the treatment is worse than the disease. This was one such occasion, doubly so since it had hurt the doctor as well as his patient.

I found a deserted spot overlooking the Bristol Channel and slept peacefully in the back of the Ford.

*

Friday, October 22nd dawned brightly. I woke as it was getting light to find the windows dripping with condensation. I had breakfast and then got down to work.

I returned to the area I had explored yesterday. Of the potential sites, one now stood out in my mind. It was an off-road track in a forest called Coed y Deifol. On reinspection it proved to be a most promising location, and it was there I spent a while hunting out a few pieces of wood of a length, thickness and resilience appropriate to the use I had in mind for them. One I put in the car. The others I hid in various places in the undergrowth. I'd probably only need one, but to have some spares seemed prudent.

The next task was to drive along the road that passed by the off-road track, fixing landmarks in my mind and practicing dummy runs. I spent two hours on that, trying it from both directions and at various speeds, counting the seconds from *A* to *B*, imagining what-ifs and how I'd cope with them.

At length it was time to show myself to the enemy. I returned to my hotel in Caerabont, filling the petrol tank en route. There was nobody obviously watching for me when I arrived.

I sought out the proprietor and explained I'd not been in overnight because of a late-running conference in Bristol. He in turn told me what I wanted to hear: that there'd been a phone call for me the previous evening. The fellow hadn't left a message beyond saying he'd get me later. I ended the conversation with the proprietor by giving notice I'd be leaving permanently the following morning. Now it was known where I was staying, I had to move out, whatever else happened.

I went up to my room at speed. It felt unsafe being on the stairs; somebody with hostile intent could already have taken a room in the hotel and be lying in wait for me. I checked all the other doors on my landing were shut before unlocking my own. I entered cautiously, but nothing was amiss.

For the time being I felt reasonably secure. There was, however, one point of vulnerability, and that was my car, sitting out on the hotel's forecourt. I was happy for the enemy to see it, but might they do more than that and tamper with it? Unfortunately my room overlooked the back of the hotel, so I couldn't keep a look out. However, I reasoned my enemies would be unlikely to approach the Ford in daylight when they could be observed by passers-by and by at least some of the hotel's occupants. Not much of a risk then, though I worried nonetheless.

Despite being very tense I forced myself to wait, going over my plan carefully. After all, it was no good spotting some flaw in it when the option of aborting had ceased to be available.

In principle the idea was simple. I'd set off in my car. Somebody would give chase. I'd lead them to Coed y Deifol and spring the trap. The big doubt was who I'd be fighting. Weight Trainer, Gerry and Anthony Hartling were the candidates I knew of. Assuming that was the complete list, would all three be present? If Hartling was, I'd try and separate him from whoever was guarding him. Then I'd have him. Otherwise I'd aim to give the opposition something more than a black eye to remember me by. Beyond that, it was a case of making it up as I went along.

Timing was difficult. I wanted to reach the forest at dusk, so that if things did go wrong I'd have a good chance of escaping under cover of darkness. By my calculation, that meant leaving the hotel shortly after four, but there were too many variables to permit any attempt at precision.

By half past three I could stand it no longer. Wearing Winston Kelly's suit and tie for possibly the last time, I walked to my car. Without doing anything to give away the fact I was on my guard, I examined the ground beneath the Ford as far as I was able while pretending to check the tyres. Nothing suspicious. Then I got in. No sign of any interference inside. Taking a deep breath I started the engine. No explosion. Nothing abnormal.

I pulled out from the forecourt, heading down the street and watching intently in the rear-view mirror for signs of pursuit. There were several candidate vehicles. None was a black Mercedes or a BMW.

Still concerned about possible tampering, I tested the brakes, steering wheel and clutch. All worked as expected.

I tried to visualize the car that had taken Miranda and me for our nocturnal swim. I'd been too distracted at the time to register even the most obvious details, but now one of the potential bad guys started to seem familiar. The car was white and bore a vague resemblance to a Range Rover, though it wasn't as large. At a guess I'd say it was an east Asian make, and designed for off-roading.

I was running seriously early for a twilight encounter and so decided to delay by heading for Cardiff. As the miles passed, the cars behind me changed, except for the white off-roader.

I could make out two occupants. The driver I was almost certain was Weight Trainer. His accomplice wasn't dressed right to be Hartling. I concluded it was going to be me versus the minders. So be it.

The adrenalin was flowing, producing a sense of exhilaration. I was too committed now to worry that I might be over-reaching myself, and perhaps it was better so. If you go into battle conceding you might lose, you probably will.

9

BATTLE

I stayed on the M4 until reaching the exit for Barry and Penarth around half past four. The white off-roader kept behind me, not close, but obvious. Leaving the motorway, I headed south for a while and then began returning towards Neath on the main road that runs via Cowbridge. The off-roader did likewise.

When I got to Bridgend I chose to go through the town rather than use the bypass. It was my first mistake and nearly disastrous. I hit a traffic jam in the town centre, there was a mix-up at traffic lights which were green for me and turned red for the minders, and I found myself leaving the off-roader behind. (If I'd tried to do that deliberately, it would never have worked!)

I took the Ford directly back to the motorway at a modest speed, keeping my fingers crossed the enemy would guess the route I was taking and catch up. Light levels were starting to drop. It was time to spring the trap. All I needed was someone to get caught in it.

Weight Trainer didn't let me down. I soon spotted him in the distance, coming up fast. That was the signal for me to take the Ford up to the speed limit. I dared go no faster at this stage because to do so might attract the attention of law enforcers, and Winston Kelly had neither driving licence nor insurance. The driver of the off-roader was less inhibited. Almost losing me seemed to have annoyed him, for he was soon within metres of my rear bumper, resuming the intimidation he had last employed in London.

In due course I led him off the motorway and towards the valleys. We began climbing into the hills. The road was still designated as an 'A' road, but that didn't stop it becoming narrower and having frequent bends. Overhead, thick heavy clouds made it dark enough for headlights. The time was approaching six.

The minders remained, I presumed, under orders to kill me by means of an 'accidental' death. It was soon clear they'd decided to try staging a car crash. I had slowed to about fifty on account of the driving conditions, when they suddenly started overtaking. I guessed they intended to force me off the road. I pulled the Ford to the right to block them. Weight Trainer countered by swinging to the left while continuing to accelerate. Again I matched him.

We were quickly doing over seventy, too fast for safety. The off-roader moved out to make another attempt at drawing level. I took no action this time because the headlights of an approaching car came into view, having rounded a gentle bend to the right a quarter of a mile ahead. Weight Trainer was forced to tuck in behind me, there not being enough room on the road for three cars abreast. I used the opportunity to slow the chase down. I didn't want to have a genuine accident.

Less than two miles to the Coed y Deifol forest track. We'd be there inside two minutes. It was going to be a close-run thing.

With the car on the other side of the road safely past, Weight Trainer tried once more to overtake. It was an insane thing to do. By now we'd reached the bend, which began gently but got sharper. If somebody came round that curve heading towards us, the off-roader was going to get demolished. If nobody did, on the other hand, Weight Trainer could force me off the road at exactly the sort of spot you'd expect an accident to occur if a driver was going too fast.

I had no choice but to block him again. We took the sharpest part of the bend, both on the wrong side, both going so fast our tyres were protesting audibly.

As the road straightened out we encountered an oncoming five-vehicle convoy. I got out of their way, swerving leftwards with no more than a few metres to spare. So did the off-roader. If that convoy had been running five seconds earlier, so that we'd met up on the bend, there'd have been a head-on collision at a combined speed of over a hundred miles per hour, plus a seven-car pile-up that would have made the number one slot on the national news. The thought went through my mind that this was madness. Only fleetingly though. There was less than a mile to go and I needed to concentrate.

While Weight Trainer was stuck behind me waiting for the oncoming cars to pass, I reduced speed as before. This time he allowed the off-roader to run into the back of the Ford, gently enough not to do any damage, but jolting enough to alarm me. Twelve hundred metres.

The road was now curving the other way; that is, leftwards. It would be pointless to overtake me here because I'd be the one able to force *him* off. He hung back, repeatedly clunking the Ford as I reduced our speed still more. Eight hundred metres.

Straight section of clear carriageway; no lights ahead, red or white. I floored the accelerator. The off-roader stayed close while working its way out to the right. Six hundred metres.

I pulled over as if I was going to repeat my earlier obstructive performance. On this occasion, as soon as Weight Trainer abandoned moving right in favour of a left-sided approach, I brought the Ford sharply back to its proper position in the road.

We were still accelerating, doing seventy. Four hundred metres. Once more the off-roader was overtaking. This time I let him do it, aiming only to match his speed. Two hundred metres. Eighty miles per hour. Three seconds. Hint of oncoming headlights around a bend a quarter of a mile distant. Not now, I thought; this could wreck everything. Two seconds.

The off-roader was level with me. One second. Our two cars were mere inches apart. One hundred metres. I hit the brakes: a classic emergency stop. My tyres screamed. The off-roader seemed to surge ahead. The approaching headlights came directly into sight. I didn't dip my own. I needed full beam to see when to turn. To get out of the oncoming car's way, the off-roader was forced to swerve sharply leftwards, mounting the roadside verge. I said a silent apology to the driver I was blinding and crossed his path. He must have been braking, and it saved our lives. We missed colliding with a second to spare.

The Ford was now lurching uncomfortably up the steep and rutted forest track that led to my destination. A hundred metres in was a right turn onto level ground. I paused there until I saw a pair of headlights behind me. As I'd been sure they would, Weight Trainer and Gerry were coming after me, doubtless wondering what sort of 'accidental' death they could inflict on me in this new setting.

I took the Ford fifty metres along the level track and halted, switched off the lights and engine, grabbed the piece of wood I'd placed in the car yesterday and ran into the trees.

It was darker than I would have liked. Seeing where I was going wasn't easy. Troublesome, since I had to move fast.

I headed in the direction the off-roader would be coming from, keeping under cover as I did so.

The enemy's car duly appeared, stopping when I was roughly level with it and about twenty metres from where I had parked. At that distance they were able to retain a good view of my car and its surroundings in their headlights.

I crouched down, one tree and a couple of metres of open ground between me and them.

They opened their doors, got out, and stood looking towards the brightly illuminated Ford.

"He's escaped again," said Weight Trainer in a voice that suggested profound disbelief.

"Looks like it," Gerry agreed. "You've got to hand it to him. For an amateur he thinks very fast."

"*Three times*. How could he do this to me!"

"We could try searching, I suppose. He can't be far away."

"We could try searching," Weight Trainer mimicked, clearly unimpressed with the idea. "Three times he's got away. The boss'll have me cleaning toilets for this screw-up. Give me your bat."

"It's on the floor behind your seat."

Weight Trainer opened the rear passenger door and took out the baseball bat, muttering: "I'll teach the little runt." (For the record, I'm five feet eight inches tall and medium build.)

"What are you going to do?"

"Pay him back for bending my BMW." (Presumably, throwing me off a cliff didn't count.)

"Your BMW? It's a company car."

"Why don't you shut up," said Weight Trainer as he set off for the Ford.

"Brain dead," Gerry said under his breath.

"I heard that," said Weight Trainer loudly.

And there the pair of them were, oblivious to the two mistakes they were making. The whole point of my locating the trap in forest was to even the odds. I was gambling my opponents would be townies, good at street-fighting but novices in countryside. It would give me an advantage to counter their numerical superiority; and sure enough they were proving me correct. Townies live in a world which is well lit and noisy, twenty-four hours a day. It never occurred to either of them that leaving their car's engine running and headlights blazing were major errors. It almost made it easy for me.

I came out of hiding. Gerry couldn't hear the faint sounds I was making because the idling engine masked them. He stood motionless, leaning slightly on his open door, watching his colleague. I crept forward, advancing on him from behind.

The Ford's rear window was the first to go. Several blows in moderately slow succession. Weight Trainer was probably imagining it was my head.

As the last piece of glass shattered I swung my length of wood. It was a bit over a metre of solid branch, probably one that had broken off a tree in a gale the previous winter. With its side twigs removed, it made a first-rate club — one so heavy it took both hands to wield it. I brought it in a wide arc over my head, and down.

Gerry belatedly sensed something amiss for he began to turn, raising his arm as if to ward off an assault from the side. It couldn't protect him from above.

Contact.

Suddenly I knew why police often describe attacks as 'frenzied'. I was terrified, absolutely terrified, Gerry would get up. I struck him again before he hit the ground, and then several times more after that, but I wasn't counting.

Or being quiet. It wasn't Gerry who'd been shouting out as I hit him. I don't think he'd made a sound. It was me. Involuntarily I'd been yelling.

I looked up to see Weight Trainer blundering my way. He was shielding his eyes with his free hand and staggering. Blinded by the headlights, he couldn't spot the ruts and the potholes. And of course he couldn't spot me.

118

Not that he was at my mercy. For one thing, I no longer had the advantage of surprise. For another, it was not yet completely dark, and once he was behind the headlights I had no idea how much he'd be able to make out visually. Could it be enough to put me at *his* mercy?

Those were the rational reasons for what I did next. But the truth is, to have someone that size bearing down on me was more than I could cope with. I fled because I was overcome by fear. I retraced my steps back into the trees and ran for it, making as much noise in the undergrowth as a small tank.

I say 'ran' but in practice I was slowed to not much more than a walking pace by brambles, stinging nettles and everything else a forest has to throw at you. And beneath the trees it really was dark. I had to hold my club in front of my face, hoping it would intercept any foliage at head height before I poked an eye out on it.

A short way in, the trees changed from native deciduous to conifers. I stopped to listen. Weight Trainer was following, tracking me by sound. I knew, in terms of sight, he'd be in a bad way. He'd been looking into headlights on full beam. It would take several minutes for his retinas to recover sufficiently to enable him to deal with the light level beneath the trees. If I could be silent, he'd lose me.

The ground beneath the conifers was bare except for countless pine needles. Progress was nonetheless harder than in the more open deciduous woodland because the trees were much closer together and each trunk was adorned with thin dead branches which stuck out horizontally and mutually interlocked.

I went a little way into the conifers, noisily snapping off the dead branches that got in my way and then, selecting a tree which had enough space around it to swing my club, I stood in wait, facing deeper into the forest.

For a while there was silence. My eyes grew more

accustomed to the darkness, which was deep grey rather than black. The moon would be rising by now and could be relied on to provide a small degree of illumination, even through the low cloud that was blanketing the sky.

Weight Trainer had heard me breaking branches. He was also aware I had stopped moving about. He therefore had a good idea of which direction to head in if he wanted to find me. He had paused for a while, I presume, to give his own night vision time to get established. I waited.

In due course he started rustling the undergrowth again. Mostly fallen leaves. I don't think he was bothered about noise. Despite Gerry's misfortune, as far as he was concerned he was the predator and I was the prey. So much the better for him if I could hear him. It might frighten me into attempting to run away, thus revealing my exact position.

His movements became quieter as he reached the conifers and there were no longer any leaves to rustle underfoot. Almost directly behind me a twig snapped. He was getting close. I began to worry. Was it possible he could follow a trail of broken branches in this light? I had my back against a tree and was facing away from him, but could he actually see me despite that? Could he hear my breathing? What about my clothes? Winston Kelly's suit was dark enough, but I cursed my lack of foresight in wearing a white shirt. Heart thumping away, I clutched my club and remained motionless.

Dead branches continued to snap as Weight Trainer forced his way towards me, more to my left than behind. I turned my head a little and he was there, almost beside me. I swung my length of wood at waist height.

His reaction was as instantaneous as being taken by surprise would permit. He'd been holding the baseball bat straight up in front of him, and brought it vertically lower so that my club hit the implement before it hit him. Even so, I knocked him off his feet. Barely pausing I swung again, this time from above downwards. He rolled to avoid me. I broke off a few dead branches but missed his head.

He was so fast in action that he was already up on his hands and knees when I delivered my next blow. In consequence, I misjudged my aim and only struck a heavily muscled shoulder. It knocked him sideways, and he fetched up against a tree.

In the time it took for me to get the club into position for another swing he was able, despite being on his side, to kick out. He missed in the poor light, but it made me delay while I stepped back. His next kick caught my calf after I had set the club in motion. I staggered, completely messing up my aim. Purely by chance I still managed to hit him, striking one of his ankles. He shouted out in pain.

I regained my balance quickly, partly as a result of falling against another tree. Seeing he had rolled away from me and was once more on his knees, I went for another vertical stroke of the kind that had despatched Gerry. He raised the baseball bat in his defence. I would never have believed a guy could have such strength in one arm. The bat gave a little under the impact, enough that my club slid along its length and off the end, but Weight Trainer was totally unscathed.

He retreated slightly and got to his feet. Very bad news. As long as I kept him down, I had a chance. But my prospects in a cudgel fight with someone his size if he was standing up were non-existent.

He lunged forward, thrusting the bat as if it was a sword, and aiming for my belly. I dodged by stepping to one side. The move exposed me to a horizontal swipe to the head, my club being too ponderous to be of much use in parrying.

The blow never materialized. Weight Trainer seemed to stumble as if his right foot had collapsed under him. He didn't fall though. For an instant we faced each other. There was no point in me standing my ground. I'd get beaten to a pulp if I tried that. The only sane thing to do was to run. I ran.

The direction I chose was downhill, deeper in amongst the conifers. I had to crouch very low in order to avoid most of the dead horizontal branches. After about a minute I halted because I realized I wasn't being followed.

I decided to change course. My aim was to return to the track, but some distance behind Weight Trainer's car. I was very worried because I didn't understand what had happened. Weight Trainer didn't seem the type to simply give up. So what was he doing? Could he read my mind well enough to know where to lie in wait? Despite my best efforts, I was occasionally snapping a twig or two. Was he following my movements by sound and using the information to position himself for a surprise interception?

Fearful of the various possibilities, I unintentionally veered further left than I'd meant to, only discovering my mistake when I encountered a dense patch of brambles. I became aware that instead of going broadly uphill I'd actually been keeping almost level. I spent some moments bypassing the thicket and then emerged onto a forest track.

There were no cars on the track, which sloped upwards to my right. I was completely disoriented. Where was I? I stood still, listening for a clue. I could hear an idling car engine but couldn't place its direction. Apart from that, all was silence.

At last, I caught a flash of headlights passing by to my left, downhill. That meant there was a road down there. And that gave it to me. This was *the* track; the one I'd taken the Ford up. It meant that a short distance to my right I'd find the turning on which the off-roader and my estate car were parked.

Keeping close to the trees, I walked uphill for about

fifteen metres. And there in the distance were the two cars. The off-roader's headlights were still on. I seemed to see a figure momentarily, silhouetted by the light reflecting back in my direction. But then it was gone. I didn't know whether to believe my eyes. It hadn't looked like Weight Trainer. Or Gerry, come to that. Someone hunched up with a spasmodic stride.

Learn from London, I thought to myself. Assume the worst. At least one of my two adversaries had entered the trees to the left of the track. He'd be lying in wait, ready to pounce when I returned to my Ford.

The choice for me now was either to settle down in the undergrowth until whoever it was got fed up and went away, or to carry out the most dangerous woodland stalk of my life. Common sense urged the former. My aim, in the absence of Anthony Hartling, had been to give the enemy something to think about. That aim had been achieved. Gerry, at least, was going to have the grand-daddy of all headaches.

The trouble I had with the common-sense approach is that it would have had me peacefully earning my living in New Zealand months ago. It was too late for common sense. Right now I was battle-happy and reckless. I opted for stalking.

I entered the trees and began the task of covering the thirty metres between me and where I judged the shadowy figure was. One very slow step at a time I crept forward, judging my position by the off-roader's headlights. Silence was essential; patience was everything. The slightest noise and he'd know where I was.

Soon I was close enough to hear movement. The guy was finding it impossible to keep still. Every few minutes I'd hear him fidget. Each time he did so, I was closer.

As I advanced, I had time to work out what was probably going on. Weight Trainer had called this evening a screw-up. He really — *really* — didn't want to have to report back that he had failed again and, worse, that he had no idea where I now was. Keeping by the cars was the only option open to him that might enable him to recover the situation. He was here; of that I was certain. As for Gerry, it was too dark for me to determine whether he was still lying where I'd left him, but I seriously doubted he remained combat-ready. If my reading was correct, I had no need to hurry. My quarry was Weight Trainer, and he would wait for me.

Eventually I reckoned I was practically on the fidgeting figure. I paused. By now it was as dark as it was going to get that night, but a degree of illumination was provided by backwash from the off-roader's headlights. My immediate vicinity was a scene of greys and deep black shadows. In one of the shadows was the enemy.

He moved once more, and I saw him. I was ninety per cent sure it was Weight Trainer, hunched or not. He was kneeling, watching the cars from behind a tree. No wonder he couldn't keep still for long. On your knees is no way to do it. He'd have made a rotten mammal-watcher.

I charged. Same tactics as before: keep him on the ground. He turned towards me. Caught between two reflexes — to wield the baseball bat and to protect his head from my club — he compromised. The bat was pointing skywards when I hit his forearm. The sideways blow had such momentum behind it that it drove his arm against his head and his head against the tree he was kneeling next to. I heard the thump of skull on bark.

The bat flew from his grasp. Except it wasn't a bat. It was too short, too thin, too dark. And he was altogether too keen to reacquire it. This was obviously the back-up plan. Don't bother with faking an accident. Just kill the little runt any old how. Use the sawn-off shotgun.

His lunge for the firearm left him exposed, but I also

124

was transfixed by the lethal firepower that had entered the arena. As he felt desperately for the weapon that neither of us could actually see, I brought my club down, not on his head, but on his hand. He only grunted, but I must have broken some bones at the very least.

From his semi-prone position he twisted his lower half in a scything motion and literally swept me off my feet. He yelled as he did so, as if something was hurting him. It finally dawned on me I'd seriously injured his ankle in our previous exchange of blows. It explained the earlier lack of pursuit and the hunched-up walking.

But now we were both on the ground. Almost as bad as both being on our feet. He made a grab for me. In scrabbling to get out of his way, I dropped my club. He succeeded in seizing a foot with his uninjured hand. I kicked out, and he let go. He didn't dare risk my injuring his one good hand. Lose both hands, lose the fight.

Given the injuries he'd sustained, his best option was to locate the shotgun. He resumed casting about for it. I got to my feet, found my club and went for him. He realized he'd lost the race to get re-armed and turned to deal with the next blow I was aiming at his head. He caught the end of the club on the forearm of the injured hand and cried out in pain. Nonetheless his reliance on brute strength paid off yet again. His forearm was forced hard onto his face, but not hard enough to disable him.

Before I could do anything else, he hurled himself on me at thigh height, knocking me over. My head struck a tree, and for a few seconds I was stunned. In those few seconds he trapped my legs under his chest and began working his way upwards. I was hopelessly overpowered.

Under my left buttock I could feel the round hardness of a metal tube. My left hand found the butt, and then the trigger of the shotgun. Keeping my fingers away from the latter working part, I managed by twisting to the right to get the short sawn-off barrel out from beneath me.

A big meaty hand closed on my throat. There was no time to think. I jammed the shotgun in Weight Trainer's side and pulled the trigger.

All the tension went from him. He started making a kind of jerking movement which shook his whole body. He coughed a couple of times but otherwise remained silent.

Utterly horrified by what I'd done, I worked myself out from underneath him and stood up. For a long time I just looked, feeling weak and emotionally numb. This wasn't what victory was supposed to be like. The gore that had splashed onto my left hand turned cold.

Eventually I got my thoughts together enough to wander in a daze over to the off-roader. Gerry was where I'd left him. If he was breathing and had a pulse he was keeping it a secret. Judging by the unnatural angle of his head to his body, I guessed I'd broken his neck. It all suddenly seemed such a pity.

A vanquished enemy doesn't appear evil; he appears pathetic. The sight of the dead Gerry made me feel sorry for him. And for his oversized companion. I can honestly say I'd not planned to kill them — putting them in hospital would have been preferable — and I was shocked by the consequences of my own violence.

But then I thought of Miranda. These two brave men had taken hold of her, a defenceless girl, and even while she was begging pitifully for mercy, had cast her into the sea to drown. I didn't think, on reflection, they deserved any sympathy. I could live with what had happened, even if they hadn't.

*

Okay, I had given two thoroughly nasty characters their well-earned come-uppance. Unfortunately, the majesty of

126

the law wouldn't see it that way. So it was essential to put my brain back in gear and do some cold calculating; specifically how to get away with what I'd done.

As a first step I emptied out Gerry's pockets, throwing everything I found onto the front passenger seat of the off-roader. The intention was to hamper identification of the body. Then I went over to Weight Trainer to do the same thing with him.

When you see people shot in fiction movies, modern directors splash a red mess everywhere, and you think: is that unbelievable or what? Now I knew, where shotguns are concerned anyway, it was at least partially true. Weight Trainer had been shredded by the shot. The mid-section of his torso was a sticky mixture of blood and viscera. I know because I got it on my hands as I struggled to roll the corpse onto its back. Blood had drenched the front of his shirt and jacket.

The contents of Weight Trainer's pockets, depending on location, were unsoiled or in a gruesome state. I carried them across and put them with Gerry's. Then I turned off the car's engine and headlights and tried to think.

I found myself with an unexpected dilemma. Because the minders were dead, I had a choice of transportation. What's more, it was still not quite seven o'clock, and it occurred to me that if I was to follow through on this triumph and waylay Hartling, I had both the time and the right car for the job. If I approached him in the off-roader, he would recognize it as a friendly car. Against that was the fact that the Ford was known to belong to Winston Kelly. In the absence of Miranda, I could have laughed at that. But people were aware she had dated the soon-to-disappear journalist, and she knew his real name. She might be able to stay silent in the face of a police interrogation, but it was a risk I dared not court. I had to keep the Ford and these two dead bodies unconnected.

Obviously I couldn't drive both cars away from the scene, but it struck me I didn't have to. The nearest dwelling was miles away, and in any case no one enters a forest after dark. The minders wouldn't be found till morning. If I could settle Hartling tonight using the off-roader, I could bring it back and swap it for the Ford before dawn. That would utilize the best parts of both options.

I was instantly sold on the idea. Everything felt like it was going my way. Perhaps I was even becoming slightly manic. I scented total victory.

To guard against the tiny possibility that somebody might use this forest track during the night for some unforeseen purpose, I dragged Gerry over to lie alongside Weight Trainer, both then being fairly well hidden by undergrowth. That made them as invisible as they could be, short of a burial. Anyone seeing the Ford would assume it had been abandoned, particularly given the state of its rear window. I doubted it would arouse suspicions.

I retrieved the shotgun from where I'd left it alongside Weight Trainer's body and put it in the back of the off-roader. I then drove as fast as the law permitted to my hotel in Caerabont, arriving a little after eight. The evening meal was over by then, and the public parts of the building were deserted. That was fortunate, as my clothes were not entirely presentable. On the way through Swansea I'd helped myself to a newspaper from a paper recycling bin, and I held that open in front of me while making my way upstairs. It would have looked odd had I been noticed, but not as odd as having blood on my clothes. As it was, no one saw me.

Once in my locked room I stripped and showered. It was a disturbing experience washing someone else's blood off my hands and getting it out from under my fingernails. Then I put on clean clothes, except for my suit. With my usual lack of foresight I hadn't brought a spare one with me. The trousers were mud stained, especially the seat, but otherwise passable. The jacket's left forearm and parts of the front were more sinisterly discoloured. Fortunately, I had the smart Winston Kelly raincoat which could do duty as a substitute jacket-cum-overcoat.

I returned to Weight Trainer's car (which I'd parked in the street rather than on the hotel forecourt, because it wasn't 'my' car) and went looking for a store that was open late. Having found one, I went in and bought a bottle of whisky, a litre of cooking oil, a packet of frozen chips, a box of matches and a pair of rubber gloves (the only kind of gloves the shop sold). I also helped myself on the way out to several carrier bags.

Back in the car I found an unlit area and set about arranging my equipment. The shotgun I reloaded from a box of cartridges in the back, wrapping its barrel in the ex-recycling bin newspaper, and turning the whole thing into a long, thin parcel by knotting some of the carrier bags round it. It then joined the various purchases in another carrier bag. It looked curious and inelegant, but it didn't look like what it was, and that was the main thing.

I drove to Hartling's street in Hillside. My intention was to force my way into his flat somehow — somehow? — or better, if I was in luck and he wasn't at home when I arrived, to wait till he showed up and accompany him inside under threat from the shotgun. There was no sign of his Mercedes when I pulled into the curb and parked, so it was a fair bet he wasn't already in residence. Of course it was always possible he'd gone back to London for the weekend, but I thought that unlikely — not while his minders were hunting me in Caerabont.

While waiting on events, I looked through the contents of Weight Trainer's and Gerry's pockets. Wallets with the usual plastic and paper money, driving licence, keys, combs, loose change. All perfectly normal except for a couple of key rings which each had two identical keys on them. I hadn't labelled them at the time, so now had to assume one pair belonged to Weight Trainer and the other to his side-kick. One key of the pair was a simple Yale key. The other was more complicated.

I puzzled over why both men would be carrying identical keys. My speculation ran along the lines that when they were in Caerabont on bodyguard duty they dossed down in the same place, perhaps a hotel somewhere like my own.

I was thus musing when a car pulled up, separated from me by several other parked vehicles. As soon as its headlights were out, I realized it was a Mercedes. I was sitting in the front passenger seat (because it had more room) and made a move to open the car door, grabbing the shopping bag ready for action as I did so.

I halted just in time. Two people alighted from the Mercedes: Anthony Hartling and a young woman. The latter was wearing long high-heeled boots to her knees; from there to the top of her thighs was bare; next came a mini-skirt so 'mini' that to call it a skirt at all was to be guilty of exaggeration; still further up was a jacket which revealed an expanse of skin below her neck; and lastly came long blond hair. She was petite and, without the high heels, maybe five feet tall. She was probably still at school.

The two of them walked towards the flats. Hartling spotted the off-roader further down the street and must have made out someone sitting inside it. Probably thinking I was Gerry, he changed direction with the obvious intention of coming over. It looked for a moment like I was going to have to blast him with the shotgun, and hope neither to injure nor seriously traumatize his female companion. Wanting to avoid an immediate decision, I reached across and flashed the headlights. Hartling waved and went indoors.

After a brief pause, a light came on in one of the first-floor windows. I hadn't known where Hartling's flat was in respect of the exterior of the house. Now I did. He came into view and pulled the curtains. The process was repeated in a neighbouring window belonging to another room.

I decided to check on a sudden hunch. Taking out one of the matching key rings Weight Trainer and Gerry possessed, I went over to the entrance to the flats and inserted the complicated one. The lock turned. Immediately I understood. The two minders had come to Caerabont only in the last few days on what was expected to be a short mission. So they hadn't bothered to find accommodation. They were sleeping in flat 4. Minders in residence. The keys were their way — and now mine — through Hartling's last line of defence.

I returned to the off-roader, put the rubber gloves on, collected the shopping bag, and let myself into the building. Reasoning Hartling was likely to be blissfully distracted, now was as good a time as any to enter his premises. From the outside of flat 4 I could hear music playing — some rock radio station. Very slowly and gently I inserted the simple Yale key into the lock. The door opened and I stepped into his living room.

My fear that he might have still been in that room — in which case I'd probably have had to shoot him immediately in front of the girl — proved groundless. The room was empty. There were three doors off the living room, and my first priority was to check on the state of play behind the one the music was emanating from. I could detect the vibrations of a male voice talking softly, and the sound of the girl moaning. They were sufficiently busy, I reckoned, to give me a free hand.

Of the remaining two doors, one led to a short hallway, and via that to a bathroom and toilet. The other opened into the kitchen. In this latter room was a broom closet. To create some space inside I removed a mop and bucket and transferred them to behind the sofa in the living room, the sofa being up against the window. I also deposited my shopping bag in the same place. The shotgun I unwrapped.

Back with my ear pressed to the presumed bedroom door, I could hear they were both now engaging in urgent non-verbal forms of vocal communication. Eventually he at least became even more animated and noisy, and then they were quiet. The radio played on. I crept to the kitchen closet, shotgun in hand, and shut myself in.

Presently I heard movement. A female voice said goodbye, and a door closed. Someone came into the kitchen, turned on a tap briefly and went out again. I left the broom closet and followed. Apart from the music, which was still playing in the bedroom, all was quiet.

Hartling was sitting on the sofa, drink in one hand, television programme guide in his lap. He'd put on a dressing gown but apparently nothing else. That meant I didn't have to worry about him having a concealed weapon.

He looked up and saw me. The expression on his face was something I wouldn't have swapped for the world — well, the world maybe, but not a lot less.

"Hello, Tony," I said with a grin that hadn't been seen since February.

"How'd you get in here?" he demanded, sounding contemptuous and not at all afraid.

"Crash course in locksmithing," I lied.

He leant forward to put his drink down on the coffee table.

"Don't!" I said sharply. He stopped in mid move. "Before you do anything, let me explain the position you're in. You're sitting down. If you get up, I'll have plenty of time to stop you. Unpleasantly. I have here a sawn-off shotgun which is currently pointing at your pretty midriff.

132

If you make a grab for me, or do anything else of a seriously stupid nature — well, it'll make a hell of a mess inside this flat.

"Added to which, as you may imagine, I need almost no provocation to pull the trigger. So for lesser infringements, like not doing exactly what you're told when you're told...." I paused, pointing the barrel at his recently used genitalia, "I'll hurt you. Do you understand?"

He just glared.

"If you don't answer my question in the next three seconds, I'll give you a demonstration."

"I understand. God, I'm going to enjoy killing you."

"In your dreams, mate. Now sit back and relax."

He sat back, though I doubted if he relaxed.

Not taking my eyes off him, I reversed to the main door to the flat. The latching mechanism needed securing so the door couldn't be unlocked from the outside. (I presume it hadn't been secured while he was with the girl in case his minders needed to get in.)

That dealt with, I approached to a distance of about two metres and told him to finish his drink and stand up. He obeyed, placing the empty glass on the coffee table. I noticed his dressing gown had a flannel belt. I instructed him to pull it free and use it to tie his ankles together. He did as commanded, though twice I had to order him to make the belt tighter.

Beginning to feel a little safer, I said: "You don't need the gown. Take it off and throw it over towards the bedroom." Not homosexuality; straightforward tit-for-tat.

As he tossed the garment across the room, he felt the need to declare: "You're dead. Whatever happens to me, you're dead."

Naked, I could see that although he was only an inch taller than me he had a bigger build. He looked stronger. In hand-to-hand combat, I'd probably lose.

I ordered him to fetch my shopping bag from behind the sofa. He turned round, reaching for the bag with his left hand. His right hand moved towards the curtain.

"Twitch that curtain and you won't have time to be sorry about it," I warned. The curtain, of course, was visible from the street, and so from the off-roader where he believed at least one of his minders was sitting guard. I wanted him to go on believing that. I wanted him to play for time, hoping they'd inadvertently come to his rescue. That way he'd do what I wanted, and I wouldn't have to use the shotgun.

He left the curtain unmoved and placed the bag on the coffee table.

"Take out the bottle of whisky. Then make yourself at home. Pour yourself a drink," I instructed.

He went through all the correct motions.

"Drink it," I said. After he had complied I told him to do it again.

"What do you want to get me drunk for?" he asked.

"Poetic revenge. You tried to drown me. So I'm going to drown you. Different kind of drowning, that's all."

He gulped the second glass down and said: "You don't want this to look like murder, right?"

"Not at all. You didn't kill me. Why should I kill you? When I've finished, you'll be free to go. Like I was."

He refilled his glass, spilling some of the whisky on the carpet.

"You know, Tony, you must be awfully keen for me to ruin your sex life. One more stupid thing like that and I will." I wasn't acting. I meant it.

He sensed that and spilt not a single drop as he drained several more glasses, taking a generous amount of time over it.

About half way through the bottle he announced, speech a trifle slurred: "I feel sorry for you. You're a loser. A total loser. Take Miranda, for example. She really likes you. You could have been the first to get her into bed. But you weren't. I was. Sweet little virgin."

I reckoned he was trying to provoke me into launching a non-shotgun physical assault. I wasn't falling for it. I ordered him to have another drink. He drank.

By now his hold on the bottle was becoming unsteady. I took it from him. Nevertheless, I kept the shotgun pointing at his head as I did so in case he was exaggerating his intoxication. He might have been hoping to lull me into giving him a chance to mount an attack. His eyes still looked sharp.

"Total loser," he repeated after downing another glass. "Take you at the trial. All upright and honest and good citizen. Whereas me? Do you know, I was well over the legal alcohol limit when you and your piece of fluff got in my way with that stupid bloody bike. Obvious I must have been. And no one at the trial even hinted at it. Not even you. I'm the winner. Always am."

He stood up suddenly and clenched his fists in an invitation to start a fight. He was a hair's-breadth from instant death now.

"Sit down and drink," I said flatly.

"Sit down and drink," he repeated. He sat down.

Still very much on my guard, I leant forward and poured. He drank.

"You aren't going to win this time either," he informed me. "My friends are outside. They'll be here any moment. Do you know what's going to happen then?"

"Drink up and tell me."

I refilled. He drank and told me.

"We'll take you somewhere where you won't be heard, and I'm going to have a lot of fun with you. I'll work on your body till you can't endure it any longer. Then I'll hang you with piano wire or something. Bleeding loser."

He emptied another glass. It was automatic now. I went to pour a refill and he made his move, grabbing the barrel of the shotgun and forcing it upwards. I didn't fire or let go. I merely splashed whisky in his eyes. He put his hands to his face, cursing.

I left him alone after that. The bottle was nearly empty.

As the minutes passed, his expression grew vacant, his movements became uncoordinated, and he fell sideways on the sofa. He took to murmuring 'total loser' intermittently, all the while groaning and making weak and uncoordinated movements with his arms and legs. Then he was sick. Ever cautious, I opened one of his eyelids with a finger and gently touched his eyeball. Nobody can fake that. He barely moaned.

Retaining the shotgun against the outside possibility of him coming to, I took the shopping bag into the kitchen. Finding a suitable pan, I tipped in some of the cooking oil I'd purchased earlier, added the chips, and set it to heat on the stove.

While waiting for the oil to ignite, I tidied up. Nothing suspicious must be left behind. The shotgun I wrapped in the discarded dressing gown so I could keep it with me without being obvious about it.

I noticed there was a smoke alarm fixed to the ceiling in the living room. I disabled it and returned to the kitchen to watch. It took longer than I expected, but eventually there was a sudden 'whoomph' and flames were almost to the ceiling. I hastened to Hartling and untied the dressing gown belt from his ankles. His legs moved slightly, so he was still alive — barely, for the moment.

I stood and looked at him for the last time. Quite an impressive physique. No excess fat. A nice face too. It seemed a waste to destroy him. Such a shame about the personality.

With grey smoke spreading across the upper part of the

living room, I unlatched the door to the flat, shutting it behind me as quietly as possible. At the ground floor I set off the fire alarm by smashing a glass plate with the small hammer provided on a chain for the purpose. I didn't want to harm anyone else. The other residents would be alerted and escape. Only Hartling would be incapable.

The bell ringing deafeningly, I stepped into the street, walked smartly to the off-roader and drove away. I saw no one.

*

The battle was over; the victory, crushing and total. But there was one last deed needing to be done before triumph and tiredness could pack me off to bed.

I returned to Coed y Deifol and was relieved to find everything undisturbed. I reversed the Ford out onto the main track, and parked the off-roader where the Ford had been. It was necessary to smash a couple of windows with the baseball bat so that the broken glass on the ground would need no second car to explain its being there. Following that, using Hartling's dressing gown as a cloth, and wearing the rubber gloves I'd had on ever since entering flat 4, I cleaned every surface of the off-roader that I might have come into contact with, inside and out.

While I was engaged in this task it began to rain, lightly at first, but gradually getting heavier. I was soon feeling damp spots inside the raincoat, which was showerproof rather than fully waterproof. The discomfort was compensated for by the belief that a good soaking would wash away evidence such as footprints, as well as possibly making estimating the time of death of my two forest victims harder.

Once I was satisfied with the off-roader's cleanliness, I retreated to the Ford. A decision had to be made about the personal effects I'd taken from Weight Trainer and Gerry, and about the baseball bat, my club, the shotgun, Hartling's dressing gown, the carrier bags. What should be dumped and what kept? It became clear to me that the best answer was to place everything in the off-roader and burn it. All the incriminating material would thereby be incinerated.

Accordingly, I put everything in the doomed car except Gerry's mobile phone. Problem: how does one start a fire in pouring rain? I concluded I needed to splash some petrol about. Unfortunately it was all in the tanks of the two cars, and I couldn't get it out of there because I had nothing that would serve as a syphon.

For a while I stood by the off-roader, looking for ideas and seeing my perfect crime scene clean-up facing ruin. Then, having got soaking wet from the rain, I went and sat in the Ford, not knowing what to do, and cursing the delay. Unrealistically or not, I feared that at any moment someone would come along, and I'd be caught.

Eventually, savage frustration made the decision for me. I took the filler cap off the off-roader's petrol tank, stood as near as I dared, and fired the shotgun at the open filler pipe. My intention was to blow the tank up, but nothing happened. (This is something Hollywood definitely gets wrong!) However, when I ventured closer I could hear dripping; and there was a strong smell of fuel. By sheer luck I appeared to have shot a few holes in the petrol tank.

Heartened, I struck a match from the box I'd bought earlier, and dropped it on the ground beneath the car. There was a whoosh of flame. I returned the shotgun to the car's interior and fled hastily back to the Ford.

The result, though, was still very disappointing. Just flames on the ground and smoke and not a lot else. All I could do was sit and watch the inside of the off-roader smouldering but failing to catch fire while the petrol burnt away underneath.

138

I started to think about my options if the car failed to ignite, but as it turned out I needn't have worried. What I didn't realize until I thought about it later was that, as the petrol drained, a small amount of air must have been gradually drawn into the tank, creating an explosive mixture. And the fire directly beneath was raising the temperature higher and higher.

When it occurred, the sudden and totally unexpected detonation was utterly stunning. I was looking elsewhere when it happened, but I caught the tail-end of it: a white-hot ball of flame engulfing the car completely. The tank must have been almost empty by then, for very little burning petrol was sprayed around. Even so, it was sufficient to set the car properly ablaze.

Having succeeded at last in burning the off-roader, my immediate next concern was about starting a forest fire. It was an unlikely prospect, given the rain, but I intended to behave responsibly. Dialling 999 on Gerry's mobile phone, and being careful to use a Welsh accent, I reported that something was burning in Coed y Deifol, and provided directions on how to get to where the fire was.

That done, I drove the Ford to Caerabont and my last night at the hotel as Winston Kelly. I was feeling elated and very pleased with myself. Everything had gone brilliantly; far better than I'd dared expect. By now Hartling would be dead, the victim of a tragic drunken accident. No police investigation. No vengeful father out for blood. Even Miranda need be told nothing.

But above all, Tanya had her justice. I could meet her gaze now without flinching. A great burden had been lifted from me. For the first time since February 14th I was at peace.

10

FLIGHT

Having had an exhausting day, both emotionally and physically, and not finally getting to bed until the early hours, I fell asleep very quickly. It was a good night's sleep. But it took only a few seconds when I woke the next morning for the reality to hit me. And hit me hard. What the hell had I done? Last night's euphoria had worn off, and I was faced with the fact that I had killed three people. I had never harmed anyone much before, and now I was technically a murderer, even if the people I had dispatched were murderers themselves.

Partly what was disturbing me was the thought that I might have overlooked something. Arrest, incarceration in a high security prison with the violent outcasts of society — I had done something which had opened that up as a possible future for me. Little wonder I was troubled.

But there was another aspect to my mental discomfort which was more deep-seated and impossible to dismiss. Had what I'd done really been necessary? Couldn't I have acted differently? Yes, Tanya had been killed, but did killing her killer make it any better? I recalled the old adage: 'Two wrongs don't make a right'. Somehow, over the past months I'd managed to convince myself that they do. But now I could no longer kid myself: the undeniable fact is that they don't. I felt better about Tanya, certainly, but what I really wanted was to have her back with me. And she was still gone forever. I wondered if Weight Trainer and Gerry had families. Even Anthony Hartling had a mother. When I had embarked on my lethal course of action, I had told myself I could worry about the rights and wrongs later if I survived. Well, I had survived, and 'later' was arriving a lot sooner and much more forcefully than I'd expected.

To distract myself from an increasingly overwhelming sense of guilt, I turned on the television in my room in time for the seven o'clock news. I needed to know if my activities had come to anyone's notice yet.

The answer, I quickly learnt, was yes. I'd made it into third place in the national breakfast headlines.

"Police in South Wales last night launched a murder enquiry following the discovery of two bodies and a burnt-out car in Deifol Forest [sic] near Neath. Neither victim has so far been identified, but both are males believed to be in their thirties or forties. Police have appealed for anyone with information to come forward. They are particularly keen to speak to a man who reported a fire in the forest at about eleven o'clock yesterday evening. Detective Chief Inspector Channon, who is leading the investigation, confirmed that it was a fire crew sent to tackle the blaze who discovered the crime. He declined to reveal details of how the two men had died, and said that at this stage he was keeping an open mind on whether the burnt-out car belonged to the victims, and on what the motive was for what he described as 'these vicious killings'."

The other item of news I was especially hoping to hear didn't get mentioned until near the end of the local bulletin.

"A flat in the Hillside area of Caerabont was badly damaged by fire last night. Firefighters arrived on the scene within minutes of the alarm being sounded, and were able to prevent the fire, started when a chip pan overheated, from spreading to other parts of the building. The sole occupant of the damaged flat was taken to hospital suffering from the effects of smoke inhalation. A medical spokesperson confirmed his condition was not life-threatening, but refused to comment on a suggestion that the man had been drinking heavily at the time of admission."

I stared at the television, no longer seeing the news-reader, no longer registering what she was saying. My unease turned into incomprehension, then disbelief, and finally anguish, all in the space of a few seconds.

He wasn't dead! He wasn't dead! He wasn't dead! As those three bitter words sank in, the future I'd only last night started planning for myself disintegrated. Simeon Hartling wouldn't, as I'd intended, be mourning the accidental death of his son while I crept safely away. Instead, one phone call from Anthony and he'd have replacements for Weight Trainer and Gerry hurtling down the M4 in my direction, bristling with hostile intentions.

My first impulse was to flee immediately, but I held it in check. There were my two successful murders to worry about. It was imperative I did nothing suspicious that could be avoided. It was already bad enough that I had a car with a window missing. If asked, I'd have to blame it on vandals. My trousers were another unavoidable difficulty. I'd spent half an hour before going to sleep last night trying to wash the mud stains out using soap and water. The effort had been fairly successful, but they were still wet and smelt of the soap. Neither of these oddities would make even a policeman say to himself that this chap has been out murdering people, but oddities they were and I was anxious not to add to them.

Outwardly calm, I went down to breakfast in the third and final shirt I had with me (both the other two being unwearable, one because of blood-stains and one because it was still dripping with last night's rain). Fortunately, the hotel was sufficiently warm that being in shirt-sleeves didn't raise eyebrows. As I entered the dining room, I

142

discreetly wiped the door handle to remove any trace of my fingerprints. I did the same to my regular chair and the salt-cellar and everything else I was likely to have touched.

After the meal I paid the hotel bill, returned to my room, and cleaned it as thoroughly as I'd cleaned the off-roader the night before. That done I took my leave, wearing the raincoat to cover for the absent jacket.

Driving the Ford, I set out for Cardiff. The plan originally had been to give Miranda the all-clear by phoning her, but things having worked out the way they had, I needed to see her. I went straight to her hotel and knocked on the door of her room.

There was a delay of a few seconds, then: "Who's there?"

"Ed."

She opened the door but didn't invite me in, saying: "I thought you were supposed to phone."

She was still hurting over how I'd behaved on Thursday. I could see it in her eyes.

I said: "Do you remember asking me to hold you because you were lonely and frightened?"

She frowned but didn't reply.

I continued: "Men can be lonely and frightened too."

The hardness left her in the instant. "Oh come here, you," she said, and embraced me as I stepped into the room.

After she'd given me one of her unforgettable kisses, she remarked: "I take it you're lonely and frightened because you had your word with Tony, and it didn't work."

"It was a total disaster."

She moved some odd items off a chair, sat herself on the end of the bed, and gestured that I should occupy the space she had cleared.

"You'd better tell me the bad news," she said.

I didn't enlighten her about Weight Trainer and Gerry.

They were very much in the no-one-must-know category, but that aside I gave her an edited version of the truth. "Basically, I got into Hartling's flat. No breaking and entering or anything like that. I just opened the door and went in. Anyway, I talked to him as I said I would, during the course of which I persuaded him to drink most of a bottle of whisky. He was unyielding, so once he was unconscious, I set fire to the flat. I meant him to die. But he didn't. He's only in hospital."

She looked at me, aghast. "Have I just heard you right? You tried to kill him, is that what you're saying? Damn it, I *knew* something was wrong when you said you'd 'have a word with him'. You never expected that would be enough, any more than I did, did you? You always intended.... Dear God, that makes it premeditated. And I'm an accessory."

"You can't be. I didn't tell you. You didn't know."

That remark unintentionally made her angry. "Don't you *dare* tell me about the law. Given what you've just said, the law requires me to immediately phone the police and report you. If I don't, I'm an accessory. It doesn't matter you didn't tell me in advance. It's called 'being an accessory after the fact'. It could even count as perverting the course of justice. When I get my degree, I've got a position lined up as a trainee with a firm of solicitors in Swansea. I don't even have to be *convicted* of those crimes. If I'm so much as remotely connected to them, that's it. I'm unemployable. Hell!"

"I'm sorry," I said. "I didn't mean to do this to you."

"I do actually realize that. But, my God, you've committed arson and attempted murder! And frankly, if I was a prosecuting barrister, I'd hang you out to dry. What do you mean, '*basically* you got into his flat'? And you got him drunk. What? Did he just stand there and knock back a bottle or two to oblige you? But no, don't answer those questions. You've told me too much already."

"I'm sorry," I said again. I didn't know what else to say. My future was in her hands.

There was an awkward silence. Then she sighed and said more gently: "I don't know, Ed. You're a case, you are. What on earth were you thinking? How can you possibly believe that what you did was anything other than insane?"

"You said yourself we had to get him off our backs. There was no other realistic way to do it. Not to mention he had us thrown off a cliff. When you fight someone like him, you either stoop to his level or you lose."

"But that's the whole point," she said almost sadly. "That's what the law is for. It's there to protect people. People like us. It means we don't have to stoop to anyone's level."

"And when it fails? It didn't protect Tanya and me. It gave us a two-fingered salute."

"All right, I concede you have a justified grievance against Tony, but surely you can see that taking the law into your own hands is what got you into this mess in the first place. And you're still doing it. You have to stop. Now."

"I know."

The expression on her face changed. At first I thought it was pity for me, but what she said next belied that impression. "What a sad comment on someone when you can't deny that their death would solve more problems than it creates. But that's Tony for you. I have to admit, all things considered, I wish you'd succeeded. It would certainly have served him right. But as it is, you've made the situation a thousand times worse. He tried to drown us, and all you'd done was harass him. What's he going to be like now?"

"That's something I hardly dare think about. I wish I'd never started this whole business."

"You're going to have to go into hiding."

"Yes, I know. I.... I want you to come with me."

"Oh Ed," she said, taking my hand, "I can't. I can't throw up everything and run away."

"I'm afraid he'll harm you," I pleaded.

"Why? I'm not the one he hates. I'm just a theatrical prop. I haven't been to the police after the drowning thing. I didn't go to them last time he misbehaved. It's you he's after. I'm no threat to him. He'll just go on being his obnoxious self. I'll outface him somehow."

I had to ask the awful question because it was worrying me, even though Hartling had already told me the answer. I said: "What was this misbehaviour? What happened?"

"It's between me and him," she said, letting go of my hand. "I'm not sure I want to tell you."

"He said you had sex with him."

"I wouldn't know. Whatever took place, I never consented."

"That doesn't make sense."

"Oh, all right," she said, looking into the distance. "You seem to have got the gist of it anyway. But please don't ever pass this on.

"It was almost two years ago. I had no special male friend at the time. Most of the boys left me cold — immature bunch. February it was. Tony Hartling asked me out for a drink. I think he picked on me precisely because I was one of the few girls who was neither promiscuous nor paired up. I quite fancied him physically, I suppose, so I accepted. I was flattered. I don't often get chatted up.

"Of course, what a surprise, it turned out he wanted to get me into bed. I refused. Hell, maybe some of the girls were behaving like the world was about to end next week, but I had this idea I wanted it to be something special. You know, I wanted to be in love first.

"He took my refusal with such good grace that when he

146

asked to see me again I agreed. We had a drink. Next thing I know, I'm on my bed, naked. It's eight in the morning, my private parts are sore, and I've got a funny taste in my mouth. At first I thought I must have been drunk, though it's never given me amnesia before. I questioned some people who saw me leave the pub, and they said I was behaving in a licentious fashion. Begging for it. Out of character perhaps, but they never guessed anything sinister was going on. Later I had a few flashbacks: being alone with Tony; him taking off my clothes; wanting to resist but being unable too. Unfortunately, by the time I worked out what he had done, it was too late to make a complaint. No trace of the drug left in my blood. And besides, look what happened to you in court. What do you think a defence barrister would have done to me? So I let it go."

She looked at me defiantly. I sensed what her virginity had meant to her. Hartling had stolen her most intimate gift.

"You once told me the guy was a crook," I said quietly. "I think you were being very generous."

"We weren't so well acquainted then, otherwise I'd have used more expressive language."

"Do you know what the drug was? I thought substances like that are science fiction."

"Probably Rohypnol. It's a tranquiliser. Only available on prescription."

"So where did Hartling get it?"

"Internet probably. Mind you, the talk on the campus is that Tony has access to other drugs too, especially ecstasy and cocaine. He doesn't supply directly, of course. Too risky for a law student's career. But a few people have indicated their interest to him, and a day or two later who should they meet up with but a dealer. My guess is Tony acts as a go-between. Probably gets paid commission for it."

"Is there no end to this?" I said despairingly. "When I started, I thought Hartling was no more than a tearaway with a rich father. Now you're telling me he's involved in drug dealing as well as everything else."

With Simeon Hartling out to protect his son, and with Anthony wanting me dead, it was clear my only hope for survival lay in hiding long-term. I urged Miranda to come with me for her own safety, but she was convinced they wouldn't harm her. They'd gain nothing by it. With me out of the way, her usefulness as a prop was at an end.

Neither of us said it, but we both realized our chances of getting together were near zero. I couldn't remain in the open; Miranda wouldn't go into hiding. It looked like I'd been right in the first place. I'd relented on being cruel to be kind, but by being kind I'd only ended up being cruel.

She told me to keep in touch by phone. I hugged her and kissed her goodbye and left. She was, like me, very upset at having to part in this fashion. Being me, I hid it the way I always do. It was best she didn't know.

*

I took the Ford to a Cardiff garage to be repaired. Not wanting to hang around, I arranged to collect it on the Monday and caught a train to London. I was soon safely in my flat in Harrow. As yet, the only people who knew I lived there were the landlord I was renting it from and my bank. This flat was my 'safe house'. I felt fairly secure there, though the possibility I'd overlooked some way of tracing me kept me feeling edgy.

That evening I watched the news with great attention. Detective Chief Inspector Channon appeared on camera personally to ask for help. The two Coed y Deifol victims had apparently still not been identified (though I was willing to bet Simeon Hartling knew who they were by

148

now), but a motorist had come forward to report a couple of cars being driven recklessly in the vicinity of the crime at about the time it was getting dark, roughly five hours before the car fire. Did anyone else see these two cars on the road? No descriptions yet, beyond that one had been an estate. The murderer would have been behaving oddly, may have been unexpectedly not at home, could have had blood-stained clothing. Was any member of the public able to point a finger of suspicion at someone? I was described as extremely dangerous and in urgent need of apprehension, which amused me since I was neither.

Sunday I partly spent reading the crime report of a so-called quality newspaper. Ten per cent fact, ninety per cent speculation masquerading as fact. It was stated as unqualified truth that one of the victims had been shot in the chest (close!), while the other had been strangled (!). Their car had been doused in petrol before being set alight (not exactly). There had been a chase on foot through the forest (correct! and useful to know that the police had detected it) which had provided vital evidence (unspecified). An arrest was expected within days. "We just need one more piece of the jigsaw," Chief Inspector Channon was quoted as saying.

This last remark, I had concluded from previous difficult headline-worthy murders, is one the police usually make when they have no idea. I suppose the intention is to frighten the criminal into panicking and revealing himself. Speaking from experience, I can state it doesn't work. It did serve though to concentrate my mind on how to get rid of the one piece of evidence that could utterly damn me: Winston Kelly's blood-stained clothes.

As a temporary measure to address this problem, I washed the suit and shirt several times until they appeared clean, if badly creased. It was as much as could be done pending disposal.

On Monday I bought a replacement Winston Kelly suit as nearly identical as possible to the original, and caught a train back to Cardiff for my alter ego's last task, which was to collect the repaired Ford. I encountered no difficulties and was able to take the car on to Swansea where I sold it to a second-hand dealer (for rather less than it had cost me), insisting on payment in cash. The official vehicle-licensing record would show a non-existent Winston Kelly, whose address was the hotel where I had been staying, had purchased the car on September 25th and owned it for exactly one month. I was confident I had dissociated the murders from the Ford, and the Ford from the real me, as fully as it was practicable to do.

Back in Harrow once more, I rang Miranda from a payphone. (For the time being, I didn't want Ed Somersby's mobile number logged on Miranda's phone. Just in case.)

It was evening when I called. Miranda answered after a few rings. She informed me Anthony Hartling was still in hospital but was expected out within a day or two. A couple of friends who'd visited him said his father had sent along some fat fellow to keep a vigil by his bedside. They'd expressed their opinion that as parental devotion goes it was a trifle excessive. But then they didn't know there was a private war in progress. She'd also taken a walk past the fire-damaged flat, and reported that repairs were already underway.

These pieces of information aside, Miranda and I had only one thing to discuss, and we took a lot longer about it than I had anticipated. When I ran out of coins for the payphone, she rang me back. What we discussed in essence was meeting again. We agreed we wanted to, and expressed it in lots of different ways, and assured each other we'd find a way to manage it somehow, some day soon. Her evident affection for me was a great comfort, and it would

150

have taken a far harder heart than mine not to respond in kind.

When finally we brought the conversation to an end, I promised to ring again in a couple of days. As I walked away from the phone kiosk, I felt simultaneously cheered up and desperately lonely. I couldn't deny I'd had enough of life-and-death conflicts. The events of the last week had totally destroyed my desire for justice. If the Hartlings left me alone, I'd not trouble them further. The cost to me in emotional terms, especially in respect of being prevented from seeing Miranda, was just too great.

The next morning I travelled by rail to Dover. The washed ex-Winston Kelly suit and shirt I put in a charity recycling bin for unwanted clothes. Gerry's mobile phone, which then became the only remaining item connecting me to the Coed y Deifol murders, I dismantled, dropping the various bits in a range of places, including litter bins and drains.

*

Having returned to London early in the afternoon, I visited John Farley at the workshop where he carried on his motorcycle repair business. As I walked in he glanced at me, stood up, and said: "Good afternoon. What can I do for you?"

"Hello, John."

The look on his face! "Ed? Crikey! What's happened? Have you joined the army?"

"No chance. I thought I'd try a change of appearance, but I've already decided I don't like it. I'll be getting the long hair and beard regrown as quickly as I can."

After some small-talk — he hadn't seen me since mid-September — and rather more bike-talk, I told him I wanted to get back on two wheels.

"About time," he said, clapping me on the shoulder. "You want another Triumph?"

"Sounds good."

"Don't go away."

He made a couple of phone calls and then suggested: "If you hang around till five we can go and look at one this evening. I presume you'd like me to check it out for you."

"Yes please."

"Okay. Since it's you, I'll do it for free. Since it's me, would you mind playing mechanic's assistant this afternoon?"

"Not at all."

He gave me an overall and set me to work. It was a fair trade, and in any case he was good company.

Of course, he wanted to know what I'd been doing over the past month or so, and of course I was evasive, though I hoped not too obviously so. I said I'd been away on holiday, touring the country by train.

At five as promised, he locked up the workshop and drove me in his van to the dealer he'd contacted by phone earlier. It was a second-hand machine we were inspecting. Same engine as my old Thunderbird but different styling, a little lighter in weight and faster. He gave it a thorough medical, told me what was wrong with it — a few things needed attention, all minor — and helped me haggle over the price.

After that, he invited me round for a meal next evening and we went our separate ways, John home to Judith and I by tube to my safe house in Harrow.

My visiting John might appear to have been taking a grave risk, but I reckoned in practical terms it was safe enough. I had various connections to people in the motorcycle fraternity, but they were known only to fellow riders. Even if Simeon Hartling made enquiries, he had no reason to single out John Farley for special attention. Not that I wasn't careful. I kept watch on who was behind me on my way home. Nothing and no one caught my eye or aroused my suspicion.

That evening my double murder wasn't mentioned in the news. I began to rest easier in my mind. The police had no reason to go searching for Winston Kelly; the Hartlings had no way of finding Ed Somersby. Not even Miranda knew where I was. I didn't feel so safe I could relax. But I did feel safe enough that I could sleep at night.

11

EXECUTION

Next morning (Wednesday) saw me greeting the day with optimism. My purchase of the Triumph was a first step in getting my life together again, and I felt good about it.

Having arranged insurance and donned my long-neglected leather gear, I collected the motorcycle from the dealer. Apparently I'd been lucky to buy it. Shortly after I'd departed the previous evening, a fellow had called in and taken an interest in the same motorcycle. A conversation had then ensued, during which my name had come up. The fellow knew me, so it seems, but the dealer's description of him didn't match anyone I could think of. Nonetheless I assumed it must have been one of my biker acquaintances, since the alternative, that it was someone connected to the Hartlings, I judged (with worrying reservations) to be fanciful. There was simply no way they could have found me.

Back on a motorcycle for the first time in eight months, I went joyfully on a spree along the roads of Kent. I picnicked on a footpath overlooking the River Medway and fed the ducks, all the while thinking about my future. The key, I decided, was to get out of London and move to some other anonymous big city. Bristol, maybe, which was closer to Miranda in Wales. I'd need to change my name officially to something new and unrecognizable, and I'd a vague idea there was a thing called a deed poll for doing that: something I had to find out about fairly urgently.

As it got dark, I returned to London and the Farley's

hospitality. I parked my machine — it was a time-honoured tradition, this — in the front garden in view of the lounge window, and knocked.

Judith opened the door. "Well at least I recognize the outfit," she said. "Come on in. How are you?"

"Fine, thanks."

"John reckons it's hero worship."

"What is?"

"Short hair and no beard."

"Who's the hero supposed to be?"

"Me, of course," said John, emerging from the kitchen and blowing me a kiss.

"You're asking for a punch on the nose, mate," I retorted.

Judith laughed.

We passed a congenial couple of hours talking and eating and talking some more. Eventually (and inevitably) we got onto the subject of my new Triumph. I suggested John might like to try it out around the block.

"I don't mind if I do," he said as I tossed him the key.

"You can make yourself useful while you're about it," Judith advised him. "You're almost out of beer. Pick up a few cans from the off-licence."

"That's what I keep her for," said John to me. "Never misses a trick. So organized. I should be back in fifteen minutes."

He put on his kit, and presently we heard the Triumph heading away down the road.

"Do you mind if I use your phone, Judith?" I asked. "I'll keep it brief."

"By all means," she said, and diplomatically began reading her newspaper.

I rang Miranda, taking care to enter the 'caller id. withheld' code first. It was eight o'clock and she'd be in her room at the hall of residence. I got no response. She's gone to the theatre or she's in the bath, I told myself. For a day or two I'd almost forgotten I was under threat of death. That unanswered ringing tone brought it all back to me. It was something unexpected; something to reawaken my fears.

It would have been an abuse of my friends' hospitality to repeatedly keep trying Miranda's number, so I abandoned the call for the evening, leaving a message: "Hello Miranda, it's me. Just checking you're okay. I'll call again tomorrow morning."

John wasn't home after fifteen minutes. He wasn't home after half an hour. "He's probably jawing with a buddy," Judith said, but I could see she was getting restive. As the minutes passed she became steadily more agitated, trying his mobile phone and getting no response. In the end, I proposed we walk to the off-licence, which was only a mile away.

We put on our coats and were literally about to step outside when someone knocked.

"Talk of the devil," Judith said, and opened the door.

The man wasn't her husband. I had enough time to think that if it was a Hartling employee on the threshold I was dead, and then I saw the uniformed woman police constable with him.

"Mrs Farley?" the man asked.

"Yes."

He showed her his warrant card and introduced himself — a detective sergeant — and the W.P.C. He continued: "Is John Farley your husband?"

"Yes."

"May we come in?"

Judith stood aside without speaking. They entered. The detective eyed me questioningly.

"This is Ed Somersby," Judith said. "He's a friend of ours."

He nodded an acknowledgement and said: "I'm afraid I have some bad news. Your husband has been killed."

No build up. No warning. Straight out with it. For a moment, Judith and I just stared.

Understandably I recovered first. I could only think it was my motorcycle. "What happened?" I asked.

"Someone shot him," the man said.

"Shot!" exclaimed Judith.

I was as stunned as she was. If it had been me it would have made sense. But not John. He was a popular man. Nobody would want to shoot *him*.

"If you wouldn't mind, sir," said the W.P.C. to me, gesturing towards the lounge.

I followed Judith, and the two police officers followed me.

Once we were all seated the questioning began, directed primarily at Judith.

"I appreciate this is extremely difficult for you, Mrs Farley, but the quicker we get answers, the more likely we are to catch the culprit. You do understand?"

Judith nodded.

Maybe I was becoming cynical, but it struck me they were also sizing up our reactions. The questions were genuine enough though. They wanted to know about her husband's last movements, anything unusual in his recent past, any enemies, any unconventional business deals, any financial problems, any sexual liaisons either of them had had or suspected — I blushed here, not out of guilt, but because I fancied the police officers thought I was guilty — any new friends, any deliveries of unaccounted letters or packages, any strange phone calls. The answers they got were as unhelpful as they were honest. They recorded it all anyway.

It was plain it hadn't occurred to them the wrong man had been shot, but by the end of the interview, in which I was almost entirely a spectator, it had occurred to me. John had left the house on my machine. With his crash helmet on he'd be practically indistinguishable from me. Even bare-headed we'd look similar enough under street-lighting for a mistake to be made. Of course it hadn't been Anthony Hartling who'd pulled the trigger. I'd have recognized him and run. John wouldn't have reacted at all, which would have told Hartling he'd got the wrong target. No, this had to be someone I didn't know. And if I'd not seen this killer before, he hadn't seen me either. He'd relied on a verbal description, possibly accompanied by a clandestinely taken photograph of Winston Kelly. Somehow he'd traced me to the Farley's house, and had followed who he thought was me when John went to buy his beer.

Not a word of this could I pass on to the police; not unless I wanted my exploits of recent months to be revealed. The effect was to make me tight-lipped and dismissive. When the two officers left, I had no doubt my demeanour had put me on their list of suspicious characters.

I had no idea how to relate to Judith at this point. And that was despite my own experience of sudden bereavement. All I could think to do was to offer her my company, but she said she wanted to be alone. She did, though, accept my offer to return in the morning so that I could be with her when she went to formally identify John's body. It was the least I could do.

I returned by tube and on foot to Harrow, taking a convoluted route in order to ensure I wasn't followed. In all likelihood there was no immediate threat. The executioner had done his job — so he thought — and got away. No one would be looking for me tonight.

I suppose I was too dazed emotionally to react to what had happened, for I slept well. It wasn't till I woke next morning that the realization hit me that the death of my good friend John Farley had resulted from a chain of events I had set in motion. I was glad I had stopped shaving. It meant I didn't have to look in a mirror.

Yesterday I had started out optimistic. Today I was overwhelmed with guilt and despair. I had to anchor my mind to something or I'd go mad. So I clung to the thought that Judith needed me. She had been there for me when Tanya died. Now it was time to repay her.

Calculating it would take some hours yet for the executioner to learn of his error and get back on my trail, I was none too careful arriving at Judith's home. Perhaps in a fatalistic way I no longer cared if I was dead or alive. In fact the Farley residence was as safe as it could be, for the police were there in force. Apparently a small sachet of cocaine had been found in one of John's pockets. The house was being taken apart. So, Judith told me, was John's workshop.

For a while she and I sat in the kitchen listening to the sounds made by a merciless invasion of privacy. At first Judith seemed crushed by it all, but as she heard them going through her drawers, her most private things, she became increasingly irate.

To forestall the explosion, I said: "Let's get out of here for a while."

"Yes, let's," she agreed.

If only it was that simple. At the front door a uniformed officer barred our path. "I can't permit Mrs Farley to leave yet, sir," he said to me.

"Is she under arrest?"

"No sir. She's helping us with our enquiries."

"Not right now, she isn't. If she's not under arrest, we're leaving."

"It would be better if you didn't."

"Arrest us or get out of the way," I said, angry on Judith's behalf.

"Let 'em go," somebody called from upstairs. The constable stood aside.

"Thanks, Ed," Judith said, once we were out of police earshot.

She was adamant John had nothing to do with drugs. I told her I didn't doubt for an instant she was right, and stated the obvious truth. The killer had planted the cocaine on her husband's body to throw the investigation off track. And the ploy had succeeded. "By tonight," I predicted, "John'll just be another casualty in the drug wars that flare up in London from time to time."

"I suppose so," she agreed. "But why would anyone want to kill him? He didn't have enemies."

"Probably it was a mistake. Somebody thought he was someone else."

It was such a sensible explanation that she accepted it without pursuing the line of speculation further — for which I was extremely grateful.

We strolled up and down the street a few times — I didn't want to go far in case the executioner showed up earlier than I expected — and finally went back indoors. The police found no drugs. Not even a sniffer dog's worth.

They put the interior in order, but nothing is ever in quite the right place when someone else tidies up. Judith had to go round and do it all again.

The afternoon was spent dealing with two chores. The first was formally identifying John's body. I was there in a supporting role.

Contrary to my expectations, the execution had been carried out, not with a shotgun, but with a handgun. The entry wound was slightly in front of the left ear, looking like a large black birthmark. I couldn't see where the bullet had exited. There was no mess and no external destruction of the skull. The main message I got from these observations was that the Hartlings had given up on staged accidents. They just wanted me dead now and weren't fussy about how that was achieved.

The second chore was an interview with a senior police officer. I offered to accompany Judith into the interview room, but was firmly told by the officer that unless I was her solicitor I was not welcome. Judith was too traumatized to argue, and I judged making a fuss would upset her more than acquiescing. So she was interviewed alone.

Absent though I was, I soon learnt what had taken place. Judith obviously needed to tell someone, and I like to think she told me because I was a person she could trust, and because I knew how she was feeling.

The officer, it seems, had not handled the interview well, being apparently somewhat lacking in sympathy. I had her crying on my shoulder for a while afterwards, the sobs being interspersed with uncomplimentary remarks about his character.

The breakdown in communication between them had been due to her questioner's belief that John had been attacked for a reason. Witnesses reported that the gunman, who they all agreed had been smoking a cigar, had walked up and shot his victim once in the head as he was preparing to put on his crash helmet after leaving the off-licence. A professional assassination. The killer had then crouched over the fallen body and taken a small packet out of John's jacket pocket — the pocket where the sachet of cocaine was later found. Mr Farley was plainly involved with narcotics, and Judith was expected, if not pressed, to reveal what she knew. Her serious, truthful answers, which inevitably portrayed her husband as entirely virtuous, had caused mounting irritation on the other side of the desk. She was branded as uncooperative and therefore suspect.

"It's obvious," Judith said later back at the house, "that that detective wasn't listening to me. Does he honestly think I don't know my own husband? If there was cocaine in John's pocket, it's because the killer put it there. Two packets in and, for the witnesses to see, one packet out again."

She'd got it about right.

We watched the early evening news, but John had already been forgotten. Not so, Coed y Deifol. The police now revealed that Gerry's fingerprints had been found on file and he and Weight Trainer identified thereby. It was reported they worked for, and the burnt-out car had belonged to, a London-based company called High Rise Nightclubs. Detective Chief Inspector Channon appealed yet again for information from the public, and repeated the 'one more piece of the jigsaw' mantra. I thought it absurdly perverse the authorities seemed to be putting more effort into catching me than John's infinitely more culpable Cigar-man.

Just after the news finished, the police brought round my motorcycle and returned it to me. They'd searched that for hidden drugs too (naturally), found nothing, and concluded it wasn't a material part of the crime.

My decision to ring Miranda in the morning had — understandably in the circumstances — slipped my mind. I remedied the oversight in the evening, once again using Judith's phone with 'caller id. withheld'. As before, Miranda's phone went to 'leave a message'. I declined to do so. The lack of response from her end, for two evenings in a row, had me desperately worried. I started mentally planning an urgent trip to Caerabont.

After a few minutes, having explained to Judith I'd not got through, I tried again. This time the call was answered, but I didn't hear the friendly voice I was expecting; only silence.

Immediately on my guard and cautious — behaviour that was becoming a habit — I said: "Hello? Is that Miranda?"

"Yes," she said. "Who's this?" Something was badly wrong. Her voice sounded unnatural. Not like her. Lifeless.

"Hello, Miranda. It's Ed."

She cried out almost as if someone had hit her.

"Miranda?"

"Oh thank God, thank God," she exclaimed and burst into tears. My stomach knotted up.

"What is it? What's the matter?" Keep cool, I told myself. Keep cool. Not least because Judith couldn't help but overhear what I was saying.

"He said he'd killed you. He said...." More crying.

"Who said? Was it Tony?"

"A man smoking cigars. He made me.... You've got to get away from there. He's after you. He's got a gun. Oh Ed, I'm so sorry. I'm so sorry."

It was like Chief Inspector Channon's jigsaw. The bits were coming down the phone in random order. Somehow I had to calm her.

"It's okay," I said as soothingly as possible. "I'm safe. You can't help me by crying. I need to know what's happened. Are you at the university?"

"Yes."

"What's your room there?"

"105 Llewellyn."

"Will it help if I come and stay with you for a while?"

A simple question like that and it panicked her. "Don't come here. Don't come near me. You've got to hide. He knows where you are."

"How does he know? Where does he think I am?"

"I didn't mean to. He made me do it. I couldn't breathe, over and over...."

I was baffled. She'd told Cigar-man where I was. But she didn't know where I was. Could I have slipped up and not known it?

"What exactly did you tell him?" I asked.

She started crying again. Let her take her time, I thought. Be patient. "You remember that phone number you gave me...."

What phone number? And then the key bit of the jigsaw fell into place. I'd given her John Farley's workshop number the night before I sprang my trap in Coed y Deifol. She'd written it down at the time, but in the course of subsequent developments I'd forgotten all about it, and I'd assumed she had too. I knew then how true it is when they say it's not the big things that catch you out; it's the little things.

"Okay. Now listen. As of now you don't leave your room without an escort. Never let yourself be alone in public. Keep your mobile with you. Call the police if anything alarms you. Have you got that?"

"I think so."

"Good. Now try not to get upset. Just answer a few questions. Will you do that for me?"

"I'll try."

"Good girl. I want to know when you had your conversation with this man. When did it take place?"

"It was Tuesday. The day before last. He hurt me, Ed. I didn't want to tell him."

"I know. It wasn't your fault. When did he give you the bad news about me?" (I couldn't be more specific with Judith nearby.)

"This morning when he came to let me go. I thought it was too late to warn you. Oh Ed...." She started to cry again.

"I understand. Now just sit tight. I'll be on my way to rescue you, tonight."

"No. No. Don't come near me. He'll come back and find you. Just get away."

"All right," I said gently. "Don't worry about me. I'll call you again tomorrow evening."

I put down the phone. My heart was pounding, I was trembling and I felt sick.

Judith said: "If you're in trouble, Ed, you know I'm here." This from a woman whose husband had just died.

"I don't deserve a friend like you," I told her sincerely.

"That's what I've been thinking about you most of today," she replied. There are no words to express the utter revulsion I felt for myself at that moment: a coward who was hiding the worst conceivable truth from someone trusting him. With friends like me, you don't need enemies.

Judith insisted on being left alone that night. I checked the house was secure before I departed and advised her to keep her phone by her bed.

Out in the street, I mounted my Triumph and roared off like the devil was after me. Cigar-man hadn't known of his blunder when he'd released Miranda this morning, but he would surely know by now. It was quite possible he was sitting in a car outside Judith's, waiting for me to leave. If that was so, I didn't give him any more chance than the barest minimum. When it comes to throwing off pursuit, there's nothing that can match a motorcycle. I used every trick imaginable. Long before I reached Harrow I was in the clear and out of immediate danger.

From my safe house I walked to a local pub a mile away and ordered a late meal, Judith not having provided one.

I was dining peacefully when a brazenly-dressed woman came in, handed some money over to the barman, and looked around. She spotted me, the only customer eating a meal who also happened to be alone and male. She approached my table.

"Mind if I join you?" she asked.

"Please." It was a genuine answer. I was profoundly depressed and wanted human contact.

She made small-talk for a while, which I responded to in an automatic, almost mindless way. It wasn't a brush-off, so she became more overt, shifting in her seat so I got a clearer view of what I admit was an appealingly sexy cleavage.

"Would you like some real girl company for a while?" she said.

I looked in her eyes. I supposed she must be as hard as nails inside, but that isn't what I saw. "I hadn't better," I answered. "Whenever I get to like anybody, they end up being hurt."

"I wouldn't be hurt, love."

"You don't know Tony Hartling."

"Hartling?" she said, followed by an ominous: "Oh!"

"*Do* you know him?"

"If it's the Hartling I'm thinking of. Not a nice man. Big fellah, late forties, filthy rich. Lives down the West End."

"That would be Simeon, the father."

"Right. Whatever. You on his hate list?"

"I think I must be."

"I can see you've got problems then."

She had me intrigued despite my mental state. "So tell me. What's he got to do with you?"

"He's offered me work in the past, that's all. A couple of girls I know do business with him. He owns a hotel down Soho. Rich foreigners use it mostly. Personal service in every room."

"You mean a brothel."

"I mean what I said. Got several nightclubs too. And a gambling joint. Has its attractions for workers like me. Job security. Protection. But you've got to perform when you're told to, and half your money disappears into Hartling's pocket. That's why I've never taken him up on it. I prefer self-employed."

I asked her how much she charged, and she told me what her prices started from. With the thought that the beneficiaries under my will wouldn't miss it, I took out my wallet and gave her that amount. "This is if you'll talk to me a while longer," I said.

She smiled. "Tell you something," she said, moving closer to me, putting her hand on mine, and speaking quietly. "Clients often want to talk more than anything else. Surprising but true."

So we talked. I told a total stranger about Tanya and the plans we'd had and the dreams, and how it was all in ruins. I watched the performance from somewhere up near the ceiling; a poor little guy with his fiancée scattered in a memorial wood, his friends all being victimized, his head in a noose, and his future prospects bleaker than an Arctic midwinter. Tanya wept for me.

When I finished, Candy — that was her working name — once again put her hand on mine, and in a tone of voice full of compassion said: "Are you sure you won't come home with me, love? It won't cost you any extra."

"I can't," I responded. "My girlfriend wouldn't like it."

I left her sitting there and made my way to the flat by a devious route, just in case. The cold night air complemented perfectly a mind-numbing despair that left me feeling like a zombie. I found myself wondering if by 'girlfriend' I had meant Tanya or Miranda. It wasn't clear to me. Nothing was clear to me any more.

I roughed up my bed to make it look like I was in it when I wasn't, fortified the main door with a piece of furniture, and settled down on the kitchen floor, a carving knife within easy reach.

It took a long time to get to sleep. The thought went round and round in my mind that I was bringing disaster to everyone who knew me. The only thanks you get for being a friend to Ed Somersby is to be tortured or shot or bereaved. The most considerate thing I could do was keep away from all those I cared about; from Miranda, from Judith, from everyone. The one consolation was that I wouldn't need to make myself a pariah for long. Cigar-man was bound to catch up with me. My life expectancy had come down to hours.

12

DUEL

There's no history of manic-depressive illness in my family, but perhaps even perfectly level-headed people can suffer from it in extreme circumstances. I had gone to sleep feeling more wretched even than in the dark days of late February. I awoke to discover I had added Cigar-man to Anthony Hartling on my tally of individuals who were going to regret the day they got into a fight with Ed Somersby. Yes of course it was irrational and questionably realistic, but so what! It was a better frame of mind to be in than last night's. Anything was better than last night.

Over breakfast I reviewed the situation. Before the battle of Coed y Deifol, the enemy must have regarded me as an irritating pest needing summary disposal but not to be taken all that seriously. Now they had found out what I was capable of, they'd be taking me very seriously indeed.

And for that reason, finding me was their top priority. Hence Cigar-man's interrogation of Miranda. Knowing she'd given him John Farley's answerphone number, I could account for how I'd been located. If you ring the number, John, or the answerphone message if he's not there, begins by giving the caller the name of John's motorcycle repair business. Cigar-man had heard that name. A browse through the London telephone directory would have given him John's business address. Someone from the Hartling camp must have been sent to locate the workshop, and had arrived in time to follow John and me to the second-hand dealer. After we'd left, the dealer had been tricked in the course of a conversation into revealing that Ed Somersby had just purchased a motorcycle. Doubtless, a careful note was made of the motorcycle's registration number. That was on the Tuesday evening. Come Wednesday, all Cigar-man had to do was go to John's workshop, hang around and follow John home. His next step after that depended on me. If I didn't show up, he could 'persuade' John or Judith to summon me or at least tell him where I could be found. If I did show up, the motorcycle would identify me. All he had to do after that was get me alone.

Assuming after his botched attempt to kill me he was still on the job, he was once again faced with the problem of finding me. And it was urgent. Anthony Hartling was in danger while I was on the loose. So how would Cigar-man go about it? Another visit to Miranda to extract further information — which she didn't possess — was one chilling prospect. More likely he would try his luck with Judith. Between them, the two women represented his only hope of coming into contact with me quickly. They were both therefore in peril. The trouble was, unarmed there was no way I could protect them, either singly or together. I scolded myself bitterly for consigning the sawn-off shotgun to the flames in Coed y Deifol. It would have made all the difference.

The other matter to consider was manpower. It appeared Cigar-man had acted mostly alone, abducting and subsequently releasing Miranda in Wales, and travelling to London in the interim to kill John. It was tempting to think he'd had no help in Wales and little in London, and that the reason was simply that none was available. Simeon Hartling probably employed quite a number of tough guys — bouncers and suchlike — but most of them wouldn't have signed up to a job description which included a clause on committing murder as and when directed by the boss.

And of those who had, two had recently had their employment terminated. 'Innocent' employees might of course be used for surveillance operations — taking the timing into account, it must have been just such an employee watching John's workshop on the Tuesday evening, for example — but even that was a risk, given they might be called on to 'assist the police with their enquiries' at some point. Thus it seemed unlikely to me I was up against a private army. If the opposite was the case and it was all down to Cigar-man, I was in with a chance. A fighting chance, I convinced myself.

After breakfast I set off for Judith's. Before I had left the previous evening, she had asked me to help her sort out the paperwork and the motorcycles in John's workshop, and I had agreed to do so.

Some of the way there it occurred to me I couldn't walk up to her front door and knock. Cigar-man might be lying in wait outside; or, even worse, inside. From a payphone I asked Judith if it would be all right to meet her at the workshop rather than at her house. She said that was fine and confirmed a time of nine thirty. I decided, without telling her, that if she didn't show up by ten I'd make an anonymous call to the police and send them round to her address.

I rode the Triumph to a location roughly half way between the Farley's house and the workshop. There are many ways to get from the one to the other, but John had normally used the simplest route, and I assumed Judith would also.

She drove past me in John's van almost to the minute when I predicted she would. There was no one else with her in the van as far as I could tell. Less satisfactorily, it was impossible to detect if she was being followed; the traffic was too heavy. I tucked into the flow of vehicles and kept about fifty metres behind her until she turned off the main road and into the narrow street, a short distance down which was the workshop. Then I closed the gap between us quickly so we arrived more or less together.

No one suspicious on foot nearby. No occupied parked cars. Nothing amiss. Judith said hello. My response was a rude: "Let's get inside."

She fiddled with the padlock. With that removed, she fiddled with the mortise lock. If some stranger had walked up to us at that moment, what the hell would I have done? It was because I didn't have an answer that I was on the verge of hysteria by the time the large multi-panelled sliding door rolled aside enough to admit us. It wasn't Judith but I who extracted the key and inserted it on the inside of the door. Grabbing the padlock so we couldn't be locked in, I slammed the sliding door shut again and secured it.

"What on earth are you doing?" Judith exclaimed as she de-activated the burglar alarm.

"I'll explain in a moment," I said. I snatched up a convenient crowbar and went round the workshop. No one. The office out the back was also empty. Through the office and upstairs. Toilet empty. Kitchenette empty. Finally, the large unused room over the workshop; also empty. All windows shut. Looking into the street: all normal. Longer look out the rear from the kitchenette: the back garden — for such it had been at some time in the past — was a collection of weeds mixed with various bits of mechanical hardware; an eyesore which John was forever going to tidy up, never had and now never would. Beyond that were a one-and-a-half metre tall wooden fence and an alleyway. No signs of life.

I began to feel more relaxed. The enemy hadn't known I was meeting Judith; they didn't know she was coming to the workshop. Maybe we'd be unmolested, at least for the time being.

As I was about to return to the office from upstairs, the office phone rang. Judith must have been close by for it only trilled a couple of times before she answered it.

"Yes," she said. "Ed? It's someone for you."

Thinking it was Miranda, I hurried into the office and said hello. The line went dead.

"Did they say who it was?" I asked quickly.

"No."

"Male or female?"

"Male. What's going on?"

I didn't reply. Judith was subject to my prime policy: *no one must know*. It meant I couldn't recount my sorry story. In any case, the attack might materialize any time from here on in. Not a good moment to launch into an explanation.

The significance of the phone call was obvious enough. Look at it from Cigar-man's point of view. You hit the wrong target. A humiliating bungle of the first magnitude. Still on the job, you decide to keep Judith under surveillance; or maybe you just hang around by the workshop. Either way, another motorcyclist comes into your sights. You see him enter the workshop. But who is he? The difficulty you face is that, kitted up, all bikers appear the same to you. You can't afford to get it wrong a second time, so you ring up and ask for Ed Somersby. Either it's him in the workshop or it's someone else. Judith had just confirmed it was me.

Considering the moderate security out the front of the premises, that out the back was awful: windows with only thin glass in them and no window locks, plus a rear door with a three-lever rim lock that a twelve-year-old could force open if he put his shoulder to it. It was better than nothing, but not much.

I made sure the back door was locked, and put the key in my pocket. Next I ran into the workshop to double-check on access from the front. Yes, nobody could get in that way either.

Judith had followed me and was staring, hands on hips and irritation in her face. True, she knew her husband had been murdered. But she couldn't begin to guess why. And of my doings since the end of August when my original stalk of Anthony Hartling had started, she was wholly ignorant. In essence she knew nothing. Nothing at all. And there was I, an erstwhile family friend, running about on her premises like I owned them and, what's more, like I'd taken leave of my senses. For no reason.

"Ed," she said firmly, "would you mind opening the door. A customer may call round at any time."

"I don't think I should," I replied.

"Oh you don't," she said in a decidedly assertive tone of voice. "I'm getting very stressed."

We had a kind of stand-off while I tried to work out what Cigar-man would do. Would he wait till I left or come in for me? Would he be alone or assisted? Would the attack be made from the front or the rear of the property? What weaponry would be used? Revolver? Shotgun? Do gangsters in London have access to machine guns, hand grenades, petrol bombs? What about Judith? While she was with me she was in the line of fire. I couldn't get away from her — frankly, I was far too scared to flee outside — so should I eject her into the street? Should I summon the police? That might protect us both, but what could I tell them? "Please come round in force to John Farley's workshop because...." Because what? Because someone had put the phone down on me?

Judith continued to stare, watching me dither. She must have been well aware I was badly frightened. "We're going to have to have a serious talk, you and I," she asserted at last.

"I know, but not now. We're in great danger."

"I don't know about 'we'," she remarked. "You will be if you don't stop...."

A sound, quite faint, came from the office. It wasn't my imagination. Judith heard it too and turned to look towards the back of the workshop. I still clutched the crowbar in my hand. It was all there was.

The intruder must have come along the alleyway, climbed over the fence, crossed the back garden, and arrived at the back entrance into the office. Had he already got inside, or was he in the process of effecting an entry? I knew I had to prevent him coming into the workshop. We'd be unmissable targets if he got that far. With that in mind, I skirted several machines in various stages of dismemberment in order to press myself against the partition wall. I signalled to Judith and mouthed the words: "Get down."

The half-open door to the office was about midway along the wall, hinged on the left and opening into the workshop. I was placed so I could see through the crack between door and frame. Nobody was in view, though a moving shadow was being cast. There were more faint noises.

Judith startled me by beginning a monologue from behind a Yamaha in the far corner. She was telling me about the problems she faced tying up bikes and invoices. It was a tactic worth trying. The intruder might be less cautious if he thought he was undetected.

I crouched, crowbar ready. A glimpse: gun in his right hand, cigar in his mouth. He turned towards the crack I was peering through. I'd been spotted.

I threw myself in panic at the door, slamming it shut in passing and coming to rest to the right of it. There was a bang after the door slammed. When I looked, I could see a chunk of the door's lower left corner had splintered — the result of a bullet fired while I was in motion.

Judith fell silent.

Very lightly I tapped the wall. It seemed solid but I wanted to be sure. My expectations were confirmed. It was easily bullet-proof.

No sooner had I reached this welcome conclusion than the door flew open, fast enough to hit the wall and rebound slightly. The executioner was just the thickness of a fifteen centimetre breeze block partition away from me.

The seconds dragged by. Cigar-man had a problem in that he didn't know exactly where I'd gone. If I was up against the right hand side of the doorframe — he had to assume I was, and he would have been correct — I could injure him if he entered the workshop body first. Alternatively, if he came in gun first I could knock the weapon out of his hand. Lastly, if he did neither of those things I wasn't going to be executed, since there was no other way for him to get at me.

I was beginning to think it was stalemate. One minute passed in complete silence. I hoped he might withdraw. He had that option, which I certainly didn't. I needed to keep all my attention on that open doorway until I knew for definite he was no longer on its far side.

Two minutes. He fired the gun. I heard a motorcycle in the centre of the workshop judder, and then the sound of a liquid running, rapidly followed by a smell of petrol. He'd punctured a petrol tank. A distraction? Had he intended to start a fire?

Another minute went by. The air was filled with the combined stench of petrol and cigar smoke. Suddenly something skittered across the floor of the workshop. It was a cigarette lighter, its flame turned up to maximum. The spreading pool of petrol ignited. My attention was momentarily diverted, as was doubtless the intention.

He came through the doorway much faster than I'd anticipated, like he'd taken a run at it. I had the crowbar raised above my head and brought it down hard. And missed. I bent forward with the continuing motion and struck the concrete floor, jarring my arm.

Even as I was moving, he fired at me. It was a hasty shot, for he was having to stop short before he ran into the flames he'd ignited. The bullet hit the wall where I would have been if I hadn't swung the crowbar.

I fetched my primitive weapon up in an arc, aiming for the gun. He had come to a halt and was bringing the firearm to bear for a more accurate shot. I struck his hand. The gun flew from his grasp. If I'd been half a second slower, John Farley would have had company.

Cigar-man gasped, and for an instant our eyes met. From the look on his face, it was news to him I had more than a fist at the end of my arm. I also detected a hint of pain.

I swung the crowbar left to right at waist height. If I struck him, fine. If he dodged, I wanted him moving away from the direction the gun had taken.

He couldn't step backwards because the flames were at his heels, so he leapt sideways. I failed to make contact. As the crowbar swept past him, he twisted round and lunged at me. I retreated but not quickly enough. Instantly in too close for me to strike him, he rammed his shoulder into my groin and I fell over. He followed me down.

Before I could recover from the shock, his left hand had gripped my right wrist, neutralizing the crowbar. I found myself on my back, pinned to the floor by his weight on top of me. His right forearm came up to my throat. He exerted as much pressure with it as he could, which fortunately wasn't a lot. It was nonetheless sufficient to hurt and stop me breathing.

My left arm was the only part of me free to move. I reached over to go for his eyes, but he forestalled me by turning his face downwards and pressing it against my chest. I grasped his right hand instead. He cried out, a sound greatly disproportionate to what I was doing. When I'd sent the gun flying, I must have produced some damage. It was why he was trying to throttle me with a forearm.

I was hurting him too much. He relaxed the pressure on my neck and lifted himself up slightly. It happened so swiftly. He let go of my wrist and brought his left fist in beneath him and jabbed it into my side. I was already swinging the crowbar over, targeting his head, but the punch forced my arm downwards by reflex action. I hit him on his upper back, fairly harmlessly.

Before I could do anything further, he punched me again, this time getting my kidney. The pain was so intense I was totally paralysed. He got off me and turned me over onto my stomach. How he planned to finish me off I don't know, for he wasn't given the chance. Judith intervened.

"Get away from him," I heard her shout. Judging by the aggression in her voice, she was deadly serious. I guessed Cigar-man was looking down his own gun barrel from the wrong end.

"Give me that," he commanded.

For Chrissake, shoot him, I thought. Shoot the bastard.

"Don't," said Judith. No sound of fear about her at all; just belligerence.

Cigar-man thought better of getting his gun from her. I was facing away from her, towards the office, and was able to watch my would-be executioner retreat. He calmly left the workshop, even shutting the door behind him.

For a few seconds it seemed that time had stopped. Then I heard the sound of dry ice being released under pressure, and guessed Judith must have grabbed a fire extinguisher. I started to pick myself up.

With the fire out, she put the heavy metal cylinder down and came over to me. By then I was on my knees, trying with limited success not to whimper. My hand still clutched the crowbar.

"Are you okay?" she asked, sounding very concerned.

"No," I whispered. I became aware my face was contorted, and made an effort to look more normal. "What have you done with the gun?"

She had put it in her coat pocket. I took it from her.

"We have to make sure he's not still on the premises," I explained. I spoke in a whisper not out of a desire for secrecy, but because it was an effort to talk at all.

She helped me get to my feet. Mercifully, standing up didn't make the pain any worse. I got her to open the office door while I did my best to cover her.

The office was empty. A window was ajar. The glass had a penny-sized hole in it against the frame. Cigar-man had made the hole, put a hook of some kind through it to lift the simple latch, and climbed in. Judith pointed out a small pile of ash on the desk. It was where he must have left his cigar while attacking me.

Gun at the ready, we proceeded to check the upper floor, returning to the office once we were certain Cigar-man really had fled.

I slumped in the chair that went with the desk. It helped a little with the pain. Judith sat in the customers' chair. She waited patiently until I began to feel better.

"I'm in your debt," I said at last. "You saved my life. But my god, I wish you'd killed him?"

"There was no need," she responded. "Having a gun pointed at his head was enough to give him the message."

"Oh Judith!" I moaned, lamenting the missed opportunity. "That was the guy who murdered John."

"It could have been. But I don't *know* that. I can't kill someone on suspicion."

"Well," I said, defeated, "it *was* him. But you're right. You weren't to know."

Abruptly Judith asked: "How long have we been friends, Ed?"

"Since you.... Since you and John got together."

"Do you want us to stay friends?"

"You know I do."

"Then I really think you'd better tell me," — suddenly she was shouting — "what the hell is going on."

I told her. As with Miranda, I didn't mention the battle of Coed y Deifol, and I gave her an edited version of my confrontation with Anthony Hartling in his flat. (I couldn't mention the sawn-off shotgun because that would have meant explaining where I got it.) And then I had to add the excruciatingly awful knowledge I possessed about subsequent events, including John's murder.

When I finished, I felt like I had been expelled from the human race. I couldn't look at her.

"You IDIOT! You stupid, self-pitying, arrogant, reckless cretin. What *is* it with you men? Why couldn't you have let it go?"

"That's all I want to do now, but they won't give me the chance."

"And because of that my husband is dead."

"If I was able to swap places with him, I'd do it." I said, taking the gun by its barrel and offering her the grip. "If you want to use this, I wish you would."

She looked at me for a few seconds and said: "Now you're being ridiculous as well as stupid."

After a pause she continued: "Okay. Here's what we're going to do. We're going to call the police and you're going to tell them what you've just told me. You tell them everything. Well, maybe not the bit about setting fire to the flat. But everything else. Let them sort Anthony Hartling out."

"Like they sorted him out before?" I retorted.

"That wasn't their fault."

180

"I don't care whose fault it was. And besides, I'd be admitting to committing the odd crime or two along the way. They'd arrest me, not him."

"Better arrested than dead."

"I don't agree. It's not an either-or situation."

"I'm not arguing with you, Ed. The police must be brought in on this."

"Not by me they won't."

"Where did you get the idea I was giving you a choice?"

There was a silence.

In my mind, the one imperative was to avoid police involvement. If Judith pressed me hard enough, given how guilty I felt over John, I'd have to do as she was demanding. So somehow I had to persuade her to stop demanding; and to let me deal with this problem another way.

"Look, Judith," I said. "Do you want justice for John?"

She didn't answer. It was an absurd question.

"How do you think you're going to get it by calling in the police? Put it all together. One: they think John's a drug dealer. Two: the cigar smoker who killed him is a professional, so I very much doubt they'll have any idea who he is. Three: to crown it all, they can't catch the killer with the murder weapon because in all probability it's this gun here — it's in *our* possession with *our* fingerprints all over it. Calling in the police isn't going to get either of us nearer to what we want. It'll drive us further away than ever."

Judith thought about that.

"And if you really want to look on the bleak side," I continued, "there's four: they think you're being uncooperative on John's drug connection. They're going to be asking themselves why. And five: they suspect there's something improper between you and me. What conclusions do you think they'll come to if they find we've got the gun John was killed with? We're not going to look like innocent third parties, not to them."

"All right. I concede going to the police won't be a passport to justice, but there isn't an alternative. You're just an ordinary man, Ed — and usually a nice one. You're living in a fantasy land if you think you can take on people like these and get the better of them."

Her assessment of me was factually flawed, but I couldn't tell her why. "That's not how I see it. You can't deny I came close in Caerabont. And there *is* an alternative. Here's the way it works. I'm going to run. If the Hartlings don't know where I am, they'll set a trap. Probably use you or Miranda under duress to get me into the open. Then I'll do what I have to do. I owe Tanya, and I owe you and John. I'm not going to hide behind the police. The time for that ended when Anthony Hartling was given a suspended sentence."

"So you set Miranda and me up as bait in order that Ed Somersby can come riding to the rescue, scattering his enemies like chaff? Is that your alternative? And you think that's realistic?"

"Something like that," I muttered.

"Why on earth should Miranda and I play along with you? How dare you put us in danger so you can pursue your personal crusade! It's not like you, Ed. It's ruthless. That's not who you are."

"Believe me, the last thing I want to do is put anyone in danger. But it's not up to me. I'm not the one being ruthless. The fact is, I'm not going to hang around like a target on a shooting range. That means I have to hide. There's nothing I can do to prevent them calling on you or Miranda. I can only deal with it when it happens."

"Look at me, Ed."

With immense difficulty I met her gaze.

"If you want me to back you on this, I have to be

confident you can deliver. And I'm not. I mean, look at your track record. Even when you managed to get Anthony Hartling at your mercy, you blew it."

"That was bad luck."

"It wasn't bad luck. That's not what saved him. It was you setting off the fire alarm. If your roles had been reversed, would Anthony Hartling have set off the fire alarm?"

"No. But I didn't have a choice. I might have killed innocent people."

"That's exactly my point. You've got a conscience. It puts you at a disadvantage when you're up against people like the Hartlings."

"I suppose so. But it doesn't mean I can't win. It just makes it harder. And now I've got this gun. That's a whole new situation. Is it so hard to believe I can get the job done?"

Judith looked away. I sensed I was making headway.

"Listen," I said. "They wanted to beat me up, and I got away from them. Since when they've been trying to kill me; and I'm still here."

"Thanks to me," she interjected.

"Thanks to you. The point I'm making is that it's not as one-sided as it appears. Of course I can't guarantee this isn't going to end with my death. But it hasn't yet, and I'm going to do my damnedest to make sure it never does."

"Okay, Ed, I'll grant that you're pretty tough. But you have to understand the one thing that matters *to me* is that the people who murdered my husband are going to pay for it. So it comes down to whether I'm more likely to get what I want by backing you or by bringing in the police? If I'm honest, I have to say it looks pretty hopeless either way."

"Then you've nothing to lose by giving me a chance."

"No, but you have. I fear you're going to get slaughtered, and I don't want to be a part of that."

"Wouldn't justice be worth taking that risk?"

"Perhaps."

I knew Judith well enough to know the signs: she was making up her mind. Time to keep quiet.

A few minutes passed, and then she said: "You're determined to play this your way, whatever I say, aren't you?"

"I...."

"Come on, Ed. Let me hear you say it. Just answer the question truthfully."

"Yes, I am. I have to see what I started through to the end. Stopping now isn't an option."

"That's what I thought. In which case, maybe it would make sense for me to keep the police in reserve. If I go along with you and you succeed, fine. If you don't, I can involve the police later. So let's take it that I agree — reluctantly — to tackle this the way you want. But be clear on one thing. What you're planning isn't heroic; it isn't noble; it isn't Boys' Brigade, comrades-in-arms stuff. It's nasty, violent, and degrading. So don't start kidding yourself I'm ever going to want to give you a medal. We're adults in the real world, and we're talking about being involved in very serious criminality. I have a lot of qualms about that."

"So do I. It's not qualms I'm short of; it's choice."

"Very well then. It's settled. There is, however, going to be one condition: we don't give them two sacrificial lambs to choose from."

"Meaning what?"

"I don't hang around like a target on a shooting range either. I come with you."

That wasn't what I wanted to hear at all. "That's not a good idea, Judith. You'd only get in the way. Anyway, I'll be on the Triumph."

"So? I'll ride pillion."

"No."

"Why not?"

I didn't answer. I was staring at the floor again.

"Why not, Ed?" Judith repeated sternly.

I still didn't answer. I'd made a vow after Tanya's funeral about pillion passengers. I couldn't go back on it. Plain couldn't.

Judith got up, came round the desk and stood before me. She put a hand gently on my forehead and ran it through my hair, making me look up. "You've been fighting demons for the last nine months, mostly in there," she said, tapping my scalp with a finger. "If you can't beat the ones inside you, how are you ever going to beat Anthony Hartling? Think about it."

She rummaged around in the office for a few items while I stared out across the weeds and rubbish in the back garden. I remained in a lot of pain, and I didn't want to 'think about it'. Heaven preserve me from well-intentioned women!

I decided the most useful thing I could do right then was sort out the gun. In a way I was fascinated, because I'd never seen the real thing before, let alone held one in my hands. According to the information on the barrel, it was a Heckler & Koch P7M8. The calibre I measured to be nine millimetres exactly. The trigger and hammer were standard, but there wasn't a safety catch such as I was expecting. Instead you had to squeeze the grip, which depressed a little plate affair, and that armed (if that's the correct term) the firing mechanism. In other words, to discharge the gun you had to squeeze the grip and pull the trigger. If you did either but not both, nothing happened. I admired the ingenuity.

I walked stiffly and slowly into the workshop and acquired a rag, some light machine oil and various tools. Judith held up a placard she'd been creating which read:

CLOSED DUE TO BEREAVEMENT.

WILL REOPEN AS SOON AS POSSIBLE.

"Fine," I said.

Back in the office, I took the gun to pieces and cleaned it and oiled it. I expected my life was going to depend on this lump of metal, so I wanted it in the best condition.

The magazine, which fitted into the grip, I found could hold eight bullets. Four remained. Three had been fired in the workshop. I had little doubt the one unaccounted for had ended John's life.

I reassembled the gun and inserted the magazine. My chances of survival and my confidence went up by a thousand per cent. I got to my feet, feeling like a gunslinger.

"Have you decided?" asked Judith. "Am I coming?"

"It's not going to be pleasant," I replied.

"Thanks," she said, and kissed me on the cheek. "Anyway, I can make myself useful watching your back."

Why was this woman able to give me a lump in my throat? Tanya never had and neither had Miranda.

"You don't hate me over John?" I said, somehow keeping my voice level.

"Frankly, I could kick you from here to Scotland, but...." She paused. "I'm thinking: what if it hadn't been you and Tanya that day, but John and me...."

For a moment, she had a faraway, heartbreakingly sad look in her eyes. It hadn't remotely occurred to me her thoughts might run in that direction.

"This is going to sound weird, Ed, considering how critical I've been of you, but I know I would have wanted John to do for me what you're trying to do for Tanya. So,

186

no, I don't hate you. I just wish you'd confided in me sooner. As of this morning, Simeon Hartling would have had one less name on his payroll if you had."

"That's easy to say, but you may not find it as simple as that when you're actually about to pull the trigger."

"That is precisely the kind of talk we can't afford. If we're going to do this, there must be no doubts, no hesitating at the crucial moment. This isn't about good and evil. It's about winning. If you're not sure you can kill someone, we stop right this minute."

"No," I said, recollecting Weight Trainer and Gerry. "It's facing up to it afterwards that's difficult. Doing it is easy."

13

RESCUE

We left the workshop about midday after sorting out a lot of paperwork. The pain in my side had decreased to almost nothing by then. I took the lead, gun in hand in jacket pocket, and stood on guard while Judith set the burglar alarm and locked up. I watched her get in the van and drive off, and followed on the Triumph. It began to rain.

Shortly before we reached her house, I went ahead so I was ready for action by the time she arrived. She opened the front door and monitored the approach to the house while I went nervously through the place, one room at a time, searching thoroughly. Once I was sure the premises, including the rear garden, were clear, she came in.

She lent me John's waterproofs to keep my leathers dry, and changed into her own rain-gear. She packed a few personal items into her pockets and we departed, exercising as much caution on our way out as we had on arrival.

Having her sitting behind me on the Triumph brought me out in a cold sweat. At first I was psychologically incapable of taking the machine up to any sort of reasonable speed. I traced an irregular route along the roads in order merely to reveal pursuit, certainly not to throw it off. There was no one following us. My surmise that Simeon Hartling was severely limited with respect to the manpower at his disposal continued to look plausible.

My first stop was at a chemist's where I bought a supply of the strongest painkillers they sold which were safe for driving and didn't need a prescription. This was a necessity. Vibrations from the motorcycle and occasional unevenness in the road surface were reviving the pain Cigar-man had inflicted on me. It was pills or bed, and I couldn't take to the latter.

After that, I called into my bank to withdraw some cash, filled up the tank at a garage, bought a pay-as-you-go (i.e. anonymous and untraceable) mobile phone, and lastly visited my flat in Harrow to retrieve my own personal items and switch on my alibi-providing auto-pilot. Then we hit the road properly.

If I was going to hide, there was only one place to do it that made sense: somewhere near to Miranda. Not Caerabont itself, I decided, at least partly because of potential complications over the ex-Winston Kelly. Nor one of the larger towns. Somewhere small where no one would think of looking. I chose Aberystwyth, a place I'd briefly passed through in September.

In slow stages I increased the speed I was doing. Judith played her part by keeping still and quiet. By Birmingham my confidence had returned, and I was handling the machine like my old self. It was as well, because the light rain that had accompanied our journey thus far turned into heavy showers as we rode through the Cambrian Mountains at nightfall. In those conditions you can't afford distractions or self-doubt.

It was seven when we arrived in Aberystwyth. Before finding us a couple of rooms for the night, I rang Miranda using my new mobile phone, mainly to confirm she was safe.

Her phone was answered after half a dozen rings. By a male voice. My adrenalin surged.

"Who's that?" I asked, trying to keep calm.

"South Wales CID. Would you be Mr Somersby?"

I was completely wrong-footed. Despite Gerry's backhanded compliment in Coed y Deifol, I can't think any faster than the average 'amateur', and the unanticipated reply I'd just been given left me at a loss for any answer except: "Yes."

"I'm glad you've rung," said the man. "Where are you at the moment?"

In the second or two he took to ask the question, I recovered. Give nothing away, I thought. Be obstructive if necessary. Find out what the damage is.

"London," I said.

"Where exactly in London?"

"I'd rather not be precise. What's happened to Miranda?"

"Miss Kettrick is fine. The thing is, Mr Somersby, you're in a lot of trouble. I'm about to issue a warrant for your arrest. You're not doing yourself any favours behaving like this. All it's...."

"I don't know what you mean," I interrupted. I wanted him to tell me what Miranda had revealed. Denial wasn't a good tactic, but it was the best I could come up with.

"You know well enough," he retorted. "Miss Kettrick has told us everything. Now, I'm going to give you some advice. It would be better if you turn yourself in voluntarily. Courts always look favourably on that. How about it?"

"I'll consider it."

"Do more than that. All the time you're roaming around, you're in great danger. Custody is where you belong, for your sake as well as in the interests of law and order. We've had more than enough bodies to clear up already. If it will help, I'll make it easy for you. Do you know Miss Kettrick's room at the university?"

I did, but I said: "No."

"It's room 105 in the Llewellyn building. Meet me there, say, eleven tomorrow. That'll give you time to get here. Then we can start sorting this shambles out."

"I'm not promising anything. Let me speak to Miranda."

190

"I can't do that. We can't allow you to talk to Miss Kettrick until after we've interviewed you. Otherwise there's a danger you'll collude together. Just be patient. Eleven tomorrow. I'll hold off on the arrest warrant till then. But not a moment longer."

I broke the connection.

"Damn!" I exclaimed as I put the phone back in my pocket. "Damn! Damn! Damn!"

"What's happened?" asked Judith, who'd only heard my half of the conversation.

"That was a man from South Wales CID. Miranda's gone to the police."

"You advised her to do that if anything alarmed her. It may be for the best."

"Thanks for the vote of confidence."

"You're welcome. So what now?"

"I don't know. I don't know. I've got to think."

"Okay. Tell me what he said. It'll help."

"He ordered me to hand myself in. I'm supposed to meet him in Miranda's room at eleven tomorrow."

"Miranda's room? What's wrong with Swansea police station? Isn't it big enough?"

"He probably wants the credit for capturing me."

"Maybe. But it's odd, don't you think?"

I shrugged. "I wonder how many years I'll get. I'll bet they don't suspend *my* sentence."

"That depends on what you're charged with."

"He didn't go into details but it sounds like murder."

"Murder! Who have you murdered?"

That brought me up short. I'd momentarily forgotten Judith didn't know about Coed y Deifol, any more than Miranda did. "Attempted murder," I corrected quickly.

Any more than Miranda...?

"What is it?" Judith asked, picking up on my sudden frown.

"Something's wrong."

"What?"

"I'm not sure. He said I'm in great danger. But I'm not. Right at this moment I'm completely safe. The only time I'm in danger is when people know where I am."

"As in eleven o'clock tomorrow in Miranda's room," Judith stated.

"Yes. Exactly."

And then I got what was bothering me. *Bodies to clear up.* What bodies were they? Miranda only knew I'd tried to kill Anthony Hartling. She also knew I'd failed. I hadn't informed her about John Farley or Coed y Deifol. She couldn't have told the police about one body, let alone bodies, plural. It was conceivable the police had connected the two dead Hartling employees in Coed y Deifol with my activities, but that would be pure speculation on their part. They didn't *know* I'd killed anyone. Only the Hartlings knew that. The conclusion was obvious. I was being set up, and it couldn't be by South Wales CID.

"South Wales police haven't got Miranda," I said to Judith. "It's Hartling."

I felt nauseous. Now it was actually materializing, it was impossible to view with equanimity the scenario I'd calmly outlined to Judith earlier in the day.

"Calm down, and don't jump to conclusions," Judith advised. "All we can be sure of is that someone's got her mobile phone. Miranda may not be with it."

"That's possible, I suppose."

"Look, if it's Hartling or one of his henchmen you were talking to, why didn't they just say 'do what you're told or we'll blow her brains out'?"

"Because I've got a gun. You may not believe it, and they might not like to admit it, but these people are scared of me. They don't want to force me to launch an attack. It's too unpredictable. If they can get me to walk calmly into a well-disguised trap, on the other hand...." I mimed cutting my throat with a finger.

"You know what I think? I think we'd better get moving."

"You want to go to Caerabont straightaway?"

Judith looked at me blankly. "You're the team leader, Ed. I'm just the bodyguard."

I grinned. "Yes ma'am. I'll try and remember that. Let's go."

We set off along the coast road to Aberaeron. As the miles passed, I realized a truth about human nature. When you're down and being kicked around and are finding it a struggle to do no more than cling to existence, that's when you get depressed and your spirits fail you. But when you're fighting back, taking the offensive, getting in control, even if the ultimate position remains grim, you feel on top of the world. Battle-happy and reckless I'd called it in Coed y Deifol. I had the same buzz now. For someone who had been nearly out of his mind with despair only the previous night, it was magic.

In a village a few miles from Caerabont, we stopped off at a pub and sat down to a meal, over which we discussed options. The vision of Ed Somersby riding up on his motorized steed and scattering his enemies like chaff had to be turned into a workable plan.

"Okay," said Judith, "we have three scenarios. One, you really were talking to the CID. Not likely, but if true, we have nothing immediate to worry about. Miranda's safe and you're under no threat."

"Except of imprisonment."

"Quite. Two, Hartling has Miranda's phone, but she's safe until we turn up at her room tomorrow at eleven. Three, she's a prisoner being used to lure you in."

I recalled my lesson number one. *Assume the worst.* I said: "Let's plan for the worst option: Hartling's got her. It would certainly make sense for one compelling reason if for no other. In the game these people are playing, seizing Miranda is their obvious next move. It's what they *should* have done. With you missing from London, she's the only way they have of finding me. They use her to bring me into the open so I can be grabbed. After that, it's a joint drug overdose or a suicide pact. And where better to stage our deaths than in her room. That's what I'd do in their place. That's where she is, and not alone. I bet you."

"And if you're wrong about location? She could be anywhere."

"It doesn't matter. We have no choice but to start with her room. If she's not there, then we have to worry about finding her."

We finished our meals. Outside it was pouring with rain, and we decided to wait for this latest shower to pass. After fifteen minutes it hadn't, and we said to hell with it and got wet.

Keen to avoid giving the slightest unnecessary advance warning of my presence at the university, I parked the Triumph at Caerabont railway station, half a mile from the campus, and we walked the rest of the way, arriving at the hall of residence at nearly ten.

At which point we hit our first snag. The entrances to the building were all locked at this time of night except for the main entrance, which needed a swipe card to open it. There was also an intercom to each room, but I doubted the trick with the flowers which I had used in Hillside would work here. Who sends a student flowers? Who would deliver them at night? Where would I get them from?

Judith told me to keep back and leave it to her. After a time, a girl approached the door. As she opened it, Judith dashed up and said something to her. The girl let her in. A few minutes later Judith reappeared, held open the door, and I was in too.

194

"I said I was a friend of Miranda's in 105 and that I couldn't get her to answer the intercom," Judith explained.

"I could have done that," I said.

"You're a man," Judith replied.

The word 'so?' sprang into my mind, but obviously not into hers. I let it go.

We explored the ground floor. Going through the entrance, you're confronted by a wall. You either turn left or right. Left, there's a stairwell. A short distance past that brings you to a right turn along a corridor, on the left side of which are rooms 1 to 8. At the far end, another right takes you past kitchen and lounge. Right again into another corridor, rooms 9 to 16 on the left side. One more right brings you back to the entrance. On the right hand side of both corridors, occupying the core of the building, were individual toilets, shower cubicles and one bathroom.

We went up the stairs to the first floor. The floor plan was exactly the same: rooms 101 to 108 on one side of the building; rooms 109 to 116 on the other. We walked casually past Miranda's room, 105, but didn't dare loiter. We retreated to the stairwell for a conference.

Judith said: "Before I let you in, I checked her room from the outside. You saw the light?"

"Around the door frame? Yes."

"I also put my ear to the door and there's a television on in there too. You do realize, if she's left things switched on but isn't at home, or she's there happily minding her own business, we're going to look complete clowns."

"I hope we do. You ready?"

She nodded.

I took out the gun and worked the action to get a bullet under the hammer. It was unreal.

"You almost look like you know what you're doing," said Judith.

I slipped the gun back into my pocket and we left the

stairwell. In fact the gun was a precaution, because this was unlikely to be a guns-blazing encounter. There were too many students about, both to get hurt and to bear witness. Killing a villain or two in front of an impressionable audience, even if Miranda testified on my behalf, was an invitation to the lottery of a jury trial. So the Heckler & Koch would be kept in reserve. We were going to pursue a less lethal course of action.

Outside room 105, I put my ear to the door. Yes, there was a television on in there.

"What are you doing?" said a voice from behind me.

I looked round. With impeccably unhelpful timing, a student had emerged from room 108. I put a conspiratorial finger to my lips and crept over to her. I reckoned some dramatic acting might help.

I whispered: "We think Miranda has an unwelcome visitor."

"Not her new boyfriend?" said the girl, fortunately picking up on the whispering and keeping her voice down.

"I'm her boyfriend," I snarled quietly.

"Wild," she said.

I decided the girl might be useful after all. A bit of improvisation occurred to me. "Have you got a heavy book we could borrow?"

She didn't ask why, but went into her room and came out with two. The larger was *Woolaston's Jurisprudence, 3rd edition, vol. 15*. Nice hard covers and weighing, I would guess, four kilograms. The smaller was *Law of Contract: Test Cases, 1951-1975*.

Judith gave me a 'what's going on?' look.

The girl put the question into words: "What are you going to do?" she said.

"Stand in your doorway and watch. But if you hear any loud bangs, get out of sight."

She thought I was joking. "Really wild," she asserted.

196

I gave Judith *Law of Contract*, nodding at Miranda's door. Judith nodded back. I kept *Woolaston* for myself, needing both hands to hold it.

The door to room 105 was hinged on the left, opening into the room. I took up position to the right of it. Judith knocked.

"Miranda?" she called.

There was no reaction.

"Come on, Miranda. I know you're in there. I can hear your TV. I've got the book you lent me. I want to give it back."

Still no reaction.

"Miranda?" Judith called again, her voice sounding slightly tipsy. She banged on the door more firmly. "Come on, sweetheart. It weighs a ton. I don't want to have to take it all the way back to my own room."

"Leave it outside," came a quiet, timid reply. "I'll fetch it in later."

Judith gave me a thumbs-up. "Are you kidding? This thing'd cost a fortune to replace if it went missing. It'll only take a moment, for goodness sake, if you're busy."

A few seconds passed.

"I'm waiting, Miranda," Judith repeated, making it clear she wasn't going to give up.

"I can't come out," Miranda called plaintively. "Please go away."

Judith gave me a hard, meaningful look. "If you don't open this effin door right now, I'm going to effin kick it in," she said, contriving to sound furious rather than tipsy, and kicking the door hard a couple of times.

There was another pause and then Miranda's door opened. Judith cheered.

Considering we'd not rehearsed the next move, it went like a dream. Judith held up the book, taking a few steps back from the door as she did so. Next moment she dropped it, simultaneously lunging at the door and hitting it with her shoulder. The door moved inwards a little, striking whoever was behind it. Judith seized Miranda's reaching hands in her own and jerked her violently into the corridor. Miranda struck the door on her way out and stumbled, so that Judith had to swing her round on her knees to get her out of the line of fire.

"Hey," someone in the room said. Definitely male. I had a sudden appalling thought it could be Miranda's father or brother or some other family member called in for her protection, and that I might hurt an innocent party. But I needn't have worried. The man who came through the door was someone I recognized: the fat guy I'd seen leaving the High Rise Nightclubs office one evening back in early September. His attention was focussed on Miranda and Judith. I don't think he even noticed me until it was too late. *Woolaston's* four kilograms of jurisprudence smashed into his face, knocking him onto the floor.

"Who is this bloke, Miranda?" asked the girl with the weighty tomes as Miranda got shakily to her feet.

"You've heard of paedophiles, haven't you?" I answered on Miranda's behalf. "Well this is a student-ophile."

"Pervert!" the girl exclaimed. Momentarily she seemed about to kick him, but by then Miranda's ex-jailer was getting up and she thought better of it. "Shall I call the police?"

"No. Leave that to Miranda and me," I said.

Fatty stood up unsteadily. Blood from his nose ran down over his chin and onto his coat. He put a hand to his face to find out what the wet was and looked at the blood. "Jesus!" he exclaimed.

I could see his expression change. His natural reaction was to retaliate aggressively. But then he saw the witnesses and hesitated.

"I'd keep calm if I was you," I said. "If you're not careful, you're going to drip DNA evidence all over the carpet."

He tried sniffing up some of the blood.

"A word with you," I said, and led him a short distance down the corridor. Speaking very quietly, I went on: "Tell your boss I want out, okay? He calls off the army, I'll emigrate. You got that?"

I could see it coming a mile off. "Yeh," he said and swung a podgy fist at my stomach. I blocked the blow with good old *Woolaston*, who kindly spread the impact over a nice big area so I hardly felt it. Fatty's fist was a much smaller area. He felt it a lot. There was a barely audible squeak as he stifled a howl of pain, and I, Miranda, Judith, and the girl from room 108 had the pleasure of watching the crestfallen individual walk, nose-bleeding and tight-lipped, towards the stairs and out of sight.

I gave the girl back her book. With my hand on the gun in my pocket, I peered cautiously into Miranda's room. There was no one else inside. Mission accomplished. I relaxed.

Miranda was regarding me with a dreamy and uncertain expression on her face. The girl from room 108 decided this was a somewhat unenthusiastic response to being rescued, and asked: "Is this all-action hero really your boyfriend, Miranda? You don't look particularly pleased to see him."

"Yes thank you, Sophie," said Miranda.

"Some of us haven't a clue," said Sophie, winking at me. "If you ever get tired of her, come and knock on my door. I love a man who really knows how to use a law book."

She got Judith to place *Law of Contract* on top of *Woolaston* in her hands and slinky-walked to her room, eyeing me in passing with undisguised lust.

"Don't you mind Sophie Alexander," said Miranda. "She's one of the end-of-the-world-next-week girls."

"The what?" asked Judith.

"It means she's not fussy," I explained.

Judith and I shepherded Miranda into her room and locked the door.

For a time I had to lie still on the bed, for I was in agony. It took several minutes to develop. The painkillers I had been taking in response to Cigar-man's assault on me in the morning were completely overwhelmed by the jarring effect of Fatty's parting punch. It was an hour before I recovered enough to be remotely my normal self. Miranda sat on her study-chair beside me and stroked my hair continuously, which was sweet of her.

My temporary incapacity settled one issue for us; namely, whether to pass the night where we were or find a hotel. I wasn't up to moving, and we agreed we needed to keep together. The only difficulty we faced was lack of space. We reckoned we could manage, but luxury it wasn't.

By the time I was feeling better, Miranda too had recovered from her latest ordeal. I was able to tell her, with occasional input from Judith, what had happened since the Monday evening, those four fraught days ago, when we had spoken by phone of meeting again. We'd neither of us imagined we'd come face to face so quickly and in such a strange fashion.

Then Miranda told us her story. She'd checked out of the hotel in Cardiff shortly after my visit informing her of my attack on Tony Hartling. The next two days, Sunday and Monday, had passed without incident. On Tuesday morning, as she had no lectures to attend till the afternoon, she'd decided to go shopping in Caerabont. She felt reassured by the continuing normality and the fact that Tony Hartling wasn't expected out of hospital until Wednesday. She was off-campus when a motorist had stopped her, threatened her with a gun, and forced her to get into his car. (I assume he'd visited Tony Hartling in hospital beforehand and been given the information he needed in order to identify her.) She'd then been taken to a building — she couldn't say what kind of building or where it was, because she'd been blindfolded the whole time — and persuaded to part with John Farley's answerphone number. Her interrogator had started by making threats and breathing cigar smoke in her face, and when that hadn't worked he'd repeatedly wrapped a towel round her head so tightly she could barely breathe and poured vinegar over the part covering her nose and mouth.

Recounting the experience she became distressed, not, I was sure, because of the suffering she had endured, but because she believed she had betrayed me, and because Judith's husband had died as a consequence. We had to break off for a time while I comforted her, and reassured her she had done nothing whatsoever that needed forgiving.

When she had recovered her composure, she went on to relate how she'd been left alone, unable to do anything more than shuffle because she was tied up, blindfolded and gagged. Cigar-man had returned on Thursday morning, driven her to a wood on the outskirts of the campus, removed her various restraints, and told her that if she said anything to anybody about what had happened he'd be paying her another visit. After that, she'd made her way to her room and shut herself in, too shocked and distraught to do anything else.

Which brought us to today. She'd followed the advice I'd given her during my Thursday evening phone call and kept to her room except for occasional visits to the toilet, which was literally straight across the corridor. That was how they'd got her. No more than an hour before I'd called her from Aberystwyth, she was unlocking her door to re-enter her room, when Tony Hartling had come out of the neighbouring shower cubicle and rushed her. And that was that. She'd been tied and gagged again and left alone with Fatty. And then Judith had knocked on her door, forcing Fatty to remove her bonds and rely instead on fear to restrain her.

Having decided to spend the night in Miranda's room, there were actions we needed to take. The lock on the door was not particularly strong, and it was the only thing stopping Hartling and Fatty returning. To remedy that, we barricaded the door with Miranda's chest of drawers.

There were also two other furnishings of importance in the room. One was a small washbasin which supplied us with drinking water, and which we contrived to use, with much awkwardness and embarrassment, as a urinal. The other was the bed. We drew up a rota so that one of us would be awake at any given time throughout the night, sitting in the study-chair. That left us one bed short. Miranda arranged some spare blankets on the floor for the second sleeper.

And so we passed the hours of darkness, unmolested but under threat.

Come the morning, we breakfasted on a collection of sandwiches which Fatty had left behind, watching the early news as we ate. The Coed y Deifol murder case got a renewed mention. ("Dreadful business," commented Miranda.) The police had realized that Weight Trainer and Gerry were employees of that same Simeon Hartling whose son's flat, only a few tens of miles distant from the forest, had been set on fire the very evening the two men had been killed. A spokesperson for the Hartlings — who were evidently as keen as I was to keep our private war private — maintained it was pure coincidence and that the fire in the flat was an accident. The police were unconvinced, however, and were appealing for anyone who saw anything suspicious in the vicinity of Hillside to come forward. They particularly wanted to know who set off the fire alarm on the ground floor. I got an odd look from Miranda, but fortunately neither she nor Judith asked me, even indirectly, whether the Coed y Deifol murders were my doing. Perhaps we all secretly agreed some dark corners are better left unilluminated.

Breakfast over, we discussed our next move. My intention of wiping out my enemies while rescuing Miranda had been consigned by events to the litter bin. I could of course sit back and hope that my offer of a peace treaty would be accepted by the Hartlings, but none of us thought it likely to appeal to them.

Judith had returned to the idea of going to the police. She had been shaken by Miranda's story, and could only think we should avail ourselves of the one viable source of help in prospect. I expected Miranda to back her up, but to my surprise my law student friend's views had changed radically.

"Suppose we do involve the police," she said, mainly addressing Judith. "We tell them Tony Hartling is trying to kill us. They'll want to know why. Ed will have to confess to stalking. Tony will pretend ignorance if questioned so nothing will come of it, but it won't look good. We can accuse Tony of trying to drown us, but we'll have to explain why we didn't say anything about it at the time." (She gave me an 'I told you so' look at this point.) "I don't think we can, and again Tony would simply deny it. We can claim Mr Hartling was behind John's murder but we've no proof, and Ed would be guilty in that case of withholding evidence. So would you, Judith. As for Ed's gun, the sentence for possession of a handgun without mitigating circumstances is five years. In other words, we can't admit to possessing it even if it is a murder weapon, since there's no way to prove how Ed came by it. And the fellow that Sophie can testify was in here last night could have been anyone. If the police find him, Tony and his father will be sure to disown him. In short, everything is our word against Tony's, and the upshot is that it won't be Tony who gets arrested, it'll be Ed.

"And there's one other thing I have to say. Ed has done some dreadfully irresponsible things this year...."

"I'll second that," interrupted Judith.

"But he doesn't deserve to go to prison...."

"And that," Judith interrupted again.

"And I'm going to stand by him."

Judith smiled. She said nothing this time, but the message was: "So am I."

I felt deeply touched by them both.

Miranda's speech settled the question of seeking help from the constabulary. The best I could hope for from them was neutrality based on ignorance. What else we could do we were at a loss to think up.

Judith declared she was disgusted with the toilet facilities in Miranda's room, and that she wanted to have a decent wash, and 'other things'. Nothing could better illustrate the severe nature of our predicament than this simple visit to a toilet which was literally the width of the corridor away from Miranda's room. The door defence had to be moved aside; not an easy job, because the architects of the Llewellyn building study/bedrooms had laid out the floor plan with obvious instructions to be economical with space. Having freed up the door, I, with gun in hand in pocket, next had to check the corridor was safe and that no one was lurking in the kitchen or the other toilets and shower cubicles. Then, while Judith was using the facilities, Miranda and I had to stand guard, she looking in one direction, I in the other. The same was the case when Miranda and Judith swapped places.

When it came to my turn, I was extremely reluctant to leave Judith with the gun, but she pointed out being constipated would be detrimental to my effectiveness. I yielded to her advice and the call of nature, though transacting the business with unusual haste.

Cleaner and more comfortable, we reassembled in Miranda's room and addressed the issue of how the Hartlings might let me know they accepted my peace proposal. They couldn't contact me except by personal call of a messenger, an option so rich with treacherous possibilities and misunderstandings that it was more likely to end up intensifying the war than ending it. It dawned on me the problem of providing an alternative channel of communication had a trivial solution. I used my mobile phone.

Directory Enquiries knew of no Simeon Hartling in London (meaning he was ex-directory) but did give me the number of High Rise Nightclubs. Although it was Saturday, a female receptionist answered my call. No, Mr Hartling wasn't in the office today. Yes, she could transfer me to his private line if I disclosed my name and the nature of my business.

"I'm a friend of Tony's in Caerabont," I informed her, "and Mr Hartling's son is in some trouble I can help with."

She told me to hold the line while she asked her boss if he wanted to take the call. 'No' would of course mean my peace offer had been rejected.

I heard a click on the line, and someone with a cultured male voice said: "Good morning, Tony's friend in Caerabont. How may I be of service?"

Surely, I thought, this had to be some public-relations junior. "I want to speak to Mr Hartling."

"You're talking to him." Not a trace of menace or venom.

"I wondered if you've received my message," I said, adopting the same civilized tone.

"Would that be the one via the man with a runny nose?"

"That's right."

"Yes, I've received that communication."

"And?"

"I'm thinking about it."

"You'll appreciate I'd like an answer fairly soon. My phone number is...."

"No need. I've got caller display."

"Great. Can you provide me with an idea of how long you'll take to reach a decision?"

"If I want to avail myself of your offer, I'll give you a call within a day or two."

"And do we have a ceasefire in the meantime?"

"I have no idea what you mean by that. Don't call me again. I'll call you. Goodbye."

The connection was broken. I put the phone back in my pocket. My hand was trembling.

"Well?" said Miranda.

"He sounded very reasonable," I answered. "Not the least how I imagined he would be. Not angry or abusive or threatening or anything."

"Hope at last!" she exclaimed. "I wish we'd thought of ringing him before. It's so obvious."

Judith was looking at us as if we'd both gone mad. She said: "Let me get this straight. His son throws you off a cliff; then you set fire to his son's flat; then he has Miranda kidnapped; then he has my husband murdered; then his henchman tries to shoot you in my husband's workshop. And he's not angry or abusive or threatening? Pardon me if I'm not impressed. It's too good to be true."

I didn't know what to say to that. She had a point.

She continued: "Tell me exactly what he said."

I recounted his responses to her.

"He's a good actor, that's all," she commented, shaking her head. "And do you know what gives it away? 'Ceasefire'. Why do you think he hung up when you said that?"

"You tell me."

"Because it's a naughty incriminating word. He's a gangster, correct? He was talking to you over an official business line. He has to reckon the phone's tapped even if it isn't. The thought in his mind is always: 'How will this sound to someone listening in?' If you think about it, until that last question of yours you could have been discussing a proposal to sell his son a box of smoke detectors. If he sounded like a Mr Nice-Guy, it's public posing. So don't be deceived."

"Okay. We stay on our guard until he calls back."

"We stay on our guard after he calls, too. No matter what he says."

I nodded my agreement. As bodyguards go, Judith was pretty on-the-ball.

Having decided to keep to Miranda's room to await developments, the question arose of supplies. Miranda had some food in the fridge along the corridor in the kitchen, but otherwise the cupboard was bare. One of us would have to visit the shops. Miranda understandably wouldn't go anywhere without me, so Judith volunteered. She asserted she was the least recognizable of the three of us, Tony Hartling having never set eyes on her, and Fatty having done so only momentarily in passing.

To be on the safe side, a change of appearance was in order. She swapped her biker clothes for a skirt and jacket from Miranda's wardrobe. Judith was taller by a couple of inches, but as long as she didn't square her shoulders the sleeves didn't stand out as being too obviously short. For a finale, she rearranged her hair in a way long-haired men don't find possible. The resulting transformation was remarkable.

Judith decided to buy the food in Caerabont rather than in the campus's general store, in case that was being watched and her disguise wasn't as good as we thought. I warned her to keep to crowded places and avoid walking close to passageways and other potential traps, gave her some money, and went through the routine to release her safely into the corridor. She said she'd be at least an hour. We agreed a code of knocks for her return, and she was gone. I re-locked the door.

"Ed, can I ask you something?"

"What?"

"You don't have to answer if you don't want to. If they'd caught you this morning how they'd intended, and held a gun to my head and said they'd kill me unless you went with them, would you have let them take you away?"

Miranda was looking at me intently, tears not far below the surface. I returned her gaze and told her the truth. "If it had come to that, yes. But...."

A tear trickled down her cheek. "I wish I'd been so brave when...."

I put my arms round her. "Listen. You're the damsel in distress. I'm the knight. It's not your job to be brave; it's mine."

"What is my job?" she said softly.

"To be your beautiful self. To be worth rescuing. And you are."

She put her arms on my shoulders and whispered: "I love you."

I felt desperately sad. "I know," I said.

"Why can't you say it?" she asked quietly.

"Because it's hopeless. At the very best I'm going to have to leave the country. More likely Tony Hartling will kill me, or I'll spend the next god knows how many years in prison for killing him. I've brought you nothing but pain and sorrow since we met, and it's all I have to offer you for the future. You're a sweet girl, truly sweet, and I can't bear to contemplate doing that. It's for the best that we...."

I had to stop. She was crying. I was being cruel to be

kind again. Damned if I was one; damned if I was the other.

"It's too late for me to turn the clock back," she said. "When the man with the cigars told me you were dead, it was like the end of everything. Nothing mattered any more except that you were gone. That was when I knew I loved you. And I thought how you'd never know it, and that was the worst thing of all. I spent the day staring at the ceiling in this room telling you things in my imagination. This, here and now, is a reprieve, Ed. Don't throw it away."

I pulled her tightly to me, exactly like I had on that cold, dark beach nine long days ago. She returned the pressure.

I couldn't be cruel any longer. If she wanted to risk going through with me what I'd been through with Tanya, it was her right to do so. She was old enough to make her own decisions.

We relaxed a bit by mutual consent after a time, and she whispered in my ear: "I want you to make love with me."

She took a couple of paces back from me and began to undress, gazing into my eyes all the while. I could feel myself getting aroused.

She was about to remove her bra when an unwelcome thought hit me.

"Hold it," I commanded.

"What's the matter?"

I took a deep breath. "Winston Kelly's generously provided condoms are currently in a flat in Harrow."

Her look of alarm was replaced by a mischievous smile. "No problem, Victor," she stated baldly. (Who's Victor?)

She got dressed again, leaving her clothes distinctly dishevelled, roughed up her hair, and bade me let her out of the room.

Gun at the ready; the usual corridor routine; it was getting to be automatic. I stood on guard while Miranda went along to room 108.

She knocked. No response. She tried again and called: "Sophie?"

The door opened, and Sophie came into view wearing an eye-wateringly short, filmy negligee. "Do you know what time it is?" she asked irritably. (It was gone ten.)

"It's an emergency," said Miranda. "We've run out of condoms."

"Hurray," shouted Sophie, punching a fist in the air. "No problem, Victor!"

"Can we have several?" said Miranda. (Several?) "He's insatiable."

Sophie — with what she was wearing it required no imagination at all to appreciate she had a beautiful body — treated me to a lustful grin so enticing that for a fleeting moment I considered a three-some. "Wild," she exclaimed.

Back to reality. I didn't return her grin. I was too busy trying to watch the corridor in both directions at once.

She disappeared into her room and returned to view with the requested items. "Can I come and observe?" she asked. "I'm a brilliant sex instructor. I could show you some classy moves."

My God! *Sophie* was suggesting a three-some!

"Hey, what a great idea," said Miranda.

That had to be a Miranda-joke. Didn't it?

"Just let me get my key," said Sophie.

Miranda followed her into room 108, and after a nerve-racking delay came out alone. We retreated to our own room, and I replaced the defensive chest of drawers against the door. I could hear Miranda undressing.

I turned to face her. I knew she was feeling very vulnerable.

"I could put on an anorak like before if it would make me more attractive," she offered uncertainly.

Was that another Miranda-joke? I could tell, unbelievably, that it wasn't. I gazed at her silently for a

210

moment, the world-class legs, the well-padded abdomen, the lovely breasts, the cuddly shoulders, the sexy mouth, and those adorable pale green eyes, and said: "You have no idea how physically desirable you are, have you. I promise you, you absolutely do not need an anorak. In case you don't believe me, I think I'd better get on with showing you the evidence."

"Yes please," she said. "That would be nice."

We kissed and then she helped me out of my clothes. We transferred ourselves to the bed. Sexual intimacy with Miranda suddenly seemed so right, so natural, so honest.

Following nine months of abstinence and with a woman new to me, the action felt like it was going to be over too quickly. As a delaying tactic, I thought about Anthony Hartling. It was an over-effective thing to do: I nearly lost it. Not a mistake I made a second time.

She lay there afterwards, her eyes closed, while I fondled her and lightly kissed her. The feeling inside me was one of overwhelming love. What, truthfully, was achieved by not telling her?

"I'm an idiot, aren't I?" I murmured.

"Hmm?"

"I've tried to keep my distance, but King Canute had more of a chance of stopping the tide coming in."

She opened her eyes. "Please say it."

"I love you, Miranda. Whether we have hours or decades left to us doesn't matter. In this moment, right now, I love you. And I shall go on loving you for whatever time we're given."

She was silent for a moment and then whispered: "Was I good?"

"You were delightful. How about me?"

She pulled me down on her and said: "Oh, that's an easy question to answer. You're far and away the best I've ever had." I looked at her questioningly, but she was smiling. It was a Miranda-joke. But then she added: "Of course, we could always ask Sophie."

"We what? I'm not going to bed with Sophie."

"You don't have to. She was listening."

"Pardon?"

"I told her she could listen."

"Miranda," I exclaimed angrily.

She put a finger to my lips. "Please don't be cross with me, my love. You don't know Sophie like I do. She was going to have her ear pressed to the door, no matter what. So I got her to promise that if Fatty or any of the boys from our year — I didn't mention Tony Hartling by name — came into the corridor, she'd bang on our door loudly a couple of times. I thought she might as well be of service while she was eavesdropping."

"Well, well. And I thought I was the clever one."

"You approve?"

"That was a bright idea."

"I'm good at bright ideas. That's a way I can help you. You know I want to help you, don't you?"

"In more ways than one," I said, and pressed myself firmly against her.

"Ooh," she said, grinning wickedly. "Are we going to do it again?"

"Sadly no. Not right now, anyway. Judith will be back shortly. And I'm afraid men are only insatiable in pornography. Asking for several condoms was a trifle optimistic."

"That was for Sophie's benefit. She flaunts her prowess at lovemaking, and I wanted to score a point off her."

"I think we can safely say you scored more than one," I said and stood up.

We got dressed, opened a window to let some of the hot air out, and awaited Judith's return.

14

AMBUSH

Eight in the evening. My mobile phone trilled.

"Hello."

"Somersby?"

"Speaking."

"Simeon Hartling. The deal's on if you want it."

"Good."

Not cultured, and dripping with menace and venom. An untapped phone, plainly.

"You and the law student are off the hook. And you can live where you like as long as it's nowhere near me and my family. There's a condition, though. You've got a piece of hardware belonging to a mutual acquaintance of ours with a smelly habit. You with me?"

"Yes."

"I want it back. I'll take its return as proof of your sincerity. Be awake at six tomorrow morning. You'll be phoned with instructions."

Before I could respond further, the line went dead.

It was clever. If I meant what I said, I wouldn't need Cigar-man's gun. Handing it over would demonstrate my good intentions. The trouble I had with Simeon Hartling's proposal was that I was getting nothing in return — no matching demonstration his intentions were equally as good. There had been no negotiation; only a diktat. It came down to how badly I wanted to be free of this nightmare. How much of a risk was I prepared to run?

Despite the apparent peace offer, it would have been

highly unwise, as Judith had pointed out, to start taking things easy as regards our security. We remained vigilant, once more arranging that at no time during the night should all three of us be asleep simultaneously.

I used my period on guard duty to think out how the Hartlings would handle the return of the gun. I ran through a range of scenarios, from being told to throw it out of Miranda's window, to having to hand it in at Throckmorten Square.

For a while, I was obsessed with the possibility they'd instruct me to take the firearm to some location or other, having first tipped off the police to arrest me when I got there. Being found in possession of the John Farley murder weapon would put me in so much trouble Anthony Hartling could forget about me for a long time. As a partial counter to this potential tactic, I cleaned the gun so that there was no way to prove I'd handled it.

On further reflection though, I doubted the police would be deliberately involved. The Hartlings preferred to deal with problems like me privately. So let me once again assume the worst: the diktat was a ploy to disarm me so I could then more easily be killed subsequently. Decision number one followed immediately: I would not hand over the gun unless there were negotiations first.

Of course, my non-cooperation risked starting the whole private war up again, but if Simeon Hartling was genuine in his offer of a peace deal, he'd agree to find a way for me to surrender the gun which was acceptable to me as well as to him. And if he wasn't being genuine, I'd still have the Heckler & Koch to defend myself with.

Another possibility was that the purpose of tomorrow morning's six o'clock phone call was to ensure we were all in Miranda's room at that time. It would still be dark, everyone else would be asleep, and we'd be vulnerable to all sorts of devilment. That brought me to decision number two: we would not be in Miranda's room at the appointed time.

I got us all up at four thirty. In case anyone from the enemy camp was on watch outside the building, I insisted we didn't turn on any lights and that we were as quiet as possible. Judith and I got dressed in our full biker regalia; Miranda wore her warmest clothes.

I told the women we probably weren't coming back — not until this affair was settled one way or another. Accordingly we pocketed various personal items and, having wrapped the gun in the carrier bag Judith had carried the supermarket shopping in yesterday, we left room 105 at five o'clock, taking the utmost care as we did so.

My big worry walking through Caerabont at that time on a Sunday morning was that we'd be stopped on suspicion by a police patrol. That would be a disaster. And not just because of the gun wrapped up in my pocket. I was Ed Somersby now, not Winston Kelly, and a man with a reason to hate Anthony Hartling. It wouldn't take a genius to suspect a connection between me and the dead High Rise Nightclubs employees in Coed y Deifol a few miles up the road. I had covered my tracks well, but was by no means sure my recent past could stand up to the kind of scrutiny it might conceivably be subjected to.

As far as practicable, we made our way from the campus to Caerabont railway station on off-road public footpaths where there would be no police patrols. Miranda's local knowledge was crucial to this, especially as the paths were mostly unlit. Where we had to take to roads, we walked together in silence. Once, on hearing a car engine, I temporarily dumped the gun and we went on without it until the car had driven off into the distance. As it turned out we saw no police patrols, but it was still a great relief to get under cover on the station platform. Apart from us the station was, of course, deserted, there being no trains or passengers at this hour on a Sunday.

The call was late. All part of the psychology, I suppose, intended to wear me down. It came through shortly before half past six, just as it was starting to get light.

"You're late," I said, reflecting a mixture of irritation and nervousness.

"Hi, loser," Anthony Hartling began unimaginatively. "Here's what you're going to do. Between Neath and Merthyr Tydfil you'll find a village called Trefdarren. It's on one of the minor roads...."

"I haven't got a car," I interrupted. I didn't like his tone, and I was minded to be obstructive.

"You got your bike?"

"I came here by train."

"Well, get a sodding taxi. I don't care. About a mile past Trefdarren there's a car park with a visitor centre and toilets. Pull in there. At this time of the year the centre's closed but not the toilets. Go into the gents and leave the gun in a bag up against the door to the cleaner's cubbyhole."

"Why can't I hand this thing over to you in a busy public place?" I asked, interrupting again. "Much safer all round."

"Because, pea-brain, you could have undercover cops posted in the crowd waiting to grab me as soon as I've got the gun in my hands. No crowds."

"Okay, but let's get one thing straight. I'm not going into a toilet. I'm not that daft. There's bound to be an outside litter bin. I'll leave it in that. And if I see you or anyone else I don't like the look of within half a mile, I'm away from there, gun and all. We'll have to negotiate from scratch."

"Who's negotiating. You do what you're told or I'm coming after you. I've got plans for you."

216

"Yeh, yeh, likewise. So let's do it right and we can both live happily ever after."

"I want everything sorted out by eight or the deals off. You've one and a half hours. Move it."

He hung up abruptly.

Miranda and Judith looked at me. I shook my head. "I don't like it." I said. "I need a map."

"What of?" Miranda asked.

"Roads between Neath and Merthyr Tydfil."

"I've got an app," she said, taking out her mobile phone.

I went over to the station's litter bin, which was full of rubbish dumped by yesterday's passengers, and took out a plastic drink bottle, a crumpled Coke can and a soggy magazine. Placing the bottle and the can side by side on the magazine, I rolled it up and wrapped the result in the carrier bag hitherto containing the gun. The Heckler & Koch went in my biker jacket pocket.

Miranda showed me the display on her phone. The obvious route from Caerabont to Neath and thence to Merthyr Tydfil was easy to trace, with Trefdarren involving a detour off the main road. But it wasn't the obvious route I was interested in. I would indeed need to 'move it'.

One of the sure places for taxi firms to advertise is at a town's railway station. We had several operators to choose from, and I asked Miranda for her recommendation. Next, using my pay-as-you-go phone, I got her to ring the firm she'd recommended. On instructions from me, she requested a taxi to go to Cardiff.

While we waited for the transport to arrive, I explained to Miranda that the taxi was for her. Very predictably, she didn't like it.

"I'm not going to leave you," she asserted.

"Listen, my sweet. While I was on watch last night, I thought of various ways Hartling could play this handover and how I'd tackle them. Every scenario had one thing in common. You have to be out of the way, somewhere safe. Maybe it'll go smoothly. But if it doesn't, things could get very rough. That really isn't your kind of scene."

"You mean I'd be a millstone round your neck," she said, starting to get upset, and recalling to my mind something I'd shouted at her in extremis on a spray-soaked ledge in the moonlight.

"You aren't a millstone, my darling, you're a lifejacket. You buoy me up. You give me courage. You're the light at the end of a long dark tunnel. And the best help you can provide right now is to get yourself out of danger. Suppose Hartling is trying to lure me away so he can grab you again. It's vital he doesn't know where you are, either at the hall of residence or with me. If I'm confident my greatest treasure can't be harmed, it will be such a load off my mind."

For once she didn't cry. She swallowed and asked: "Where exactly do you want me to go?"

"Cardiff Central railway station. You'll be able to get breakfast there. Tell the taxi driver you missed the last train last night. Oh, and if you think you're being followed on the way to Cardiff, go to the main police station, not the railway station."

I got Miranda to swap our mobile phones and show me how to work the app on hers. I wasn't familiar with the roads and would need the map display. That settled Miranda.

Judith I wanted to request a second taxi, ideally to pick her up round about seven. Her destination was to be Merthyr Tydfil. I was asking her to put herself in considerable peril, but she didn't let me down. I knew she wouldn't. "Tell the taxi driver your lift failed to show up. That will explain the biker gear. When he's gone past Neath, insist on him taking that road," I said, pointing out the route on

218

the map displayed on the phone. "Get him to pull into this car park north of Trefdarren. If he looks like he's going to get there before eight, tell him you want to enjoy the scenery, and try to persuade him to drive more slowly. Offer to pay him extra, or even double, if you have to. Take this package," — I gave her the bottle/can/magazine ensemble — "and leave it in the car park litter bin. Then tell the taxi driver you've had enough of the scenery and want to get to Merthyr Tydfil a.s.a.p. And keep your gloves on. I don't want your fingerprints on anything."

Having given both women enough money for their fares, Judith and I watched from out of sight as Miranda's transport drew up.

I didn't want an emotional goodbye from Miranda. She sensed that. We touched hands and that was all.

As soon as she had gone, I came out from cover, swallowed a painkiller, wished Judith luck, mounted the Triumph, and set course for Trefdarren. Quickly leaving Caerabont behind, I took to the alternative route I'd worked out. Once out on the open road, I let the machine rip. One hundred miles an hour and then some. At that speed, you hit a pothole, a modestly-sized furry thing crossing from one side to the other, a patch of oil, and your chances of getting up again after a spell in orbit are near zero. It requires intense concentration, skill, luck and, in normal circumstances, a fair amount of fatalism on the part of the rider.

But these weren't normal circumstances. The plan I had in mind required I get to Trefdarren well ahead of Judith's taxi. Furthermore, to guard against being ambushed on the way there, I intended to approach the handover site from the wrong direction; that is, heading south *towards* Neath. Consequently I was on an indirect route involving slower roads, extra miles, passing — at a lawful speed — through several towns, and stopping once in a while to check my route against the app on the phone. Speed on the rural stretches of road was therefore essential. If I arrived late, I'd be unable to do what I wanted to do, which was to observe the handover proceedings (conducted by Judith on my behalf) from behind the scenes. If nothing happened beyond collection of the package, the peace deal was probably legitimate. If anything hostile happened, I'd draw the opposite conclusion and take whatever action was necessary, firstly to protect Judith, and secondly to strike at the enemy. It was a neat plan, though inevitably it left far too much to chance. Hatched in the space of a few minutes after Anthony Hartling's phone call, how could it do otherwise? For no better reason at the time than a desire to be obstructive, I had tricked Hartling into expecting me to show up in a taxi. The plan had been crudely cobbled together on that deception. It was woefully ill-considered and, as such, an invitation to misfortune.

Initially at any rate, luck was with me. The motoring conditions proved favourable: the weather was dry; and being early on a Sunday morning in late October, there was no other traffic. The several towns notwithstanding, I made as good time as I could hope for.

The byroad through Trefdarren runs along a valley. On the south-east side of the road is a large stream flowing along the valley floor and, beyond that, the main 'A' road to Merthyr Tydfil. On the north-west side of the byroad is a hill covered in fir trees. I needed to get into this forest. Roughly two miles short of my destination I slowed to a quieter twenty miles an hour in order to search for a track or firebreak. If there hadn't been anything suitable, I'd have had to get the Triumph out of sight and force a passage, which would have been time-consuming and difficult. However, I stayed lucky. Less than a mile from the car park I found the track I was praying for and took the motorcycle up it. I trusted the trees would deaden the sound of the engine in the still air, and hoped that any residual noise would be confused with a powered saw such as foresters use (even if it was a Sunday).

Five hundred or so metres off the road, and after a considerable increase in altitude, the track was joined by a footpath from the left marked by a small post with arrow symbols on it. These indicated it was a forest walk — one which almost certainly started at the target car park. I rode down this path for maybe three hundred metres, pulled into the trees where a severed horizontal trunk made a landmark, and continued my approach thereafter on foot. The trend was downhill, which made the going easy, and the path was also crooked enough to restrict visibility so I couldn't be seen at any great distance. That meant I could opt for speed rather than caution.

I doubted in fact that there was anything to be cautious about. Not yet. There would be no in-depth posting of sentries. The Hartlings, I was confident, had no army to call on, and in any case this wasn't the marines they were taking on; it was a pea-brained loser. So, assuming the worst and that an ambush had been planned, I reckoned it was down to Fatty and Anthony Hartling and they'd both be at, or close to, the handover site.

I reached an otherwise unremarkable minor kink in the path and saw below me, and about a hundred and fifty metres away, a sliver of tarmac. On the right side of it I could make out a brick wall. Presumably that was the information centre and toilet block. Now was the time to start being cautious. I stopped running, and entered the trees on my left. I also thought to take out Miranda's phone and switch it off. That way it couldn't start innocently ringing and give me away.

I was sure someone would be watching the car park from under cover. Even if the handover of the gun was being played sincerely, it couldn't be left lying about for more than a few minutes. Quick retrieval required a collector on the spot. Not a person I wanted to stumble over.

When I had fifty metres to go, I went deeper into the trees, completely out of sight of the path. The time was 7.45. From here onward, it was essential to move silently. Underfoot the ground was springy and leaf-free, which helped, but littered with dead twigs, which did not. In contrast to Coed y Deifol, the individual trees here were well-spaced, permitting a certain amount of undergrowth, mostly mosses and grass and occasional bushes. Moving soundlessly was difficult but not impossible, though it took an age.

After ten minutes of the most meticulous care in advancing, I heard a car arriving. I was close enough by then to be able to make out the roof of the information centre well off to my right through the tree trunks, but the car park itself was still not within view.

As I listened to the noise of tyres scrunching grit, I caught the unmistakable whiff of cigar smoke. Oh God, Cigar-man was here! My fear level instantly jumped up a couple of notches. The source of the smoke wasn't pinpointable. Out in the open the wind had been light; inside the forest it was non-existent. Logically the fumes had to be coming from somewhere ahead, but beyond that it was guesswork. I drew the Heckler & Koch.

I heard the car come to a halt and a door open. If that was Judith dumping the package, she was five minutes early — my watch showed 7.55. I wasn't in position yet. I needed more time.

The car door shut. The engine engaged. Wheels turned. Bang. There was a flapping sound I couldn't identify. Brakes squealed. The engine returned to idling. A car door opened.

The bang had been a gunshot coming from the edge of

the trees a little to my right. It filled me with alarm. Assuming it was indeed the taxi in the car park, Cigar-man had opened fire on it. He wouldn't have shot Judith, would he? Not Judith! When I'd assigned her the role of courier, it was with the conviction that there was no gain to the enemy in killing her. Could I have got that wrong? Had I made a terrible mistake?

As I continued to creep forward — haste might be lethal — I heard talking: Cigar-man using a mobile phone or a two-way radio.

"You can come in, but it isn't him. It's the Farley woman.

"....How do I know?

"....Could be. I heard a bike not long ago. Quite a way off. Might have been him.

"....Staying put. You want to grab her?

"....Leave that to me."

He set off for the path I'd been walking down earlier. I caught sight of him briefly, but not for long enough to take aim.

Knowing Cigar-man's whereabouts permitted me to move a lot faster. I was quickly at the edge of the trees, with a good view of the car park. The taxi was there, its left front tyre completely flat. Judith — undamaged — was sitting in the front passenger seat. The driver had his door open, and was reporting the mishap over the taxi's radio.

I watched as he went unconcernedly to the boot and unloaded what he required in order to change the wheel. He could be forgiven for not realizing his flat tyre had been shot out. It's not the sort of thing one associates with rural Wales.

Now I knew the handover had been no more than a tactic to entice me into the open, anybody from the Hartling camp who came into my sights was a legitimate target. Unfortunately, of the two people I could currently see, one was an innocent bystander and the other was on my side. All I could do was wait.

I was unsure if Judith had correctly identified the nature of the bang. She was certainly ill at ease, looking round repeatedly. She sat tight, not knowing what was happening or what to do.

Another car drew into the car park and pulled up twenty metres or so from the taxi — a nice safe distance that wouldn't attract the attention of the fellow fixing his wheel. It was the ex-Weight Trainer's BMW.

"Get out of there, Judith," I whispered, angry at myself for having never described this enemy car to her. Unaware the lions were closing in, she continued to stay where she was.

I was positioned a metre to the rear of the taxi, which was broadside on to me, and all told about fifteen metres from it, looking down from behind a tree at the top of a steep two-metre high bank. It was an excellent vantage point for passive observation, but felt too remote to generate confidence in my ability to intervene. And intervention was rapidly becoming essential. Cigar-man came into sight, strolling towards the taxi.

"Having a spot of bother?" I heard him ask the driver as he came up on the left side of the car.

"Weirdest puncture I've ever seen," came the reply.

Judith realized she was in trouble. When you've pointed a gun at someone, you don't forget what they look like. In one move, she swung her legs across and almost threw herself out of the driver's side of the car.

The BMW's doors opened.

Judith ran.

Hartling, alighting from the BMW, shouted: "Wait," at her.

At the same moment, Cigar-man eliminated the one neutral participant in the action. I don't know what he did to him, but the poor man sprawled either unconscious or lifeless alongside the wheel he'd been replacing.

I would have shot Cigar-man there and then, but I held back. Having never discharged a pistol before, I had no confidence I could hit the target at a range of fifteen metres. I knew that if I took on a trained killer I had to be sure not to miss, because if I did, he certainly wouldn't. The range was simply too great.

Hartling had set off after Judith, who'd disappeared from view. There were only two places she could have made for: the forest path or the ladies' toilets. The sensible option and the stupid one. I had confidence in Judith. She wasn't stupid.

My priority now became the protection of my friend. As I turned to leave, I saw that Fatty had also got out of the BMW.

I ran obliquely towards the forest path, meaning to emerge onto it perhaps fifty metres from where it left the car park. Cigar-man probably detected the noise I was making. I couldn't help that. Speed was vital now, not surprise, and I had no time to be silent.

I reached the path sooner than I'd intended. And practically ran into Fatty. He was chasing after Hartling, who was a way off to my right.

Fatty had a shotgun. I had the Heckler & Koch. The range was less than four metres. It was just a question of who fired first. He raised the shotgun; I sighted along the pistol's barrel. I think I screamed as I fired. I was surprised to find the handgun had quite a kick to it.

Fatty's shotgun went off, but by then he was already falling backwards. None of the pellets struck me. He hit the ground face up and lay still.

I looked to my right. Judith was two thirds of the way to the slight bend that would take her out of sight. She was running for her life. Hartling had come to a halt. Having heard the commotion behind him, he had no choice. He turned and saw me.

Our reactions were identical. We both dived into the trees.

I stopped worrying about Judith. As a bit player, she was now safe. I was the one Hartling wanted. I knew he'd leave her and come after me.

What unnerved me was I didn't know Cigar-man's whereabouts. Imagining the worst, that he was heading rapidly in my direction from the car park, I threw myself down in a handy non-prickly bush and listened intently.

Someone — it had to be Fatty — had started swearing loudly, interspersing the obscenities with shouts of pain. Apart from him, all was quiet. No sounds of movement. That made me feel more secure. I doubted if either Cigar-man or Hartling knew how to move silently in a forest. Even if they did, time was against them. They had to expect a local person or two would chance on the scene at any moment. Silence and speed are incompatible in woodland, and they had to choose speed.

I waited. Fatty continued to cuss. The sound was changing direction though, heading downhill. Was he alone or being helped?

Not knowing where the enemy personnel were was severely disturbing, especially Cigar-man. Although it was forty-eight hours since the duel in the workshop, the kidney pain was still with me on and off, and right now it was getting to be markedly on. I couldn't help being extremely fearful of him. As long as I stayed where I was, it would be virtually impossible for him to detect me. To play safe was tempting.

But I'd assured Judith I could 'deliver'. You don't do that by cowering when there are targets within range. Gathering up my courage, I came out of hiding. Keeping low I moved quietly, but too fast for complete silence, towards the car park. That's where they'd all be, sooner or later.

Fatty shut up at last. A new sound filled the air: three blasts on a car horn.

I gambled on moving faster. When the BMW came into view, it had been repositioned. It was now at the centre of the car park, pointing at the exit. Both the front doors were open. Cigar-man was standing on the driver's side, looking by chance almost directly at me over the car's roof. His right hand — bandaged, I noticed with some satisfaction — was resting on the roof, clasping a gun. There was someone on the rear seats. I assumed that must be Fatty. No sign of Hartling.

I guessed the horn blasts were a signal recalling Hartling to the car. Cigar-man had readied himself to provide covering fire as necessary.

Two things occurred to me. One was that Cigar-man was no longer an immediate threat. His professional judgement presumably told him the ambush had failed and that the best course was to get away, regroup, and try again some other time. The second was that Hartling had a big problem. I was between him and the car park. And I was armed.

I reasoned his most likely course would be to parallel the forest path, keeping just within the trees. If I was correct, I could position myself to intercept him.

I had barely started on the manoeuvre when there was a movement to my right. Ten metres maybe. Something in the corner of my eye. I threw myself flat. The sound of the gunshot reached my ears before I reached the ground. I rolled onto my stomach, Heckler & Koch in front of me, petrified. Hartling and I had damned nearly run into each other.

Facing towards where I now knew him to be, my head was so low my chin was touching the grass around me. I couldn't see him, but I didn't dare so much as twitch to get a better view. I'd have to rely on hearing.

As far as I could judge, he had hit the ground too and seemed to be heading away from the path. Definitely not on foot. If he'd been standing or crouching, he'd have been visible. Nonetheless I could detect clear sounds of movement — rustling sounds like something heavy was being dragged through the undergrowth. It was a good bet what I could hear was him crawling on his belly, crocodile fashion. It meant he wouldn't be able to open fire instantly if he saw me. Thus it was safe to raise my head. Even then I still couldn't spot him. The matted long grass and the weeds were growing too high and too thick.

Moving on elbows and toes, I positioned myself to get a better line of sight on where he seemed to be heading.

He stopped.

I don't know if he was trying to answer Cigar-man's summons by going round me, or if the idea was to attempt to come at me from the side. Either way I was blocking him, covering the space between him and me and the car park. He knew that.

The problem we both had was that while you're taking steps to see your opponent you can't open fire. It's spot the target first; fire second. But while you're adopting a firing stance you become visible and can be shot at. So neither of us could initiate the action. The first person to make a move gets his head blown off.

The advantage was mine. Hartling was in a hurry. I wasn't. It was just a matter of keeping still until he made a mistake.

And then a new player entered the arena. A third car drove into the car park. Cigar-man let off two blasts on the horn. It was a relief to know he was continuing to man the BMW rather than coming to Hartling's rescue.

All at once several shots — at the time it seemed like a

fusillade, though I think on reflection it was only three —
were fired in my direction. Instinctively I turned my head
to one side and pressed it to the ground.

Hartling was running. Not at me but directly for the
BMW. He could see me now he was standing and fired
twice more. The intention, I suspect, was not so much to hit
me (except by chance) as to stop me shooting back. It was
an effective tactic.

He dropped out of sight. I heard stones rolling down the
bank that marked the boundary between trees and tarmac.
Two doors slammed. An engine revved, tyres screeched,
and there was a hasty motorized departure: towards Neath,
judging by the way the sound of the engine faded.

Cautiously I raised my head. Having got away with that,
I stood up. Nobody shot me. It wasn't some cunning feint.
Hartling really had gone. Quickly at the edge of the trees, I
saw the BMW had been replaced by a Range Rover and a
gentleman with a couple of yapping dogs. He looked
distinctly nonplussed. The taxi driver looked dead. I fled
the scene.

I backtracked, rejoining the forest path once I could do
so without being visible from the car park. I ran up the hill
calling Judith over and over. I was almost at the place
where the Triumph was hidden, and getting worried, when
she came into the open.

"Did we win?" she asked grimly.

"One down."

"Who?"

"Fatty."

"So that was him I heard hollering?"

"Yeh. I shot him. That should put him out of
commission for a while."

"Well done; though we're going to have to improve on
that next time. I want that cigar-faced butcher in a
mortuary."

I didn't necessarily agree with the 'we' but I couldn't fault the statement in any other respect.

Having retrieved the motorcycle, I variously pushed and free-wheeled it down to the road. I kept the engine turned off because it seemed like a good idea to avoid giving any unnecessary indication of our presence.

Judith had left her crash helmet in the taxi. That meant she wasn't legally dressed for motoring on two wheels. It was, however, important that we get away from the area as quickly as possible. She agreed, on my absolute insistence, to wear my helmet.

I started the engine and set course for Merthyr Tydfil.

15

RETRIBUTION

We travelled slowly and, where possible, on minor roads and tracks, and in some places off-road completely. On the outskirts of Merthyr Tydfil, as soon as I had a good signal, I called Miranda and told her we were okay, and that the peace deal was a sham. It had occurred to me the police might trace the other of the taxis we had summoned to Caerabont railway station, and for that reason it was advisable for Miranda to leave Cardiff Central urgently. With Hartling's resources deployed at Trefdarren, I was fairly confident she'd be unmolested. I instructed her to catch a train to Rhymney, a town in the next valley east of Merthyr, and we'd meet her there.

Still keeping off main routes, Judith and I managed to reach the proposed rendezvous ourselves fairly easily. We were fortunate not to encounter any zealous policemen to add to our troubles. Without a helmet on, I felt like I was riding along with a large 'arrest me' placard over my head.

We found a cafeteria and had a late breakfast while waiting for Miranda. This being Sunday, the first train didn't arrive till gone eleven, and I had time to become quite anxious before it pulled into the station. It was a great relief to see Miranda walking calmly along the platform. The three of us then went and found somewhere quiet where we could discuss the situation.

It was clear the Hartlings had never intended to give me a break. The Trefdarren exercise had been designed solely to get me into the open in an isolated place. If it had been me in the taxi instead of Judith, Cigar-man would have shot me dead without ceremony. But it was Judith they had found themselves dealing with, and they had tried to seize her precisely because they didn't know my whereabouts. She would have become a hostage: someone whose life they might conceivably have persuaded me to exchange with my own. It was a conclusion which reinforced my belief that she and Miranda were both in grave danger, and would remain so for as long as the Hartlings pursued their vendetta against me.

We agreed we had to get out of South Wales. To that end, our first problem was how to leave Rhymney. For me it was simple: the Triumph. Judith and Miranda had no such easy option. I was keen for them to stay together, and insistent they should not travel via Cardiff, because it was an obvious place for the enemy to keep watch. We settled for a taxi once again, this time to convey them to Abergavenny. From thence they should catch a train to Birmingham, followed by a second train to London. I gave them the keys to my safe house in Harrow, checked that Judith remembered where to find it, and issued dire warnings about taking great care on approach and entry to guard against the possibility it wasn't as safe as I thought.

The only matter outstanding was that of money. Since I didn't want to be traceable to Wales, all my transactions there had to be in cash, and I was running low. Miranda volunteered to make a withdrawal from her account via a cash machine. That done, I sent them on their way.

Once I was alone — I'll confess to being relieved that it was so — I could start seriously planning what I myself was going to do next. The main thing I was clear about was that it was essential I avoided ever again being reduced to the kind of miserable state I'd been in when I poured out my troubles to prostitute-with-a-heart Candy. The way to prevent that, as I knew well, was to be continually taking action, hitting back. Therein lay the only remotely credible route out of the mess I was in: to strike at the Hartlings, and to do so repeatedly, until they concluded I was more trouble than I was worth. Then it would be in their interests as well as mine to negotiate a peace deal. And I'd snap it up.

So what to do? I'd told Miranda and Judith that I had a few things to sort out, and that I'd join them at my Harrow flat tomorrow afternoon. They'd questioned me, of course, about what I was going to be up to in the meantime, but had had to be content with my assurances that it wouldn't involve any danger to me, nor anything in the way of arson and/or murder. What it did involve was twenty-four hours of untrammelled freedom in which to arrange some mayhem.

As a start I rang High Rise Nightclubs, which was the only certain phone number I possessed connected to Simeon Hartling. I'd intended to use my pay-as-you-go phone, but found it was Miranda's phone (with the app) I had in my pocket. So I used a payphone instead. This being Sunday I got an answering machine, and as directed left a message after the beep. Using my Irish accent I said: "Okay Hartling. If that's the way you want it! Now I've got nothing left to lose, next time that slime-bag son of yours shows his face in Caerabont when I'm about, I don't care if he's got a hundred bodyguards and there are a thousand witnesses. I'm settling his account with me. Permanently."

The Triumph took me to Birmingham, where I booked one night in a city-centre hotel and hired a standard 'white van' for a week. I spent the evening dozing in my room.

Around eleven I set off in the van for Caerabont. When I arrived, I hurled a couple of large stones through the living room and bedroom windows of Anthony's flat — just to make sure the Hartlings got the message. That accomplished, I returned to the Birmingham hotel, slept for a couple of hours, had breakfast, loaded my motorcycle into the van and checked out.

Of course, threatening phone calls and broken windows were mere flea bites to hard cases like the Hartlings, but they were simple blows I could strike, primarily on Miranda's behalf. She had been forced to abandon her studies at Deheubarth University. In that case I intended to force Anthony Hartling to do the same. If successful, the tactic had the advantage of being cheap and almost risk-free, while imposing a serious inconvenience on the enemy.

That was my first bit of mayhem. But a much more ambitious project had also occurred to me, one requiring a certain amount of equipment. To begin with, recalling the problem I'd had with wearing a white shirt in Coed y Deifol, I bought a black one. I followed that with a large holdall and some clear plastic gloves of the kind dentists and other health workers use. Finally I purchased forty metres of insulated single-core wire from an electrical retailer. Everything else I needed was in my flat, so I bade farewell to Birmingham and headed for London.

The two women were at home when I arrived, though something wasn't right. I'd been expecting, perhaps not a hero's welcome, but at least some enthusiasm, whereas what I got was restrained to the point of politeness.

We discussed lunch and decided to fetch our requirements from the nearest supermarket, which was only a hundred metres up the road. Miranda offered to go, and I said it ought to be me or Judith. The latter woman gave me a glare of such ferocity it could have felled a lesser mortal at twenty paces. It was explained to me they'd been constantly watching the street for the past eighteen hours, and nothing the least suspicious had happened in all that time. Furthermore, if their whereabouts had been discovered, they'd have been attacked long before now. In short, Miranda was going to the supermarket or we'd stay hungry. When I disagreed, it was pointed out the road was a straight one, and if I really wanted to I could watch her walk from door to door. Very reluctantly I climbed down. Miranda went for the shopping.

"I gather you've been talking about me," I remarked to Judith after Miranda had left.

"We've been talking about a lot of things. You were one of them."

"So what have I done wrong?"

"She worships you. You know that, don't you?"

"That's not my fault. Anyway, I wish she didn't."

"I've explained that to her. I've told her you want a partner, not an acolyte; that she has to get you off your pedestal so she can stand at your side instead of at your feet. That's right, isn't it?"

"Yes Judith, it is."

"Good. She's going to try and do that, but she needs your help."

"She does? In what way?"

"Ed, you have to stop shutting her out. She spent most of yesterday in tears over you."

"That's just her way. She's like that."

"Oh is she really? I'd say you must be the most insensitive man on the planet, except that's how most of you men seem to be. So you listen to me. Miranda is not 'like that'. You remember the day you visited her in the Cardiff hotel after you'd set fire to Hartling's flat, and she told you he'd once raped her? She says when you left her that morning she'd never seen a man so desperately unhappy and alone ever before in her life. And you just walked away. Have you any idea what that did to her? And I know what she means, because you've treated me to a similar display. After John was shot, I spent twenty-four hours watching you tearing yourself to pieces, not knowing why, or how I could reach you. In heaven's name, we had to come face to face with a nutcase intent on murdering us before you'd confide in me. Good old Ed; chin out, squares his shoulders, never cries in front of the girls. You obviously reckon we're blind. You've done some stupid things this year, but thinking you can hide your feelings from people who care about you.... well, that's the stupidest thing of the lot. Don't you see behaving like that *forces* Miranda to put you on a pedestal. You're not giving her a chance to put you anywhere else."

"I'm only trying to protect her, Judith; trying to keep her from being hurt. Not just by them; by me too. If I told her how I really feel, it would add to her troubles."

"Why is that a problem? As I've just explained, she already knows how you feel. By not telling her, by not sharing your feelings with her, by shutting her out, you're making it worse. You're making her think she's failing you."

"That's ridiculous. She's not doing anything of the kind."

"Then share that with her. You have to realize love is a two-way process. You talk to each other. You trust each other. And yes, sometimes you add to each other's troubles. That's what being partners means."

"You really think I should tell her when I'm unhappy?"

"*Yes*."

"Okay."

"There's more," Judith continued, detecting that I thought the lecture was over. "You told her her job is to be beautiful and worth rescuing. But it's not only your opinion that counts here. *She* has to think she's worth rescuing too. And I don't think she does. Given what's happened in the past she needs, really needs, to prove herself to you; to help you with more than moral support."

"No," I said firmly. "If I take her along with me, it'll get us both killed."

"I'm not suggesting you send her into the front line. Of course she wasn't the right person to sit in that taxi at Trefdarren. But surely you can see that to exile her to a railway station in Cardiff was downright cruel. You have to give her a role which is more active than worrying herself sick while she darns socks by the fireside. *Involve* her."

There was a long silence.

"I've made a real hash of this relationship," I said eventually.

"I don't agree. You've captured the heart of a charming girl who'll be a great credit to you if you let her. And it's obvious you love her dearly. That sounds like a success story to me. All I'm suggesting is how you can turn the good job you've done so far into an excellent one."

I went to the window and looked out, watching for Miranda's return and taking the opportunity to fight down the latest lump in my throat that Judith had given me. It was such a beautiful dream, Miranda and me and a peaceful future. And there, standing over this vision of Eden like a primed nuclear arsenal, was Anthony Hartling. I damned him to hell.

Miranda came into view at last, making her way to the flat, a vision of conscientious wariness. I understood she hadn't gone for the provisions merely to let Judith batter my ears. She'd gone because it was a small risk she could run for me. It made me smile, for she'd be about as much use in a punch-up as a teddy bear. And I loved her for it more than ever.

When she entered the flat, she glanced at Judith as I went up to her. I took the shopping out of her hands, put my arms around her, and whispered in her ear: "Can I be pleased to see you now?"

"Yes, Ed, you can," she replied, and gave me one of those kisses of hers I sincerely hope I never get used to.

We had lunch and discussed our options for the future.

Judith, particularly, was in an impossible position. She agreed she didn't dare return to her home, yet at the same time insisted she couldn't stay in hiding for longer than a few more days. There was John's funeral to attend to, his business affairs to sort out, and her supermarket job to return to. (She was currently on two weeks' compassionate leave).

I was unable to offer advice or hope, not because I thought our position hopeless but because, despite Judith's remonstration, I couldn't tell her and Miranda what I had in mind for the evening. Like the two Coed y Deifol murders, it was something I wanted to keep firmly in the no-one-must-know category. I couldn't stop the women suspecting, but I didn't want them to become accessories — before the fact, or after it — in what might prove to be a bloodbath.

Just after four we heard a phone ringing. Miranda found her jacket and took out the one in the pocket. It was my pay-as-you-go phone, so she reached across to pass it to me.

I had a sudden inspiration. "Would you like to answer it?" I said. "Let's confuse him." (I knew it was one of the Hartlings calling, because they were the only people, other than Miranda and Judith, who had the number.)

"Hello," said Miranda.

"....Your fairy godmother.

"....No. He's busy. And don't you call him that.

"....Slime bag? He must have been feeling kind. Rat faeces would....

"....And I've just about had it with you!" She held the phone away from her ear and looked at it, frowning. She resumed listening for a few seconds, said: "I suggest you go and wash your mouth out, preferably with industrial strength bleach," and hung up.

I went straight over and hugged her. I was completely at a loss for words.

"That was Tony," she said. "He's awfully angry. I'm sure I've never heard so much filthy language before in such a short time. I think he wants to kill me. How did I do?"

"I couldn't have done it better myself," I answered, and hugged her again.

We swapped our two phones so they were back with their rightful owners.

"Did he say anything about where he is?" I asked.

"Not directly. But I think he's had to leave Caerabont. That's what's made him furious. Did you throw a brick through his window last night?"

"Yes. It seemed like a good idea."

"He was there then by the sound of it."

"Smashing," I said, and was disappointed neither woman reacted to my little pun.

I'd been up half the previous night, and needed to sleep for a few hours. I gave Miranda the keys to the hired van, pointed out she wasn't insured to drive it so she'd need to be especially careful, and asked her to reconnoitre Hardiman Terrace and see what cars were parked at no. 47. A black Mercedes would particularly please me. I also suggested she take a look around Throckmorten Square. I warned her these were the lions' dens, there were CCTV cameras about, and that under no circumstances should she leave the van or drive in any way that might arouse suspicion. I wanted to send Judith with her as a sort of minder, but wasn't sure how the suggestion would be interpreted, so I left them to decide between them whether Judith stayed with me or accompanied Miranda. They got it right without my help. A return knock-on-the-door code was agreed, and I was left alone.

Before going to bed, I got out a few of my electrical tools and the replacement dark blue Winston Kelly suit I'd purchased to wear when collecting his repaired Ford in

Cardiff. Excepting the suit, everything went into the pockets of my biker jacket. The suit I put in a carrier bag and left by the bedroom window. As an afterthought, I filled an empty one-litre plastic milk bottle with water and left it by my biker jacket. Then I slept.

Judith and Miranda got back at eight as we'd arranged, bringing three take-away fried chicken portions to eat. I was getting too on-edge to be hungry, but I joined in the meal for the sake of appearance.

They reported seeing the black Mercedes in the drive of no. 47, but didn't spot the gold Rolls Royce either there or in the vicinity of Throckmorten Square. They said the lights in the High Rise Nightclubs office were still on in the first-floor windows when they last cruised past the building at seven o'clock.

After the meal we watched television. By quarter to ten I was so hyped up I could stand it no longer. I went into the bedroom and dropped the carrier bag containing the suit out of the window and then, as casually as possible, put on my biker jacket, picked up the water-filled milk bottle and the van's keys, and announced: "I'm going out for a while. I want to give the lions' dens a look-over and see if there's anything going on. I don't know when I'll be back."

As I was leaving, Miranda called my name and I had to pause by the door. Our eyes met and some wordless message crossed the deep but narrow gap between us.

"Be careful," she said.

"Don't worry," I replied, forcing a smile. "Aren't I always?"

Out in the open, I picked up the carrier bag from where it had fallen, and got in the van. I felt reasonably confident I had given neither woman any intimation that I was going to do more than give the lions' dens a 'look-over'. After the telling off I'd had from Judith earlier in the day, though, I was nowhere nearly as sure about that as I would once have been. I just hoped my acting was good enough. There was no sense in the two women worrying. What happens, happens.

I drove to Regent's Park. The lighting is quite dim there in places, and I was able to change into the black shirt and Winston Kelly's dark suit without being observed. I put on the plastic gloves, stored my tools and the forty metres of insulated wire in the holdall, and gave the Heckler & Koch a careful check. Then I drove to Throckmorten Square.

There was no problem parking. As expected, the cleaners were still at work.

I waited.

In due course all the floors were in darkness, and the cleaners began to file out. Carrying the holdall I rushed to the front door, taking care to keep my face turned away from the CCTV camera monitoring the entrance. I entered the lobby as the head cleaner was preparing to set the burglar alarm.

"Hey!" he shouted. "What you doin'?"

"Sorry," I said in my best Dublin brogue. "Mr Hartling sent me over for some papers. Don't worry about locking up. I'll do that on my way out."

"Right," he said, sounding very unsure.

"Telephone him if you're worried. Tell him the man who gives people nosebleeds is here."

"Gives people nosebleeds, huh?"

English clearly wasn't his first language. My accent was probably wasted on him. "Now go on. Clear off. I'm in a hurry."

"Maybe I wait."

"Call him," I said, pretending to be angry. "Now get out. Or he'll find someone else to do the cleaning."

That did the trick. He stepped out of the building. Before he could change his mind, I slammed the front door and bolted it.

Five minutes to familiarize myself with the building layout. I began running.

Viewed from above the offices are L-shaped, the short arm of the 'L' fronting Throckmorten Square, the long arm running along Carrington Place. In the angle between the two arms are the lifts, toilets and carpeted stairs. On the ground floor the room overlooking the square contained the security desk, CCTV monitors, and telephone switchboard; also an external door leading to the courtyard behind the building. Upstairs the matching rooms on first and second floors were open-plan areas with desks, computer terminals, telephones, cupboards, filing cabinets. The top floor was locked and I couldn't gain access to it.

The Carrington Place wing had a similar set-up. No access to the top floor, open-plan second and first floors. The ground floor was a conference room. Each floor had a way out at the end of the Carrington Place wing: an internal fire-escape consisting of concrete steps running from the locked third floor to a pushbar operated door on the ground floor. The door could not be opened from the outside and had no alarm fitted.

The fire-escape steps — and also the carpeted stairs — continued down to a basement, which was the place I checked out last. So far the streetlamps had provided sufficient illumination — better than a full moon — but below ground level I had to turn the lights on. The Throckmorten Square wing down here was a junk room: cardboard boxes full of computer printouts, all sorts of broken office furniture. Its counterpart on Carrington Place was what I wanted: a concrete-floored utilities room containing central heating boiler and, against the wall near the fire-escape, the electricity consumer unit.

I looked at my watch. Fifteen seconds early. Good. Another five minutes for the next stage.

The electrical supply was routed through a couple of

RCDs and two banks of MCBs. An RCD's function is to disconnect the power supply in event of a leakage to earth, and my first job was to disable the two in front of me. I clipped the master fuse tag and pulled out the fuse. That of course plunged the basement into darkness. Using my head-mounted torch for light, I bypassed the RCDs.

The next task was to sort out the MCBs. The role of these devices is to switch off individual circuits in the event of a power overload. And the electrician who'd installed them, bless him, had thoughtfully labelled each MCB in the two banks with the circuit it controlled. That saved me quite a bit of time and guesswork. I set to OFF the one controlling the basement socket outlets, and then unscrewed the faceplates of two of these power points, one at each end of the room, connecting the live terminal in each case to a length of the insulated wire I'd brought with me in the holdall. The other end of the wire I stripped bare and coiled around the nearby door handle. Thus the door from the fire-escape and the door from the carpeted stairs were connected to the mains. All I had to do was switch the MCB to the ON position and the handles would be live.

But I wasn't finished yet. The basement door leading to the carpeted stairs opened into a carpeted hallway. I poured half the water in the plastic milk bottle onto the place on the carpet where someone would have to stand in order to open the basement door. All it needed was a human holding the door handle to complete the circuit by providing a route from the live handle to the earth.

At the fire-escape end I couldn't rig the same set-up because there was no carpet. However, I did the next best thing. I wetted the floor *inside* the room where someone would tread while pushing the fire-door open.

I looked at my watch again. This time I was running late. I replaced the master fuse, causing the basement lights to come back on, thereby confirming the electricity supply was properly restored. Then I hastened to the front door on the ground floor, turning off the basement lights in passing. I had bolted the door when I arrived. Now I unbolted it. From that moment on, anyone could walk in.

The CCTV monitors had been left on when the building was locked up for the night. They showed three views: one of the courtyard, one looking towards Throckmorten Square, and one showing the front entrance. No one was in sight in any of them. I had set the trap. Now it was a matter of patiently waiting to see who, if anyone, got caught in it.

The reaction of the cleaner was the first of the big unknowns. If he did nothing beyond quietly going home, I would have to ring Simeon Hartling myself. His phone number was printed at the top of a list by the telephone switchboard, as I'd expected it would be, so no problems there.

If, on the other hand, the cleaner called the police, I'd be compelled to write this particular plan off, flee as best I was able, and think up some other stratagem.

But my intuition told me the cleaner would do what I wanted, alerting Simeon Hartling to an intruder on his premises. Which led to the second big unknown. How would Simeon Hartling react?

I was certain he wouldn't summon the police. That would be totally out of character. I was equally certain doing nothing wasn't an option open to him. So he'd send someone after me. But who? I'd timed my raid to coincide with when the brothel, the nightclubs and the casino would be at their busiest. There was a good chance he'd have no one to spare. Suppose, though, he did have some surplus manpower. Bearing in mind they'd be coming to murder me, or at the very least convey me to my death, I'd seriously injure or kill them. I didn't expect him to send more than two men for the simple reason I was a mere unemployed electrician. A greater number than that and he'd make himself the laughing-stock of the underworld. And I reckoned the Heckler & Koch and the electrified doors the would see me all right. I could cope with two adversaries. If there were three or more I'd be in serious trouble.

But assuming I was correct and no one was available, it would be Cigar-man who would soon be paying a call. For several reasons. Firstly, he was one of those on the payroll with a 'willingness to commit murder' clause written into his job description. Secondly, with Anthony Hartling in London, Cigar-man would be in the capital also and on call. Finally, he had three times botched attempts to kill me, so he was probably facing toilet-cleaning duties. He'd be keen to redeem himself. Despite my fear of him, I prayed he'd be the one to show up on the monitor. I owed John and Judith.

While waiting for something to happen, I checked out the CCTV data storage system. The monitor images were recorded onto a drive in a box beneath the screens. I didn't want any more information left lying about for the Hartlings or the police than was unavoidable, so I prepared to disconnect the drive. Fortunately, that would plainly be childishly simple to accomplish.

As nothing continued to happen, I picked up the phone to dial Simeon Hartling. Briefly I hesitated, and there on the screen was the Rolls Royce pulling into the square. I doubted the boss would lend his fancy car to one of the hired hands, so it looked a real possibility he was coming to sort me out personally. If so, I was honoured.

I watched as one of the rear doors opened. Cigar-man alighted — so who was in the front passenger seat? — and the Rolls drove out of the square and off-camera. It was time to get moving. I disconnected the drive; no more CCTV images would be recorded this night.

I left the security room and rushed past the front door.

Cigar-man was already cautiously opening it. I entered the conference room and headed for the fire-escape at the far end, making as much noise as possible. I didn't intend Cigar-man to waste precious seconds being circumspect. I wanted him to know where I was so I could eliminate him before anyone else came on the scene.

I pulled open the door to the fire-escape loudly and glanced back. Cigar-man burst into the conference room at the other end, ducking sideways and down. I went through the fire-door, leaving it to close itself behind me. (All the fire-doors were self-closing.)

The next bit was going to be tricky. Would a professional like Cigar-man fall for it? I rammed down the pushbar on the fire-escape exit leading to the courtyard, but instead of going outside I crept silently down the steps to the basement. Crouching in a corner, I aimed the Heckler & Koch at the place where Cigar-man would have to stand in order to peer into the open air. I wanted him to believe I'd left the building. If he thought along those lines, I'd be able to shoot him in the back.

I heard fire-door hinges creaking, but no one came through them. My opponent was assessing the situation.

There was the sound of wheels on tarmac. It had to be the Rolls, and it was entering the courtyard. Damn! If the Rolls was out there, then I couldn't be. Not without an immediate exchange of gunfire. Cigar-man would know I was still in the building.

I could picture what he'd do. Enter the fire-escape, gun at the ready. The first steps he'd come to led upwards. He'd look, tensed to fire. No sign of me. Take a pace forward towards the steps leading down. See me. Fire. It was his expert reaction against my unpractised amateur one. I didn't fancy my chances.

I fled into the basement proper, taking care that the door shut behind me. Cigar-man inevitably heard. The sound would tell him I had left the fire-escape, and he could safely descend.

Barely seconds passed before the fire door opened a fraction. He was plainly opting for overwhelming speed. However, the situation was different from that in John Farley's workshop. This door was sprung, and so couldn't be thrown open. It slowed him and gave me the second I needed. I switched the MCB to ON.

There was a stifled cry, and the door opened further. Cigar-man, left hand rigidly gripping the live metal, came into sight. He fell to his knees on the wet floor as his weight and the rotation of the door carried him forward.

Before he could crash to the ground completely and possibly unhook himself from the current, I strode up to him, put the barrel of the Heckler & Koch against his temple, and executed him. Even in the darkness there was no mistaking the shock of the bullet's impact. Justice for John Farley.

Cigar-man's body toppled over. As his right hand hit the floor, the gun he was holding discharged. The loud and totally unexpected bang unnerved me so badly I thought for a moment I was going to faint.

To my surprise, Cigar-man's left hand was so tightly clutching the handle of the door that it remained attached, even though it was now supporting some of his weight. Only a minor nuisance. Seizing an insulated part of the live wire, I yanked it free from its connection to the socket outlet. The left hand plummeted to join the rest of the corpse. The ex-cigar smoker was safe to touch. I extracted his gun from his grasp and put it in my pocket. It added what I hoped was an almost full magazine to the two bullets remaining in the Heckler & Koch.

I had won the first round. If I was to win round two as well, it was essential to work out the enemy's dispositions. Who was where and doing what?

I could hear someone whispering — someone who had come in through the opened pushbar door. That meant there were at least two people remaining to be dealt with. The whispering quickly stopped. I heard a fire-escape door opening. Then silence.

My guess was that the plan had been to trap me in the building. There were three exits from the High Rise Nightclubs office: the locked door into the courtyard, the pushbar door, and the main front door. I had no key to the locked door, so it was only necessary to guard the two remaining doors. That needed two people. So the third man — Cigar-man — was free to come in after me.

Assume the plan was now in place: one man at the front door, one man at the pushbar door. But the plan had gone wrong. The two men guarding the doors had heard the shooting in the basement. Cigar-man hadn't declared victory, so they'd be assuming I was still alive. But what about Cigar-man? They didn't know what had happened and they needed to find out.

The man by the pushbar door was the only one in a position to do that. He'd look down towards the basement. What would he see? Answer: the basement fire-door being held open by a body. He'd know the third man had to sit tight by the front door. The man guarding the exit to the courtyard would therefore realize it was up to him to enter the basement and flush me out, assuming I was still there and not already trying to leave the building via the front door. If my analysis was correct, the danger would come from the fire-escape. No one was going to be opening the door from the carpeted stairs — which was still electrified in any case.

My immediate adversary had a physical difficulty to overcome. He could only get into the basement by treading on the dead body. Doing that would slow him down. The fire escape had low-level emergency lighting which couldn't be switched off, with the consequence that for the second or two it took him to get through the doorway he'd be an unmissable target. So he dared not take the one action that was required of him. Pause for thought.

I used the lull as an opportunity to consider where best to locate myself. Perhaps understandably, though it wasn't rational, I felt intimidated by that partly open fire-door and the enemy lurking silently on its far side. I decided to increase my distance from it. I backed away and approached the other exit from the basement. All the while I had to keep my attention fixed on the space above Cigarman's corpse. The basement windows, tops level with the pavement outside, let in a small amount of light, but it wasn't really enough to discern anything more than large moving shapes, and then only vaguely. It gave me confidence that I was virtually invisible, and that anyone coming at me from the fire-escape would not be able to see me as long as I wasn't moving.

Minutes passed. Total silence. I kept my eyes focused on the open doorway, Heckler & Koch at the end of outstretched arms, ready to pull the trigger. Strange dark nebulous clouds began to affect my vision. I became unsure I could see anything.

Someone touched the handle of the door at my end of the room. I was certain of it. The front door guard must have run out of patience. Or maybe my picture of the enemy's dispositions was wrong. Either way, this time the result was disappointing. Perhaps it was asking a bit much to expect the same trick to work twice. The electrified door remained shut. I had no idea what had happened. Was the guy gripping the handle on its far side, paralysed and dying? Absence of sound or movement suggested not. Possibly he had thick rubber soles to his shoes. Possibly he'd gone so tentatively about opening the door he'd felt a warning spark. Possibly.... anything.

Put it down to bad luck. At the precise moment my attention was distracted by what was going on behind me, the guy in the fire escape made his move. He came in low and fast over Cigar-man and was out of sight in the darkness before I was ready to fire.

That had me close to panic. One antagonist separated from me by nothing more than a 230-volt door; the other now in the same room as me. I had to resist a sudden urge to scream.

The man now in the basement with me didn't — couldn't — know where I was, but he was closing in. I could hear him. He was somewhere near the central-heating boiler. I had rejected it as cover myself because the spaces around it were too small to get fully into, and would serve only to hamper movement. His view of the matter was probably that it was better protection than nothing.

I could vaguely make him out: an ill-defined black shape moving against a black background. Not on his feet. Perhaps on an elbow and calf. I didn't fire. It would give my position away. Not a problem if I hit the target, but if I missed, it would be the end of me. In the absence of light I just wasn't sure I could pull off a coup like that.

When he was well into the room, he stopped. It proved he truly had no idea of my location. I hadn't bolted as he'd doubtless hoped. Indeed, he couldn't even be sure I was in the basement at all. By keeping my nerve and remaining motionless, I had gained an advantage. Unlike the enemy, I knew where to point my gun. If it wasn't for the absence of light....

I wish I could claim that what I did next was calculated audacity. It wasn't. It was panic. The lights could be turned on by switches at either end of the room. There was a switch right by my ear. I reached up with my left arm, and flicked it down.

The instant illumination revealed a big man on the floor

adjacent to the boiler, lying on his side. The gun in his hand was already being brought to bear.

Suddenly icy calm, I sighted along the Heckler & Koch's short barrel and fired.

The big man — Simeon Hartling? — slumped forward onto his chest. His enormous revolver, and the hand holding it, fell to the floor. In the centre of one of his eyebrows was a small black spot from which blood was trickling. As I knew from a distressing past observation, it was the entry wound made by a nine-millimetre projectile. The bullet's trajectory would have taken it through his brain stem and down into his neck. He was dead.

It would have been nice to have a few seconds to savour winning round two. However, I wasn't permitted the luxury. Somebody else had entered the fire-escape. Being uncarpeted, even quiet sounds, made in what was in effect a concrete shaft, were sufficiently magnified to be clearly audible. It was either the person who'd touched the live handle at my end of the basement trying the alternative route down here, or there'd been four people in the Rolls, not three. Dear God, not four of them. Please not four.

Panic overtook me worse than ever. I snapped off the lights. Desperate to flee at any price, I gripped by its insulation the wire attached to the handle behind me, pulled it off and tossed it away.

I flung the door open and threw myself down on its far side. There was no one there. I ran the short distance to the carpeted stairs and bounded up to the ground floor. Out of immediate danger my panic subsided. Self-control returned.

My intention now was to quit the building. I had dealt the Hartlings a severe blow on their home territory. That had been the whole point of the operation. Objective attained. Time to run and hide. I'd had enough for one night.

I was also worried about the gunshots. The property adjoining High Rise Nightclubs on Throckmorten Square was another white-collar office and would be empty at night, but the one adjoining it in Carrington Place might be residential for all I knew. A few loud bangs, muffled by the basement but amplified by the fire-escape, probably wouldn't alarm anyone. After all, who'd think a gunfight was in progress? But the danger was there, and the arrival of armed police while I was on the premises was the last thing I wanted.

The fact that I had escaped from the basement pretty well proved there was no fourth man. Just in case I was wrong, and to check on pursuit, I paused to listen. At which point, the one functioning body newly arrived in the basement made his greatest mistake. (Leaving his post by the front door was his other grave error.)

"Dad?" I heard him say, far too loudly.

And then he howled. Pure uncontrollable horror. It confirmed my assumption that the big man I'd shot in the basement was Simeon Hartling. And it put a name to the third man. Anthony. He was in the building. Out in the open. Alone. Unguarded. It was a chance to settle this affair once and for all. Just him and me. To the death.

All thought of clearing out left me. All thought of armed police intervention was instantly dismissed. I continued to listen, standing in the semi-dark by the carpeted stairs.

My enemy chose not to chase directly after me. Instead he ran noisily up the fire-escape and thereby into the conference room. Presumably his intention was to cut me off at the front entrance. I aimed the Heckler & Koch at the door he was going to come through, and waited for him to open it. I hoped and believed shock and grief had made him irrational, and expected behaviour to match. I'd only need one bullet.

So much for my expectations. An eerie silence

descended on the building. No one came out of the conference room.

I became uncomfortably aware of the drawback of losing contact with the enemy. He could be anywhere. The fire-escape gave him access to all the floors except the top one, and maybe he even had a key for that. Where I was standing, with my back to the carpeted stairs, was not a sensible place to be.

I was clear on one thing: it would be folly to take up position in the dead-end wing, the one looking across Throckmorten Square. It only needs one person to trap you in a cul-de-sac. The Carrington Place wing, with an exit at each end, was the rational choice to go for.

Treading silently I ascended to the first floor, but found I was no better off. Anthony Hartling could already be in the office I wanted to enter. I was exposed on the stairs, yet I couldn't leave them until I knew where the enemy was.

I tried to get inside his mind. What would he do? I could think of three options: bail out, send for help, or attack. The second was the least worrying. Anyone coming to the rescue would need to be prepared to kill or be killed. Even if Simeon Hartling had a few people like that left on his payroll, would such an employee take orders from the son without being told to by the father? I doubted it. I'd face up to option two if it arose.

Considering the third option — attack — it occurred to me his situation was the same as mine. If he was on the fire-escape, he couldn't enter any of the offices either. I might already be in the office he chose. We were both confined to our respective flights of stairs.

Then I knew what he'd do — or at least what he ought to do. If he had a key to the locked third floor, he could safely enter that and come at me from above. Failing that, he'd cross the dark basement and use that route to my stairwell. Either way, he wouldn't be in the first-floor office. Conscious I was gambling my life on my reasoning, I went through the doorway as swiftly as possible. No one shot at me.

I shut the door loudly behind me. That was so Hartling would know where I was. He'd find me sooner or later anyway, and giving him a clue would speed things up. I didn't want this business to take all night.

A glance out of the window into the courtyard revealed the Rolls undeparted. I took that to mean Hartling's first option — bailing out — had not been utilized. If he'd wanted to flee, he'd have made off in the car.

Still making occasional help-him-to-find-me noises, I squatted down between two desks midway through the office. It was up to him now. All I could do was wait and see.

A few minutes passed. I had to assume that Hartling was by now positioned outside the office at one end or the other. I really wanted him to grow impatient and try coming in. Otherwise the stalemate might continue indefinitely.

I waited, but again silence and the dim illumination provided by the streetlights shining in from outside were all my senses perceived. He was waiting for me as much as I was waiting for him.

Some new ideas were needed to break the deadlock and give me an ascendancy. One thing that occurred to me was that the enemy didn't know how many bullets were left in the Heckler & Koch. Nor was it likely, given his emotional state in the basement, that he'd noticed Cigar-man's latest gun was missing. If I could convince him I'd run out of ammunition, it might lure him into exposing himself. To that end, I removed the empty magazine from the Heckler & Koch, and worked the spent-casing ejection mechanism to get the one remaining bullet out from its position under the hammer. I inserted the bullet back in the magazine and put the latter in my left jacket pocket. I now had an empty gun which would click nicely if I pulled the trigger. I swapped it with Cigar-man's 'number two' (the Heckler & Koch being his 'number one'), deciding the empty-gun trick was one to keep in reserve for the time being.

There was another idea in my mind which appeared more immediately usable. If Hartling was skulking behind one of the doors, I could leave the office by the other, go up or down a floor and attack him from behind. The only problem was choosing which door. It was fifty-fifty. Or nearly so. What swung it was that the carpeted stairs were quieter. That's where he'd be. I made my way down the centre of the office, a row of desks on either side, towards the fire-escape.

It seemed advisable to keep a low profile, so I crawled on hands and knees. Somehow I missed a telephone cord trailing from the last desk. As I passed it unknowingly, it got under my leg and I knelt squarely on it. It wasn't so much the pain in my knee, but the sheer surprise that made me twist round. In regaining my balance, I fouled up the cord even more, and the phone clattered to the floor.

Hartling took the sound as a signal. Or more likely he couldn't contain his impatience any longer. A door flew open and he was in. I scurried behind the end desk. The only redeeming feature of my bungle was I'd guessed the right door. He'd been down by the carpeted stairs. We were now at opposite ends of the office. By slow stages we were closing with each other.

It was clear neither of us wanted to waste bullets. I don't know what his reasons were. For my part I was worried about ricochets, about being the first to run out of ammunition, and above all about the noise and the consequent police involvement. There were, after all, two dead bodies in the basement thanks to me. It made me very keen not to open fire unless there was a good chance of scoring a hit.

The silent waiting resumed. I used the pause to examine Cigar-man's no. 2 gun, primarily by touch. It was another semi-automatic but was shaped differently from the Heckler & Koch. I didn't know how many bullets it contained, but I reckoned there ought to be more than enough to kill Hartling.

My plan to get behind him resurrected itself in my mind. If I could sneak out to the fire-escape while making him think it was merely a feint to get him to expose himself, I might yet take him by surprise.

As a first step, I needed to move the desk that was shielding me so it masked the lower part of the fire-escape door. It was impossible. A fully loaded desk without castors and resting on a carpet won't budge. I tried pulling the drawers out to reduce the weight, but they proved to be that unhelpful type which extend only so far before they stick. Thwarted!

All was not totally quiet at Hartling's end of the office. He was sniffing every once in a while. Very reassuring for me, since it told me he was still there, and not embarked on some subterfuge of his own.

Keeping myself below desk height, I emptied out the lower drawers. Still the desk refused to slide over the carpet. Angrily frustrated, I lay on my back, braced my feet against the underneath of the desk's top surface, and pushed upwards. The thing tipped over with a thump, augmented by the sounds of a PC monitor and keyboard falling to the floor.

If Hartling had run at me then, firing as he did so, he would probably have got me. But he must have learnt by now that as pea-brained losers go I had a nasty habit of coming out ahead of the game. He continued to play his part cautiously, possibly wondering if I was trying to tempt him into making a frontal assault. I heard him sniff yet again.

With its weight reduced, and with a large, smooth surface in contact with the carpet, the desk was just about slide-able. I could move it, centimetres at a time, towards the fire-escape door.

Eventually I was satisfied it was in a position to obscure my exit from the office. Lying almost flat on my back and with my right hand pointing Cigar-man's no. 2 in the direction Hartling would have to attack me from, I prized the door open with the fingers of my left hand. A spring held it shut, which made the task difficult, but I was able gradually to prevail.

The next moves were critical. Having created an aperture wide enough to get through, I took the biggest of my electrician's screwdrivers from my pocket and used it as a wedge to forestall the closing action of the spring. Turning over and round, I wriggled through the gap until only my head, arms and chest remained inside the office.

I heard Hartling sniff down the far end.

At which point, I changed my whole battle plan. As I mentioned earlier, the fire-escape was permanently illuminated by dim emergency lighting. Hartling therefore knew I'd opened the door. What he didn't know was whether I'd gone through it or not. If I could convince him I had, he'd come after me. I could wait by the entrance to the second-floor office; when he came into sight, I would pull the trigger of the empty Heckler & Koch; that would be my cue to flee; he'd give chase, thinking I was now defenceless; and bang: goodbye Anthony Hartling courtesy of Cigar-man's no. 2. To that end, I put the latter gun back in my right jacket pocket, swapping it with the empty Heckler & Koch.

How to convince him I'd retreated to the fire-escape? Simple: make a noise.

But before I could do that, he made a noise of his own. The door down the far end of the office opened, and he went through it. In my prone position behind the toppled desk, there was nothing I could do to stop him — even had I had a loaded gun in my hand, which I didn't.

My plan was in ruins. I could stand up safely, and did so. But what now? Time for another panic. Was he breaking off the action? Had he decided to call it a night? Or was he going to come at me by entering the fire-escape from above or below?

I began to creep up towards the second floor. I had arrived at the fire-door and was dithering about what to do next, when the door opened. Fast. We collided as he rushed through it, both of us falling over.

Next moment, we were wrestling on the concrete fire-escape steps, me on top, my head level with his chest. I gripped his right wrist, trying to prevent him pointing his gun at me. His left hand grasped the Heckler & Koch. That didn't bother me of course. I let him turn the weapon so it was aimed at me. Somehow he got a finger under the trigger. He duly heard the click I'd wanted him to hear, though not in these circumstances.

He tried to bring a knee up between my legs, but that was predictable and easy to block. Then he tried to roll me off him, but my weight proved too great, given he had to push against the sharp edges of the concrete steps. So it came down to a struggle for the two guns: his because it was lethal, and mine because it could still deliver a wounding blow.

Since I was pinning him down, I had a slight advantage. I attempted to use it to move higher up his body. He countered by trying once more to get out from under me. Neither of us succeeded. His firearm though was getting very close to being aligned on my shoulder. I cast the Heckler & Koch away, bringing my right hand across to join the left in the struggle to point his gun anywhere but at me.

He struck me a couple of blows with his liberated left arm. He had no room to build up any speed, so the tactic was ineffectual. In the meantime, I'd got his right hand up against the iron railing that ran down the inner side of the steps. Several times I forced his knuckles onto the metal posts. The gun remained locked tight in his fist.

He tried a new approach, getting his left forearm under my chin and pushing my head back. It strained my neck and meant I couldn't see what I was doing, but it wasn't a decisive move. I endured.

Momentarily I felt him relax, and then another attempt was made to throw me off, not this time towards the wall, but against the railing. He achieved an ironical success, for as my back rammed into the metal posts and his own body turned in pursuit, his right hand and the gun got trapped against a railing and pulled so badly out of position he had to release the gun or break his wrist. He let out a grunt of pain and the gun was gone, falling vertically three floors to the basement.

He made a left hook to my groin, which I blocked with my right. There were a few moments of unproductive scrabbling. I managed to push myself off the bars. He used the momentum I'd created to roll me across the top of him and over towards the wall. I partly got up, he partly followed, we twisted round somehow, and found ourselves tumbling down the fire-escape sideways.

That separated us. He came to rest on the first-floor landing, whereas I succeeded in halting a few steps above him. I was on my feet before he was and sprinted to the second floor, past the empty Heckler & Koch, and into the office there.

Desperately I pulled Cigar-man's no. 2 out of my jacket pocket. Hartling pushed open the fire-door fast for the second time. He thought I was unarmed. I had him! He was in the room. A metre away. Impossible to miss. I pulled the trigger. Nothing happened. Nothing. I didn't know why. Automatics can jam. Maybe this one had. Maybe something else. With the exception of Heckler & Koch P7M8s, I knew damn-all about handguns. It was my worst mistake of the night to forget that stark fact. Cigar-man could probably have fixed the problem in one second flat. I couldn't fix it in less than ten. Meanwhile Hartling already knew where I was standing. I did the only viable thing. I hit him with the gun barrel.

It wasn't well judged. He ducked away as the blow made contact, glancing off his upper arm.

He aimed a fist at my face. I dodged under it and jabbed him in the stomach with an elbow. That made him double up. I dropped the useless gun back into my pocket and ran to the nearest desk, grabbing an office chair. As he lunged at me, I swung it round and hit him with it. There wasn't enough time for it to gain height, so it struck his thigh.

The chair was a standard sort of design: short straight back, thinly cushioned seat, central metal supporting pillar, and at the base five radiating spokes, each tipped with a castor. As he fell following the impact with his leg, he managed to grip one of the spokes. I tried unsuccessfully to jerk it away. He grasped a second spoke. We pulled the chair back and forth between us, him on his back, me standing.

Eventually our feet got tangled. I was sufficiently unprepared that I lost my balance, letting go of my novel weapon. I staggered, regained my poise, and dodged as Hartling, swiftly on his feet, thrust the seat-back in my face.

Rushing to the next desk in the office, I seized a second chair and brought it up to meet him. He wasn't as quick to attack as he should have been. I detected a limp. But that was the only noticeable damage I'd inflicted on him so far, and it didn't amount to anything disabling.

For a few seconds we were both at bay, breathing heavily, clutching the seats of our unorthodox battering rams. He'd turned his round so that, like mine, it was spokes foremost.

And then the medieval combat began. He thrust at my face. I parried. Metal clashed and locked briefly together. He pulled back and took a swipe at my legs. Again I parried. So it continued. There are only a limited number of ways you can wield a chair, and we tried them all.

Gradually I found myself taking more steps backward than forward. I was further handicapped by the pain in my back — Cigar-man's 'revenge' — which the exertion was reawakening, and which grew steadily more excruciating. Hartling began to achieve a psychological and physical superiority. I lost track of time.

As we fought our way down the office, the hollow crumping of metal on metal was once in a while supplemented with the sound of PC towers being written off, and screens and keyboards and other items being swept off desks. The windows only survived because the furniture kept us away from them.

Was it ten minutes or half an hour this chair-fight had lasted? I was tiring, finding it harder and harder to control what was becoming more of a leaden shield than a weapon. I had mounted counter attacks several times, driving Hartling into retreat, but now it was as much as I could do to fend off the blows. My arms were hurting along the whole of their length. I was soaked with sweat.

Eventually I fetched up against the door leading to the carpeted stairs. There was no way I could open it. Nor could I stay where I was. I was unable to absorb the impacts with a hard surface behind me.

Calling up my last reserves of strength I pushed him

back and tried to turn the fight through a hundred and eighty degrees. I only achieved half that. I was caught between a desk and the wall. He swept his chair across the desktop, which latter got in the way of my attempt to intercept the blow. I was knocked sideways, falling onto one knee. He withdrew slightly, causing a spoke to hit the back of my head and pull me further towards him. I was too groggy to react in time. He thrust the central pillar of his chair squarely at my head. It hit me on the jaw.

I was dazed. Face down. I tried to get up, but he was suddenly on top of me, kneeling on me with both knees, using all his weight. He pulled my head back by my hair with one hand and covered my mouth and nose with the other. I thrashed about uselessly until I blacked out.

Consciousness returned. A cold liquid was running over my face: an office worker's left-over cup of coffee the cleaners hadn't bothered to remove. I found I had been dragged into the open beside the door to the carpeted stairs. I was lying on my back with my hands fastened behind me by means of a plastic-coated cable of some sort. Hartling was standing over me.

He wiped his face. Sweat maybe, or tears. "You killed my dad," he said in a voice choked with emotion. He sobbed involuntarily.

I watched as he took off his jacket and cast it to one side. Then he knelt astride me. One at a time he undid the buttons on my shirt.

Underneath, I was wearing a vest. He picked up a pair of large office scissors that he'd placed beside me, pulled the vest free from my trousers and cut it, bottom to top.

He opened the scissors up and slowly brought one of the blades down, pushing it into my exposed chest just far enough to puncture the skin. "You killed my dad. I'm going to break your bones, one at a time. But first I'm going to carve you up." He drew the blade horizontally,

262

slicing a short groove in my chest. I couldn't help crying out.

"You killed my dad," he repeated. "Let's do that again, shall we."

He brought the blade down in a slightly different place and repeated the action. Again I cried out, louder.

He held the scissors above me for a few seconds. Then he slowly brought the hand gripping them lower. "I'm going to get a cloth to stuff in your mouth in a moment. I want to hear you scream, but I don't want the rest of London to. First, though, let's have it full volume one more time, shall we. The night has just begun."

He was about to cut me yet again when there was movement at the far end of the office. The lights came on. Hartling looked as startled as I was. If it was his friends, I was shortly going to die in agony. If it was the police, I was going to spend a lot of the rest of my life in prison. I prayed for it to be the police. But it wasn't them. Or his friends. It was worse. It was Miranda.

"You'd better stop that, Tony," she said, her voice calm, level and feminine.

Hartling got off me. I raised myself a little and could see her down by the fire-escape, wearing, of all things, a white cloth on her head, and holding a gun which was aimed roughly at Hartling. I could only think she must have guessed where I was going, had followed, and had entered the building by the courtyard and the fire-escape exit I'd opened before killing Cigar-man. She'd found my discarded Heckler & Koch on her way up to the second floor. She obviously wasn't aware it was empty. Oh Miranda, my darling, what are you doing here?

"I didn't know he'd brought you along," said Hartling. "That solves a problem."

He advanced on her quickly. I heard the gun click.

"Nice try, darling, but it's empty," he said as he got hold

of her. She didn't make a sound. He took the gun and threw it in my direction. It came to rest by my feet.

Miranda was manhandled roughly and forced to sit on one of the office chairs.

"Stay," said Hartling as if he was talking to a dog.

She did as she'd been ordered, plainly tense and very frightened, but also somehow expectant. Why didn't she run? Had she summoned the police? What did she think she was achieving?

Hartling unplugged a telephone cord from its connections. I made a frantic effort to stand up. With your hands tied behind you, it's not easy at the best of times. And these were very far from the best of times. I couldn't do it.

Miranda jumped up from the chair and pressed herself against the adjacent window. "There's no need to bind me, Tony," she said. "I won't run away if you let Ed go." She pulled her blouse out from her jeans. "You can have me if you like."

If I could just free my hands from their fastenings, I'd be able to reload the Heckler & Koch. I tried. God, how I tried.

He advanced on her. As he closed in with the cord, she began to scream. Not the real thing. A strange loud sort of vocalization.

And then I understood. It was all a ruse. She'd got his attention, and manoeuvred him so the fire-escape door was out of his sight. I watched Judith, who, like Miranda, had a white cloth covering her head, slip into the office. Unheard. Unnoticed.

"Let her alone, Hartling," I called, doing my bit to keep him distracted.

As he reached her, Miranda put her arms round him and pulled him onto her. He was so surprised he went with the movement. She became silent.

264

Recovering his balance he slapped her face and said: "You're nothing but a tart. Now, I told you to sit still."

He gripped her shoulders and turned her round, presumably intending to tie her arms with the telephone cord. Before he could begin, Judith dropped her own loop of flex over his neck and pulled it tight.

Hartling lost interest in Miranda. His hands went to his throat.

"Miranda," I shouted. "Here, quickly."

She pushed past Hartling. I was still on my back, propping myself up on my elbows, and she ran to my side.

Judith knew what she was doing, walking Hartling backwards so he couldn't use his greater body-weight against her. The trouble was, she'd soon run out of places to walk to. Once she was halted by a wall, she wouldn't be strong enough to hold him.

"Pick up the gun," I commanded, referring to the Heckler & Koch at my feet. Miranda obeyed.

Judith reached the wall. Hartling head-butted her, missing her nose by a fraction. She hung on. His face was crimson.

"In my left jacket pocket," I continued. "Take out the magazine. The square thing." Again Miranda obeyed.

Hartling reached back and grasped Judith's hair, forcing her head sideways and causing her to reduce the tension in the flex round his neck.

"Push it up the handle," I said. "Not that way round. The other way." Miranda followed my directions.

Hartling thrust himself to one side. Judith lagged behind, enabling him to turn and lock an arm round her head. He bent her double, ramming her face onto a nearby desk. Then, twisting round, he tripped her and threw her to the floor.

"Hold the handle with *all* the fingers of your right hand. The top of the gun slides back. Do that with your left hand." Miranda got it right in one, thus bringing the bullet in the magazine into the firing position.

Judith had half risen. Hartling wrapped his arms round her waist, lifted her off her feet, and hurled her against a tall filing cabinet. She rebounded and slumped downwards. He jerked the flex she was still holding out of her hand.

"What's sauce for the goose," he remarked.

"Just squeeze the handle hard and pull the trigger," I said to Miranda. "And get up close so you don't miss. There's only one bullet left."

She began walking slowly and purposefully towards Hartling.

Judith was on her knees. Hartling got behind her and put the cord round her neck and pulled it taut. "How's it feel, huh? How's it feel?" he said. I could see he wasn't using all his strength. He wanted her to suffer.

As Judith began struggling helplessly, Miranda came to a halt less than four paces from him, the gun pointing at his chest. "Tony," she called, her voice quivering, "please stop. *Please*."

"You don't give up, do you," he said glaring at her. "I'll deal with you when I've finished with this bitch."

Miranda said: "I'm very sorry, Tony," took two steps towards him, and shot him.

Hartling gasped.

The gun dropped out of Miranda's hand and she shrieked. She ran to me, and I told her to help me stand up.

Hartling let go of Judith, who slumped to the floor. He picked up the Heckler & Koch and examined it. Empty. "I don't get it," he muttered, pointed the gun at Miranda and pulled the trigger. Click.

By now I was back on my feet. I braced myself. Our enemy still seemed very much alive, and I didn't know what to expect. Miranda had shot him from the side, slightly below his armpit. The bullet would have entered

266

his lung. To some extent it was where the bullet had gone after that which would determine how seriously injured he was, and that was anyone's guess.

He walked towards me, clutching the gun. He was half way there when his legs buckled and he sagged to his knees. Looking up at me he said: "You had help. That's cheating."

"No it isn't," I responded. "Three a side."

He coughed, bent forward, put out his arms, and lay down as if he was going to bed. I saw then the exit wound in his back over his right kidney. It was bleeding heavily.

He partially rolled over and stared at me again. "Looks like you win this round," he said. "But next time I'm going to take you apart. And your friends." He coughed, and blood from his mouth spattered the carpet.

Judith picked herself up and came over as Miranda severed the cord binding my hands, using a pair of wire-strippers from one of my trouser pockets.

Physically exhausted, in agony from kidney-pain, and feeling like I wasn't going to be able to keep myself going much longer, there was only one coherent thought left in my mind, and I expressed it in seven monosyllables. "We've got to get out of here." It never occurred to me the women might argue.

"Kill him first," said Miranda, as Hartling, now gasping for breath, coughed out more blood.

"We don't have the time," I replied. "There's been too much shooting. The police could be here at any moment. And anyway," I added, looking at the blood soaking the back of Hartling's shirt, "it's not necessary."

I took a few weak, unsteady paces towards the fire-escape.

"Are you okay, Judith?" I asked.

"I'm alive," she replied hoarsely. "Miranda's right. Finish him off."

Somehow I found the energy to be exasperated. "I can't," I said. "I've nothing left to shoot him with." What did they want me to do? Stave in his head with an office chair?

"He's come back from the dead before," said Miranda, standing her ground. "We have to make sure."

More gasping and coughing from Hartling.

I picked up the Heckler & Koch from the floor. Miranda's fingerprints would be on it. Moving stiffly, I cleaned it using my ruined vest, and placed it on the nearest desk. There was no point in taking it with me. Without ammunition it was useless. Both women watched. I also picked up the scissors and pocketed them. They had my blood on them.

When it was obvious I wasn't going to do anything further about Hartling, Judith and Miranda exchanged glances and Judith said: "You two go ahead. I'll do it."

She picked up her makeshift garrotte.

I didn't move.

"Go on," she repeated more forcefully.

I was so tired of it all. I switched off the office lights and let Miranda help me down the fire-escape and into the courtyard where the golden Rolls Royce was parked. Once in the fresh air, I collapsed. Miranda took the keys from me and went to fetch my hired van. By the time she pulled into Carrington Place, Judith had joined me and was able to help me get in the back.

We drove to the flat in Harrow. There we spent the small hours bathing our wounds and wondering if our private war really could be over.

*

From one of the London evening papers, dated Tuesday, November 2nd:

THREE DEAD IN WEST END MASSACRE

A scene of carnage was discovered this morning when employees of High Rise Nightclubs, Throckmorten Square, arrived for work. Police were called and quickly sealed off the building.

It was confirmed that the body of Mr Simeon Hartling, 50, managing director of High Rise Nightclubs, was found in the basement, along with that of another man who has so far not been identified. Both victims had been shot in the head.

The body of Mr Hartling's son Anthony, 20, was discovered on the second floor. Police declined to disclose how he had died, but workers who saw the scene all agreed he had put up considerable resistance.

It is believed three firearms were recovered from the premises, and also other items of an electrical nature.

Detective Superintendent Wheeler, who is leading the hunt for the killer, announced at a news conference at 2 p.m. today that Mr Hartling was suspected of involvement in organized crime.

He added, in answer to a reporter's question, that he was keeping an open mind on whether these might have been gangland killings. He warned that the Metropolitan Police would not tolerate an outbreak of gang warfare on the streets of the capital.

He appealed for anyone who saw or heard anything suspicious during the hours of darkness last night in or near Throckmorten Square to contact the major incident room on....

16

LOOSE ENDS

I

Narrative by Judith Farley describing her and Miranda's part in the events at the High Rise Nightclubs office.

Sometimes I don't know why I bother with Ed Somersby. I spell everything out patiently to him. He seems to get it. And then what does he do? He carries on like I'd be talking Venusian.

We, Miranda and I, sit there watching him eat a tasty meal for which he shows no enthusiasm at all. We try talking to him, and he's so distant we give up. We turn on the TV and he only pretends to be paying attention. Then he gets up and announces: "I'm going out for a while. I don't know when I'll be back." And he leaves us.

The crazy thing is that both Miranda and I distinctly heard him say 'when' — but the tone of his voice, his gestures, the look on his face, they all cried out with 'if'. We both knew it. And he didn't think we would. After all I'd told him!

After he'd gone, poor Miranda was frantic. As for me, to be honest with you, I was highly pissed off. I thought Ed and I had agreed when we had that heart-to-heart in John's workshop that we'd tackle the Hartlings as a team. People on my team don't go freelance. End of discussion.

I calmed Miranda down and asked her if she wanted to go after him.

"Can we?" she says.

I rolled my eyes at that, so she changed her answer to yes.

I told her to get dressed. We had come from Wales with only the clothes we were wearing at the time: my biker gear, and the casual outfit she wears when she goes out walking. Neither of us had a hat of any sort, and she had no gloves. The gloves we could do nothing about, but the head coverings could be improvised. Ed had two tablecloths, one in use and one, slightly stained, waiting to be washed. I folded them both and gave the cleanest one to Miranda. I asked her if she'd ever worn a shawl. Her answer was no. I explained why we needed to cover our heads. Ed had warned us there were CCTV cameras about, and we didn't want our faces on them.

While I was sorting these things out, I asked her to get up the app on her phone and find the nearest tube station. It turned out to be Harrow on the Hill. We set off at a run.

I'll say one thing for Miranda. She may not look the athletic type, but she can move when she wants to!

We had a long wait for a train at that time of night. While we were standing about on the platform, I asked Miranda for the nearest station to Hardiman Terrace. It was St John's Wood. So that's where we got out, running again. Hardiman Terrace was the first of Ed's so-called lions' dens, and the nearest one for us to check on. We ran down the road, wearing our tablecloth shawls. No sign of anything going on at no. 47, and no sign of Ed's hired van.

We were running back to the tube station when we had a bit of luck. A taxi drove past us, and we flagged him down and got him to take us to Baker Street. (I thought it unwise to be dropped too close to Throckmorten Square.)

Running down Baker Street wasn't really an option. There were too many people about to notice us. We had to settle for walking fast. Even then, we attracted unwelcome attention from a few of the evening drinkers, catcalling.

At last we got to Throckmorten Square. Success! One hired van.

We found the gate giving access to the High Rise Nightclubs courtyard open and sneaked in, headscarves on and heads kept low. As the door to the fire-escape was also open we entered the building. We could hear something going on upstairs, vaguely like someone hammering metal tubes. Neither of us could make sense of it.

Before going any further, I glanced down into the basement — checking our rear, so to speak — and could see at the foot of the steps something which I thought at first was a roll of carpet. It looked odd, so I told Miranda to wait while I investigated. It proved to be a dead body; one that smelt of cigars. It was hard to be sure in the poor light from the fire-escape, but it looked to me like the man from John's workshop. There was satisfaction in that. "Well, that's saved *me* the bother," I muttered to myself.

I reported to Miranda that Ed had been here. And maybe still was.

Following up the hammering noise, we ascended the fire-escape. All was quiet by the time we found Ed's gun, which I picked up. By then we were almost to the second floor.

We could hear something going on in there. I pushed open the fire door slightly and could make out somebody down the far end of the office sobbing and talking, though what he was saying was inaudible. No one was replying. Miranda said the voice was Tony Hartling's.

There was a sudden cry of pain.

I asked her if that was Ed.

I didn't need broad daylight to register the look on her face. "Give me the gun," she whispered.

I'd seen Ed work it, so I did the same. No wonder he'd discarded it; the thing that held the bullets was missing.

Then Ed screamed. There was nothing I was going to be able to do to stop Miranda intervening, so I gave her the gun and whispered: "It's empty, but Hartling may not know that. In case he does, keep him distracted. Don't let him look at this door."

I left her to get on with it while I went searching for a weapon. Fortunately, the first floor fire-escape door was propped open, so I could move fast into that office without making any noise. In the heat of the moment I settled on a garrotte. It wasn't one of my more inspired decisions, mainly because I badly underestimated how long it would take to work. I thought ten seconds, twenty seconds at most. And perhaps that's all it would have taken had I possessed a man's strength. But alas, I don't. Thank God Miranda was there to come to my rescue.

Anyway, from the time I returned to join the fight, Ed describes pretty accurately what happened, I think.

II

The state of police investigations. (Narrative resumed by Ed Somersby.)

As I write, three months after the event, I am still a free man. There has been no knock on the door. Obviously, I'm not kept informed about police inquiries, but this is how things stand so far as I can tell from close attention to the news media.

A) *The Coed y Deifol murders.*

By the time the police realized Anthony Hartling's fire-damaged flat warranted inspection, it was too late. Their examination proved fruitless because the place was already being redecorated.

At the forest murder scene the Ford had left tyre tracks, and my footprints were also found, but the heavy rain had blurred both to the point where they were useless to investigators. Cloth torn off Winston Kelly's suit was recovered from brambles, but that too led nowhere, as the material was of a common type.

About a month into their investigation, a wide-awake detective asked himself the same question as I had about the duplicate keys, both of which had survived the car fire. By then, the lock giving access to the dwelling where Hartling lived, and the lock giving access specifically to flat 4, had been changed. However, a relative of one of the other occupants still had an old main door key for the police to compare. That established a definite connection between the murders and the fire at Hartling's flat. But as leads go, it appears to have been a dead end, taking the police no further forward.

Neither Ed Somersby nor Winston Kelly has been associated with this crime by anyone. By good judgement as regards timing, by sheer bravado, and admittedly with quite a lot of luck, I appear to have got away with this particular piece of extra-judicial punishment.

B) *The ambush at Trefdarren.*

It transpired the taxi driver was not killed. However, he lay in a coma for several days as a result of a blow to the head. Injuries of that kind are almost always accompanied by a degree of amnesia, and the unfortunate man was unable to recall any of the events of that morning. He didn't remember Judith. He is still not recovered sufficiently to be able to return to work.

Cigar-man had robbed the fellow of his valuables in order to make the assault look like a violent mugging — an example of his professional thoroughness — but there had been little to steal. Judith sent a postal order to the police officer leading the investigation, together with an anonymous note printed in a London public library on A4 paper. The note informed him she had not been harmed, and that the money was to cover the fare she'd had no chance to pay. Since this sum exceeded the amount stolen by the supposed mugger, the police would have been stupid to continue suspecting (as they doubtless had until then) that the passenger had set the mugging up. Miranda posted the envelope containing postal order and note in a Swansea letterbox. Police appeals for the passenger to come forward have not been answered!

The police were aware a firearm had been used because of the bullet hole in the taxi's tyre, and for that reason expended more effort on the case than a mugging, even a violent one, would usually receive. A fingertip search revealed the bullets Tony Hartling had fired at me and the spent casings. These finds became significant later (see below).

They also found and interviewed the driver who had taken Miranda to Cardiff. He produced a vague likeness of her. But no one at Cardiff station remembered her, and the taxi driver was unable to definitely point her out in CCTV footage recorded in the station on the morning in question. Furthermore, there was no reason to connect the young lady specifically with Deheubarth University. Miranda has never been called on.

The gentleman with the Range Rover and the yapping dogs proved very helpful, furnishing a full description of the BMW, including its registration number. It seems the number plates were stolen, the car they belonged to being traced to a scrapyard on the outskirts of London. I do not know if the scrapyard owner was prosecuted for this. The BMW has never been found. I presume it was re-sprayed and disposed of.

Nor do I know what happened to Fatty. Perhaps he

recovered. Perhaps he died and the Hartlings got rid of the body somehow.

No connection has been made between the supposed mugger of Trefdarren and the dead cigar smoker in the High Rise Nightclubs basement.

I doubt if the police are still devoting resources to this crime.

C) *The High Rise Nightclubs murders.*

At Throckmorten Square, in contrast to Coed y Deifol, I was unable to tidy up the crime scene. Even so, despite the clues I left lying about, the police have little that would enable them to home in on the perpetrator.

As far as I know, I left no blood on the second floor. Nor did I leave any fingerprints, as I'd worn the plastic gloves throughout. Judith similarly left no fingerprints either. Gloveless Miranda's prints must have been found, but none of them would have been on anything directly incriminating. Even if the forensics people managed to single them out from those of the office staff, there is nothing on file by which she can be identified. Furthermore I and, after I'd left, Judith did manage to partially clean up the scene on this floor.

On the first floor there was only one upended desk to examine. My screwdriver propping open the fire-escape door was pocketed by Judith on her way out.

The basement was, of course, what worried me. The holdall, the wire and the plastic milk bottle were all standard untraceable products. But the electrical tampering pointed plainly to an electrician. I don't know what the police made of this, as it isn't something they've given any publicity to. I suspect, for reasons enlarged on below, they took the view they were dealing with a killer who knew a bit about electricity, rather than with an electrician who knew a bit about killing.

Of witnesses there were only two. The head cleaner, to whom I had spoken briefly, described me as best he could. He laboured under a couple of difficulties: he only saw me in poor light for a few seconds, and his grasp of English was limited. (He turned out to be Portuguese.) The other witness was the security system; that is, the CCTV cameras. The one monitoring the front door took a picture of me, but it was worthless. Not even computer enhancement could make anything of it. As I'd switched off recording of the CCTV images before fleeing to the basement, none of the subsequent comings and goings were stored for later viewing. There was no record of Judith's and Miranda's presence. Judith's trick with the tablecloths was sensible, but turned out not to be needed.

Curiously enough, the simple act of stopping the CCTV recording was described by the police as indicating the killer was a 'professional'. They thought it an important clue. To me it had been a minor point. It seems I created a beneficial false impression by accident.

On the ballistic front, the Heckler & Koch was soon identified as the gun John Farley had been shot with, as well as all three High Rise Nightclubs victims. This was a 'breakthrough'. Add John's supposed drug dealing to the Hartlings' involvement in organized crime, and you have a motive the dimmest policeman could understand: a drug-related gangland feud with four casualties (or six if the Coed y Deifol two are included).

And that was followed later by another ballistics revelation. The two guns used in the Trefdarren mugging were identified as being guns linked to the High Rise Nightclubs crime scene; the bullets found amongst the trees, fired at me by Anthony Hartling, were from the gun discovered at the bottom of the fire-escape where it had fallen after Anthony Hartling had dropped it; and the bullet used to shoot out the taxi's tyre matched a bullet found in the basement wall (the one fired by the dead Cigar-man as he hit the ground). Having announced the connection, the police have fallen silent on the matter. My guess is that they are mystified. What possible link could there be between a mugging in Trefdarren and a massacre in the West End of London? Given poor Weight Trainer and Gerry, and of course Anthony Hartling's presence at Deheubarth University, there is certainly strong evidence of a Hartling crime connection to South Wales. But then again, perhaps the guns used in the mugging, regarded as 'hot' by the mugger(s), had been sold to the Hartlings subsequently. But really, without more to go on, I don't see how the police can be anything other than baffled.

To add further confusion to their investigation, the police also found a recording of the message I'd left for Simeon Hartling in which I'd threatened Anthony. The Irish accent I'd used led to media speculation that Anthony might have got involved with a dissident terrorist group which had turned to more mundane criminality following the peace settlement.

The linking of all these goings-on to organized crime and drug dealing and 'professionals' (and maybe Irish dissidents too) seems to have been a lifesaver for me. You see, I am a link between Anthony Hartling and John Farley; someone both men knew in common; and I could have rigged the High Rise Nightclubs basement; and I have a motive of sorts. But as I'm unconnected to organized crime and drug dealing, with no criminal record, and I am in fact (officially) an exemplary law abiding British citizen, and not remotely plausible as a candidate for the role of professional hitman, my hope is that the police will continue declining to take a Somersby connection seriously. That's if they've spotted it at all

Of course, I will never be entirely in the clear. Murder cases are reviewed from time to time, and some bright detective may one day check me out thoroughly enough to establish grounds for an arrest. If that happens, I have my story ready. I will admit to being in the building. I will admit to tampering with the electrical installation. I will confess it was an attempt to get revenge on the Hartlings. But I will also insist that I left the offices straightaway thereafter, before anyone arrived and got shot. I am confident the police would not be able to prove otherwise. Whether that would save me from prosecution and conviction is a moot point.

The mystery which at first puzzled me, that no one had reported the gunshots — four in all — was soon explained. Several neighbours had heard them sure enough, but every last one assumed they were fireworks let off by kids, Guy Fawkes Night being later that same week.

One happy consequence of this lack of concern by the local residents was that nobody was looking out of their windows when Miranda drove us away. My hired van never came into the investigation. Despite my injuries, I was just about physically able, with Judith's help, to return it to Birmingham the following Saturday as arranged.

There remains one matter of excruciating embarrassment to confess to, and that concerns Cigar-man's no. 2 gun. It says a lot about how ill and far-gone I was when I left the High Rise Nightclubs building that I not only forgot I had it, but failed to register the weight of it in my jacket pocket. It wasn't till I was back at the safe house that I realized I'd inadvertently kept it with me, and was able to examine it to find out why it hadn't worked. What I discovered left me numb with horror. The safety catch had been set on! I prefer to think this somehow happened when the gun went off in the basement, rather than that I set it on myself unintentionally while examining the gun in the dark on the first floor. (That's all I'm going to say about that!) Either way, it meant that from the moment I emptied the

Heckler & Koch onwards, I was depending on a weapon that couldn't be fired. My life had been hanging not by a thread but by thin air and bluff.

I have the gun still, though not in my immediate possession. As I became more and more confident neither a surviving Hartling nor anyone else was after me any longer, I decided to store it in a secure location. If I ever need it again one day, I know where to find it.

The Hartlings must have played their war with me like a state secret (probably out of embarrassment!). My name seems not to have reached the ears of a single underworld police informant. If Mrs Hartling was told of me, she has kept her mouth shut. She now lives with her daughter and son-in-law in Cyprus. Her husband's empire is up for sale.

III

Letter to Tanya Matheson.

15th February

My beloved Tanya,

As yesterday was the first anniversary of your death, I thought it right to visit the copse on your dad's farm where you now reside. I wanted to see the plaque your mum and dad and I put there in your memory. Miranda came with me. It was bitterly cold, with an icy wind blowing. The weather seemed fitting somehow. I stood there for a long while, taking

in the scenery, holding Miranda's hand and feeling so very
sad, remembering the many good times, and the awful way
you died, and how empty my life became without you.

After a while, my thoughts were interrupted by someone
calling my name, and I saw your dad was trudging towards
us across the field. He had watched us from the farmhouse
with his binoculars. Miranda and I went back with him and
spent a while in his warm home, drinking tea with him and
your mum.

He remarked how strange and unfathomable the ways of
the Lord are, in that if Anthony Hartling had received a
proper punishment from the judicial system he would still be
alive.

The statement is true of course, but what could I say? You
and I know the Lord had nothing to do with it. If there's ever
a divine judgement day, I'll be condemned for what I did. Of
that I have no doubt. I can only plead that if this country's
legal system was less hog-tied to medieval tradition elevated
to the status of a religion, to the clearly absurd notion that
theatricality and high-flown eloquence are the way to
determine guilt and innocence, then there would have been
no need for me to take the law into my own hands, because
the court would have given us the justice we had a right to

expect. In other words, if I have much to answer for, so do those who sustain the current judicial regime. Genuine justice can only be achieved by an inquiry which aims to separate the truths from the lies; never by an adversarial contest which is the verbal equivalent of a Dark Age trial by combat. The senior law officers and the legislators are intelligent enough to know this. In my eyes that makes them culpable. What a bunch of complacent, self-serving hypocrites they are!

You must by now be thinking I sound like a very angry young man. In one respect that's fair comment. I do still feel our betrayal by the courts deeply. I do not think though that I am bitter about it any more. Why should I be bitter? I got you justice in the end without their poxy help.

Has it made the world a better place that I did so? Has it made me a better man? I really don't know. I can only say I am who I am and I did what I did. I am not ashamed. Nor am I proud.

Miranda is gradually taking your place in my life. She was badly traumatized by the part she played in Anthony Hartling's death, but seems now to be increasingly free of the nightmares and the sense of dread that haunted her for weeks afterwards. It was particularly hard for her to return to university pretty well straightaway, but Judith and I convinced her that was the least suspicious course to take.

Judith — remember those happy, sociable evening meals with just the four of us! — is coping well, as far as I can tell. I think what happened in the High Rise Nightclubs office that night was, for her, more a matter of dark satisfaction than something to be overly troubled by.

As for me, I was just relieved it was all over. Initially I was confined to my flat by illness. My body was covered in bruises, the slashes in my chest took weeks to heal, and there was blood in my urine. But apart from a couple of scars, I recovered fully some time ago. As soon as my beard was back and my hair was long enough, Miranda was able to announce she'd got a new boyfriend. Ed Somersby replaced Winston Kelly; long-haired biker took over from neat and tidy journalist. (Not as long-haired as I used to be though. Miranda prefers men without flowing locks!)

I have an electrician job in Swansea now. Houses are cheaper in this part of the country, and I was able to buy a modest one outright with our capital, despite the drain on it caused by the war with the Hartlings. Miranda is soon to complete her degree course and will then start work as a trainee solicitor in the same city, so we will be able to live together full-time instead of only at weekends. I was surprised to learn that her degree isn't enough; she'll next have to pass a Law Practice Course in order to be properly qualified. Electricians have it easy!

There's just one more thing I must say to you, Tanya, and it's a vow. Though Miranda may take your place in my life, she will never take your place in my heart. I shall never forget you. You were my first love, and I miss you terribly even after all this time. In my mind I see you sometimes here in Wales: sunbathing on Gower's beautiful beaches or walking in the picturesque Black Mountains. Perhaps one day it won't only be in my mind. Perhaps one day it'll be for real, and we'll meet again on some other plane of existence. It's a sweet dream and I hope it's a true one.

Rest in peace now my precious darling.

My love to you always and forever.

Ed.